Bottom of the Map

~ an urban novel ~

Steven L. Brown

Bottom of the Map

~ an urban novel ~

S.H.A.P.E.

Self, Health &
Personal Empowerment

www.shapepublishing.com

Dedication

Time is the most precious commodity known to us human beings... once it's spent, it cannot be duplicated, replenished, or reproduced. I've lost 12 years of my life, 12 years I could never get back...and during those 12 years, I endured some of the most excruciating pain I've ever felt. I lost my mother, and two women that were like mothers to me. See, when you don't have nothing but time to sit and think, you start to reflect and look at self because you have no other choice but to.

While I stewed in my own shit for 12 years, I constantly thought about how bad of a son I was, on top of being a horrible father. I have one son and three daughters and didn't have a relationship with any of them. As I watched them grow and I started to mature, I realized how significant it was for me to be in their lives *and* how significant their mothers were.

God has blessed me with four wonderful children: Ashlee, Niko, Leeyah, and Nyaja. I love y'all unconditionally. I can't go back and erase the past, but I can rectify my wrongs and be a better father from here on. I lived my life; I live for y'all now. I promise to be here from there this day forth, to love, protect, and guide you by all means necessary. Ashlee, Leeyah, and Nyaja... I'm sorry for all the daddy/daughter dances we missed, and the proms and graduations and...

I'm sorry. Please forgive me.

Niko, I missed the most essential part of a young man's life. We can never get that time back. All we can do is move forward and make the best of things *now*. I love you son... I love all of you. Y'all are the air that I breath...

Andrea, Danielle, and Dina...the magnificent mothers of my beautiful children. I would like to take a moment to acknowledge you, *and*, everything you've done to become the women you now are. I appreciate you so much and worship the ground y'all walk on. I know it's not easy being a single mother...playing *mama* and *daddy*. It takes a strong woman to raise a child alone, and not only did you do that, you raised them to be strong, intelligent children... it's not easy, but y'all make it seem like it's a walk in the park. While I was being irresponsible and immature, you picked up the pieces. You held down the fort and protected my cubs and did what you had to do to take care of my children...with no help...no assistance...no child support...

No pressure.

For what it's worth, I will always be here for you. Through all we've experienced, after all we've been through, I love, respect, and appreciate y'all so much. I'm sorry for leaving you alone. I'm sorry for all the time I've spent locked up. I'm sorry for the pain I caused, and for being the half-ass man I used to be; let that be the reason why I will always love you and be there for you...

I know y'all are up there smiling down on me... You're not here in physical form, but I *know* you're here in spirit; I can feel it. I love and miss y'all so much. I wish you were here to see the man your son has become... You would be so proud....

Yesterday is a memory. Tomorrow is a mystery. Today is a gift, which is why it is called the "present". What the caterpillar perceives as the end, to the butterfly it's just the beginning...

R.I.P.

Brenda *"Starr"* Brown

Audette *"Red Eyes"* Walcott

Yvonne Harris

I love you...

P.S. I told you I was gonna make you proud, mama.

Table of Contents

Acknowledgements 11

Prologue 19

Part 1

1 How it All Started 23
2 Love at First Sight 49
3 Back Down Memory Lane 56
4 And the Game was Told 94
5 Going In 139
6 Ready or Not 154
7 Opposites Attract 164
8 Déjà vu' 188
9 A Raw Deal 199

Part 2

10 It's Going Down (excerpt) 215

Acknowledgements

First and foremost, I want to give thanks *and* recognition to my Higher Power: THANK YOU FATHER!!! Thank you for keeping me. All that I do is because of you. All my life, You've taken all the things that were meant bad for me and turned them into the stepping stones of the foundation I'm now standing on. My gift is not mines...it is yours, and I thank you for letting me utilize it. Thank you for all the tribulations I've endured, *and*, all the lessons You've taught me through the people You've brought into my life...

No man is your enemy. No man is your friend. Every man is your teacher....

Thank you, Father, for giving me the wisdom to understand the virtue of this saying.

Secondly, I want to give a big thank you to Joycelyn Wells Moore: THANK YOU!!! None of this would have been possible without you. As some of you know, and some of you don't know, in "2005", I'd got the bright idea to go to Georgia and rob a jewelry store.... I know, I know, it wasn't such a bright idea (but it seemed real good at the time). Anywho, I got away but got caught in Lake City, Florida on the way back to West Palm Beach (that's a whole 'nother story by itself; stay tuned). Long story short: I got caught, got extradited back to Georgia, and was sentenced to a 20- year, split sentence (this means I had to do 12 years in and 8 out on paper). It was during this bid I started reading "urban novels" and thought: *Hey, I can write a book way better than this bullshit I've been reading!*

I finished writing B.O.T.M. December 21, 2007 (one day before my daughter's birthday). I was in Rockdale County Jail at the time...in "high max", 23- hour lock down. As soon as I finished, I sent the hand-written manuscript upstairs to Marcus Pennant, a good friend of mine, and he and his cellmate, Robert Smith, took turns reading it. I spent the next two days listening to them laugh their ass off and arguing over who's turn it was to get the book. Then finally, on the second night, after Marcus read the book, he stood to the bars upstairs and clapped and whistled and said, "Aye, Palm Beach, this one of the best books I've ever read!" And like that, B.O.T.M. caught fire in the Georgia Department of Corrections. For 10 years, B.O.T.M. has been locked in whatever box I was assigned to along with all my other prized possessions. And in 10 years, hundreds have read this manuscript, and everyone said the same thing(s): they couldn't put it down; it was like watching a movie; it was one of the best books they've read. And for 10 years, B.O.T.M., as good as it was, sat in my box...in hand-written form...collecting dust...doing me no damn good...

Until I got out and got in contact with Joycelyn.

She had just self-published her first book, *The Virtues of Joy,* and I asked her if she could help me out. She told me to send the hand-written manuscript to her and she'll see what she could do. Two weeks later, she called me and told me she really loved my manuscript, and that we need to publish this ASAP... And the rest is history.

I hadn't heard from Joycelyn for about a month after that, and I was starting to think she brushed me off and sold me a dream. Then one day, I got a call from her and she tells me I need to start getting my acknowledgements and dedications together, and I was like, *"what?!"* I don't know how she did it, but she managed to read and convert a 500 page hand-written manuscript into digital form, on top of formatting, getting an ISBN number, making sure I was satisfied with the cover, *AND,* doing book readings and signings for her own book, *The Virtues of Joy, AND,* began writing the sequel to *The Virtues of Joy, AND,* as if all this weren't enough, she got up 5 days a week, 4 a.m., to go do her "real" job: teaching middle school kids.

I don't know how you do it, but you do it. We've spent many hours on the phone, making corrections, building, and making this manuscript into its present form. Thank you for your time, patience, and insight....

THANKS AGAIN, JOY!!! I love you, sis. I will forever be in debt to you. You have a loyal soldier on your team. Let's sell these books, get that check, and run that sack up!!!

I'd like—no—I have to give a shout out to my inspiration of this book: *PALM BEACH COUNTY*!!! I do this for you! Da Raw, West Nam, Downtown, 21 Jump St., Stacy St. The White Houses, Tamarind Ave., Lake Worth, Boynton Beach, Delray Beach, (them *"muck boys"*) Belle Glade, Pahokee, and South Bay. It's too many cities to name, so shout out to the whole county!!!

Jeter Skeeter, wussup big homie?! Marlow, what da lick read fam? Charlie Brown, what dey do? A shout out to all my day ones: Big Ike, Adrian, Falecia Bell, Pat and Eddie Chamberlin, Jeff, Donyell, and

Michelle Jamason. A shout out to my second family: Aunty Jennifer, Alison, Amanda, Mikeaay, Jade, Sade, Nanny (I love you, Nanny!), Aunty Bev, Casey Walcott, Mike Walcott, my boo "Icy, Cake", Miss Mull, Pam, Clesyl, Granny, Dae-Dae, Richie, Delores, MK, Dee, Deja, Brittany Jackson, Ray Ray, Hervie, Kristy Chambers, Fantasia Cook, Nicklous Anderson (Flip), Helen, Clair, Marcus Pennant and the Top Shotta Elite, Carolyn Myrick, Justin Head, Niko, Maria, and my personal, Justin Hall...

To Kwadwo (pronounced Kwa-jo), iron sharpens iron. Thank you for the critique and helping me master my craft. You are one of the most intelligent brothers I have ever known. Thank you for the jewels. Life is a chess game, so make your next move your best move (I switched lanes on they ass 'cause ain't nobody lookin' 😊).

2-15-19 to them Gangsters: Tyke G, Knowledge, Chris Sheppard, Cash, Train, Tank, and all y'all I forgot.

To all my nieces and nephews: I LOVE Y'ALL!!! Stormee, Rob, Chank, Josh, Shyanne, T.J., Amaree, Jordan, Samara, and Icy Cake.

To my big sister, Dawn: I love you so much, sis!!! Mama always taught us that we are all we got; family over everything!!! I don't know what I would've done without you. Since day one, right or wrong, win, lose, or draw, you've been right there by my side. No matter what, you've always loved your little retarded-ass brother. Even after I used to steal and wreck your cars when I was younger, lol!

To my brother Bernard: I love you, bruh! My mother thought the world of you and loved you like a son, therefore you *are* my brother. Thank you for all you've done for my family and I. You put me in a position to be where I am now. I will never forget that—never!

To my brother Adonis: I am my brother's keeper... No matter the time or distance that separates us, I will always love you. Thank you for the help during my bid. Thank you for sending me *Existentialism and Humanism;* I've read it numerous times. You don't know how much it helped shape and mold my mind into its present form.

Shout out to my baby brother, Seth (Dirty Redd World got Atlanta fucked up!!!). Even though shit ain't Gucci with us, I still love you, *and,* I'm proud of you, lil bruh. Keep doing your thang. Keep the City in the headlock while I keep clutching on this 5th in the 4th quarter...ain't no fouling out though; where they do dat at...?

To my brother, Fullyloaded Kurt: I love you, my nigga!!! From my heart, I love you bruh. Real niggas do real things... when I left the streets in "2005", you was a lil nigga with the heart of a lion... I got jammed, and you rode with me the whole bid. You caught fire and ran with it, now you the next to blow. I never had to ask you for shit; damn near every time I called you had a Green Dot for me. I'll never forget the day I got released after 12 long-ass years, how when I called you the first thing you said was: how can I send you some money to get you some clothes, shoes, and a phone...and the very next day you put $400 on the wire no questions asked... Kurt, you are my family no matter what; your enemies are my enemies....

To my other brothers, Isaac Smith and Michael Walcott: love y'all through thick and thin! If I got, y'all got, if I eat, y'all eat—bottom line!!!

If I forgot you, I'm sorry...

Oh yeah, I almost forgot...to all the haters, doubters, and nae sayers: THANK YOU, 'CAUSE I COULDN'T DO WHAT I DO IF IT WEREN'T FOR YOU!!! Y'all muthafuckers counted me out, but I'm still in the race; y'all just bet on the wrong horse. Some of you had a 12-year head start, but I'm still on that ass, coming from behind, about to win the race...

Everybody loves a good comeback story.

This is a comeback story for your ass...

Now...without further ado...I present to you *Bottom of the Map*.

Thank You and Enjoy.

Author Steven L. Brown.

Welcome

TO THE

Gunshine State

Prologue

South Florida

"All rise..." the bailiff announced, "Court is now in session. The Honorable Stephen Cohen presiding."

Judge Cohen said, "You may now be seated...First case on the docket please."

The state attorney approached the podium. "Yes, Your Honor, that would be an arraignment for the State of Florida versus Trevon Jenkins, case number CF200761F016: Possession of a firearm by a convicted felon and count two: Possession of counterfeit money.

Trevon approached the podium, shackled down as Judge Cohen read over the probable cause affidavit. "Defense?"

Trevon's public defender spoke: "Yes, Your Honor, Mr. Jenkins is currently employed and needs to return to work so he could help support his child. He's been a resident of Palm Beach County for the past 20 years and has strong ties to this community. We ask the court to set a reasonable bond, so Mr. Jenkins could return to work and take care of his child."

Judge Cohen looked at the prosecutor, "any objections?"

"Yes, Your Honor. Mr. Jenkins has an extensive criminal history. Records show that his last conviction was in 2003 for aggravated assault with a firearm and possession of a firearm by a convicted felon, when he was sentenced to a three-year minimum mandatory commitment. He was on community control for..." The prosecutor flipped through some papers, "ten months when he was released from the Department of Corrections, November 16, 2006. The termination date of his community control is today, Your Honor, and Mr. Jenkins was arrested two days ago, therefore violating the terms of his community control agreement. I haven't contacted the Department of Corrections yet, but when I do, I'm sure they will be filing for a violation. Mr. Jenkins has an extensive criminal history. In the past ten years, he's been arrested numerous times for drug and weapons possessions. Kidnapping, aggravated assault, and several armed robberies. He hasn't been out a full year and is already back in trouble. It would be a big mistake to give him another chance to get back on the streets. Mr. Jenkins is a threat to the community and needs to be locked up. The state strongly objects to a bond of any amount due to the fact he was caught with counterfeit money."

"How many times has the defendant been to prison?" Judge Cohen asked.

"My records show twice, Your Honor," the prosecutor replied. "The first time was in 1996 for armed robbery with a firearm, and the second commitment was in 2003 for the charges he's on parole for now."

There was a short silence as Judge Cohen read over some papers.

"After reading the probable cause affidavit and hearing the state's testimony about your criminal history, I'm going to set bail at none... This case is assigned to Division R, Judge Berman, for all purposes... Next case please."

Trevon looked at the public defender. "You're not about to say nothin' else? Are you fuckin' serious?"

"Mr. Jenkins!" Judge Cohen snapped. "I advise, you to watch your mouth or I'll hold you in contempt!"

"FUCK THAT!" Travon yelled, "And fuck you, too!"

"Deputies! Place him in confinement! Judge Cohen ordered.

The bailiffs grabbed Trevon by the arms and practically lifted him off his feet, dragging him out of the courtroom. "Get'cho mufuckin' hands off me, bitch!" He said as he was being escorted out of the courtroom. "Fuck y'all! Fuck all y'all!"

Once Trevon was gone, Judge Cohen banged his gavel and said, "order in the court!" eliminating the giggling, whispering and mumbling. "This is a courtroom, not a circus, and I will not tolerate any more disturbances, and I hope I'm making myself perfectly clear about the matter..."

There was a short silence as Judge Cohen stared out into the courtroom. "Next case, please."

Bottom of the Map

~ an urban novel ~

How it all Started

September 30, 2007 ~

"I don't believe this shit," Trevon said to himself while he was lying in his bunk in solitary confinement inside the Palm Beach County Jail. "You had two days left — two days you stupid muthafucker!"

It had been two weeks since he'd been arrested and spoken to anyone. The first week was bearable because he was able to sleep through it. Now he was too rejuvenated, had too much sleep in his system, and had too much on his mind. He spent hours staring at the ceiling, thinking about the mistakes, about the embarrassment of the past, about the realization of the present, and the fear of the future.

Trevon sat up and walked to the sink, which was connected to a stainless-steel toilet and looked in a plastic mirror. Trevon was a handsome man. Besides having his mother's high cheek-bones and light complexion, he was the spitting imagine of his father. Standing at 6'2", with a medium build and strong facial features, he was what a lot of women called "very attractive." At the age of 28, Trevon still had a baby face that now looked old and scruffy with a two-week old beard.

Trevon sat back down and buried his face in his hands as images began to cloud his mind: His son wondering where he was and why he hadn't called. Then, of Desiree, his son's mother; What was she saying about him getting locked up again? Then he thought about how she slept with Chris, his best friend, when he was in prison the year before. He thought about Tina and Fresh...

Were they trying to get him out?

Was Tina mad at him for getting locked up again?

Did Fresh still have to rest of the counterfeit bills?

Trevon laid down as tears began to well up in his eyes. "Where did I go wrong?" he asked himself. He closed his eyes and began to reminisce, floating back to the day he was released from prison...

November 16, 2006 - 10 Months Earlier

"Jenkins! Pack it up, you're outta here!" The C.O. yelled. Trevon was already packed though, and had been since the night before. He'd dreamt of this day for three years. Now, it was finally a reality. He couldn't wait to see his son and actually be able to sit down and enjoy a good meal without being rushed to eat.

He couldn't wait to see Tina either. For three years, he watched her leave visitation looking so good, his boxers full of pre-cum from their nasty conversations. He's spent so many nights masturbating, thinking about her. Trevon missed feeling her, smelling her. He missed her sucking him up and cummin' in her mouth, and feeling her legs shake as she came in his. Never in a million years did he think he would be fiending to eat some pussy...

He missed the way it tasted.

The way it smelled.

The way it looked.

And the way it felt... Now, he was finally about to get his eat on.

Trevon looked at the palm of his right hand and said, "Well Mary, it's been real, but it's time to move on..." Then he changed his voice and acted like his hand was talking back to him, *"Oh, I see how it is. Go back to that heifer, and I hope this pussy was good to ya, 'cause you won't ever get it again..."* Back to his voice, "Damn, Mary! Why you actin' like that?" Back to the other voice, *"Go nigga! Gone!"* Back to his voice, "Fuck you then, bitch! I just used you for the time being..."

"Jenkins!" the C.O. yelled. "You better come on or you're waiting for the next shift to be released!"

"Be easy," Trevon yelled back, "I'm coming!"

As Trevon walked across the compound, he thought about the last three years he'd spent here. He had some bad times; he had some good times too. Still he didn't look back. "Never again," he told himself. "Never again..."

When he got to the property room, they handed him the clothes Tina sent. He opened the box and a big smile swept across his face. The first thing he saw was a fitted, white Miami Dolphins cap (his favorite football team), a white t-shirt, a white wife beater, a pair of white Phat Pharm sweatpants, and a pair of all white Reebok Classics. After getting dressed he noticed how strange it felt to wear free-world clothes and new sneakers; he felt like a new man.

When Trevon got to the window by the lobby door, they handed him five twenty-dollar bills, a paper with the results of his HIV test (negative), a paper with directions to the community control office in Palm Beach County and was told he had forty-eight hours to report there.

As he approached the lobby door he heard it buzz open but hesitated for a moment before opening it. His heart raced as he began to, and when he finally did, he walked through it like a well-trained dog. When he stepped into the packed lobby he scanned faces looking for Tina...

She saw him first.

"Aaaaaaagh!" she screamed as she ran across the lobby. "There-go-my-baby!" When she reached him she jumped up and straddled her legs around him and Trevon dropped his bag to catch her. Tina's skirt raised up, revealing a pink G-string running up the crack of her ass.

Every man in the lobby was glued to the sight.

Tina shoved her tongue in Trevon's mouth, kissing him passionately. He grabbed the globes of her ass and began grinding her onto his rock-hard dick. They stopped kissing long enough for her to say, "I missed you baby."

"I missed you, too," Trevon, replied.

"I've been a bad girl, daddy. Are you gonna spank me?"

"Don't I always spank that ass whenever you're a bad girl?" Trevon said, slapping her ass, making it jiggle.

"Mmmmh," Tina moaned, "spank me again," she purred before sticking her tongue back in his mouth. Trevon slapped her ass so hard her caramel skin turned bright red. They were in their own little world, not caring that everyone in the lobby was watching them put on their little freak show. When Trevon put Tina down, nine inches of rock hard dick was bulging out the front of his sweatpants.

Tina wrapped her hand around the bulge and began stroking it, "Ummm, damn, baby, I miss this dick."

"And this dick miss you," Trevon replied. "Let's get up outta here."

Tina looked at the lady sitting next to them and said, *"Giiirl,* I hope you have as much fun as I'm about to have tonight."

The lady looked at the bulge sticking out the front of Trevon's pants before looking back at Tina. "Sheiit," the lady replied. "I hope I do, too."

"Where's your car?" Trevon asked when they reached the parking lot.

"Right there," Tina replied, disarming the alarm on a new 2006 black Acura Legend.

"Daaaamn!" Trevon exclaimed, rubbing his hands across the trunk. "You doin' it like this now? Steppin' up in the world, huh?"

Trevon leaned against the trunk and Tina wrapped her arms around his neck and pecked him on the lips. "Do you like it?" she asked. Dexter put the down payment on it for me last month. I wanted to surprise you."

Trevon smiled. "Yeah, I like it... It's nice to see that you're handling your business."

Tina smiled. "Well... I had a real good teacher."

"Oh yeah?"

Tina shook her head, "Um-hmm, real good, the very best."

Trevon opened the back door and threw his bag on the back seat before getting in on the passenger's side; the car smelled like new leather. He noticed that Tina had a picture they took at the fair on the speedometer display.

"I don't think Dexter would appreciate you having that picture of up."

"Fuck Dexter!" Tina quipped. "He can't say nothin' about that and he be fuckin' around with all them hoes...But I still take it down before I go over there. He makes me damn sick, with his ugly-ass! He think he has so much game and that I'm so stupid. I let him think he got all the sense...as long as he keep cuttin' that check, it's all good."

"All right now, you know them Jamaicans crazy?"

"Yeah, I know..." Tina said, "but you know what?"

"What?"

Tina smiled. "My baby...he crazy, too."

"Is he?"

Tina leaned over and pecked Trevon on the lips. "Um hmm, he's a *baaaaad muthafucker*! He don't play no games... One time, I seen him give a Tylenol a headache, and watched him beat the shit out of an Ex-Lax."

"Damn!" Trevon said. "Now that's a bad muthafucker!"

"That he is," Tina replied, rubbing the side of Trevon's face. "I missed you so much, Tre. I'm so glad you are out."

"I missed you, too-"

"Oh..." Tina said, reaching into her Coach bag to grab her cell phone. "Fresh said call him as soon as you got out. He done called a hundred times since this morning — see?"

Trevon grabbed the phone and seen there were 16 missed calls. He went through the call log, found Fresh's name, and hit the call button.

"Put it on speaker phone," Tina said, hitting the button to turn on the speaker phone.

Fresh answered on the second ring, screaming at the top of his lungs: "WUSSUUUUUP?!"

"WUSSUUUUUUP?!" Trevon responded.

"WUSSUUUUUUUUP?! Fresh yelled back.

Trevon: "WUSSUUUUUUUP?!"

Fresh: "WUSSUUUUUUUUUUP?!"

In unison: "WUSSUUUUUUUUUUUUUUP?!"

"Will y'all stop all that damn yellin'!" Tina barked, covering her ears.

"Shut up, hood rat!" Fresh barked back.

"Fuck you, nigga! And quit blowin' up my phone! You act worse than a bitch! I told you I was gonna have Tre call yo stupid-ass!"

"Wasn't nobody blowin' up your phone, you dick junkie! I was callin' to talk to my dirty, so clear the line — Tre? What da lick read, son?" Fresh asked as Tina began to kiss Trevon on the neck. He could hear a female in the background saying something and Fresh said, "Hold on dawg..." and started yelling at whoever it was: "Wait, bitch! This my muthafuckin' mans on the phone — fuck wrong wit'choo?" Fresh got back on the phone. "Hello?"

"Yeah", Trevon answered.

"My bad, son...these freaks can't get enough of Young Fresh."

"Still the same ole Fresh I see."

"Ain't nothin' change but the day, homeboy; same soup, different bowl."

"So wussup, nigga?" Trevon asked as Tina reached over to recline his seat before untying his sweatpants. "Why you ain't never come see ya boy?"

"I'll talk to you about that when you get back to Palm Beach, son. I gave Tina pictures and money to send to you. Did you get it?"

"Yeah, I got it. Good lookin' homeboy."

"Don't mention it, son. You know I ain't forget about you. It's been crazy out here, especially after I got shot..."

Tina pulled out Trevon's dick and begin stroking it while licking inside his ear. "Tell Fresh you have to go," she whispered.

"What's up with them niggas that shot you?" Trevon asked.

"Oh, you didn't hear me?" Tina whispered. She squeezed around the bottom of Trevon's shaft and stroked upward, making pre-cum ooze out. She used the tip of her finger to rub it around the head of his dick.

Trevon closed his eyes and laid back, catching the last part of what Fresh was saying: "... so I'll talk to you about that when y'all get here. Are y'all coming straight back?"

"Yeah," Trevon answered just as Tina started licking slowly around the head of his dick while stroking his shaft.

27

"Mmmmh," she moaned, *"this dick taste so good."*

"I'll call you when we get there," Trevon said, trying to stay focused.

"Hang up the phone," Tina whispered before swallowing Trevon's dick.

"Ooh shit..." he moaned. "I gotta go, bruh!"

Fresh burst out laughing. "Heeeell naw! Aye, Tina?"

"Hmmm?" She answered with a mouthful of cock.

"Spit my dawg dick out — nasty bitch!"

"Fuck you, Fresh!" Tina exclaimed. "Ole bitch-ass nigga!"

"Naw, for real though, Tina," Fresh said, trying to catch his breath, "are y'all coming straight back? I wanna see my homeboy."

"Fresh..." Tina replied casually, "believe me, Tre coming...matter-of-fact, he about to cum right now — bye Fresh." Tina took the phone from Trevon and hit the END button, cutting Fresh off: "Aww, you nasty bi -." *Click.*

Trevon sat up smiling. "Why you hung up on my dirty like that?"

"Fuck Fresh," Tina answered. "You wanna talk to Fresh, or do you want this..." she leaned over and swallowed half of Trevon's dick.

"Fuck Fresh." Trevon replied.

"I thought so," Tina chuckled. She pushed Trevon back into the seat and continued deep throating his rock-hard dick. He started to cum almost immediately and Tina could feel small squirts gush in her mouth.

"Mmmmh, I taste it, baby," she said, rubbing his nuts with the tips of her fingernails. "Cum, baby..."

"Ooh, shit," he moaned, his pelvis feeling like it was about to explode.

"Mmmmh, cum in my mouth," Tina said teasingly. "You do wanna cum in my mouth, dontcha?"

"Yes...don't stop...please don't stop," Trevon pleaded.

"I'm not, baby," she said, making slurping noises as she sucked. Trevon's legs began to tremble. Long hard gushes of warm semen flooded Tina's mouth. Her head bobbed up and down as she stroked his shaft, sucking and swallowing as he throbbed and skeeted. She didn't stop until after the last spasm.

Trevon came so hard he almost ripped the door handle off. His body rocked with each pulse. "Shit!" he exclaimed, trying to catch his breath.

Tina stroked his shaft and more cum skeeted out and webbed her fingers. "Why didn't you tell me you weren't finished?" She asked.

"Because I thought I was."

"I'm sorry, baby," Tina said, licking the cum off her fingers. She grabbed Trevon's dick and began deep throating him again until she felt him go soft in her mouth. She sucked on the head, stretching his limp cock, popping it like a rubber band.

"Damn, I love you, girl," Trevon sighed.

"You finished now?"

"Yeah, for now."

"I-I-I-I-got a surprise for yooou," Tina sang.

"What?"

"Close your eyes."

"What'choo up to?" Trevon asked suspiciously.

"Just close your eyes, nigga — *damn!*"

Trevon closed his eyes and moments later he heard the glove compartment open, followed by something cool being placed around his neck.

"Okay...you can open them," Tina said excitedly.

Trevon opened his eyes and looked down at a 24-inch 14-karat gold Cuban link with a medallion of the Virgin Mary embellished in diamonds.

"It was your birthday gift...you got locked up before I had a chance to give it to you. Do you like it?"

"Aww, baby — I love it!" Trevon said, flipping down the visor so he could look at it in the mirror.

"It's a token of my appreciation..." Tina said. "It's my way of saying 'thank you'."

Trevon shook his head. "For what?"

"For believing in me. For showing me who I am and what I'm worth. For loving me when no one else did. For teaching me how to love myself. For always telling me what I needed to hear and not what I wanted to hear... I wouldn't be where I am today if it wasn't for you, Tre, and I want you to know that I will never forget it... never."

Tears welled up in Tina's eyes and one ran a rivulet down her cheek. Trevon wiped it away with his thumb. "There's no doubt in my mind you would've made it with or without me..." he said, grabbing Tina's hand. "The first time I saw you dancing in that drive-thru window at McDonald's, I knew you were something special... You were a seed... a seed that was bound to sprout regardless of what. All I did was plant it... nourished it... gave it what it needed to grow..." Trevon rubbed the side of Tina's face, "and what sprouted from that seed turned out to be something beautiful. I'm the one that needs to be saying 'thank you'."

"For what, baby?"

"For allowing me to grow with you, girl... For being ten toes down.

29

For being by my side. For the letters. For the pictures. For the collect calls. For the money. For the visits — I'm proud of you, baby. You stood up like a real soldier these past three years."

A big smile swept across Tina's face. "Because I am a soldier..." she said, "I'm your soldier, baby. I'm ten toes to the pavement, like this here..." Tina sat up like a soldier at attention and saluted.

Trevon laughed. "Ten toes to the pavement, huh?"

"Yes, sir!" Tina punctuated with another salute.

Trevon grabbed her by the neck, pulled her to him, and kissed her passionately. "I love you, girl," he said afterward.

"I love you, too, Tre... You're my everything, baby..."

Tina pecked Trevon on the lips and smiled.

"What's so funny?" He asked.

"How your dick taste?"

"So, what, it's my dick — no homo."

"Well, how your dick taste then — no homo?"

"Like sugarcane."

Tina smiled harder. "You ain't lying, 'cause it sho is sweet..." She reached behind the seat, pulled out a bottle of Grey Goose, and placed it on Trevon's lap before cranking up the car. "It's a store up the street... we'll stop there to get you some Newports and orange juice — and I'm telling you right fuckin' now, Tre: don't make me have to fuck you and Fresh up! You're not going anywhere tonight. Get whatever you need before you get to the crib, 'cause once we get there, issa wrap!"

"That's cool."

Tina looked at Trevon, eyes squinted, and said, "I'm not playing with you, Trevon Jenkins... I took the whole weekend off to be with you. We can pick Lil' Tre up tomorrow and take him to Boomer's. I haven't seen him since you've been gone. I know he done got so big — I miss his lil' bad ass.

Trevon started pushing buttons on the CD player, trying to figure out how to turn it on. "How you turn this shit on?"

"Use the remote."

"Where is it?"

"In the armrest," Tina said, reaching over Trevon to grab her T-Pain CD from the glove compartment. "Put this in," she said, handing him the CD. She took the remote from Trevon and skipped to "I'm Sprung." "Every time I hear this song; I think about you."

"Oooh — that's my shit," Trevon said, clapping his hands and bopping his shoulders. He tilted his hat to the side and sang along with T-Pain: *"I'm spruuung — I'm spruuuuung/she got me doin' things I never do, if you ain't been I'm telling yooou..."*

Trevon was still singing and acting foolish when they pulled into the 7-11. Tina grabbed her Coach bag, leaned against the door, and looked at him admiringly. "You're so fuckin' cute," she said, pulling him to her.

"*Cute?*" Trevon snapped. "I ain't cute. Puppies are cute. Teddy bears are cute. Monkeys are cute. I'ma Pitbull...a grizzly bear... a fuckin' silverback gorilla – KING KONG AIN'T GOT SHIT ON ME!" he yelled, trying to sound like Denzel Washington in *Training Day.*

"You're so damn crazy," Tina said, pecking him on the lips. "Does the silverback gorilla want anything else besides cigarettes and orange juice?"

"Yeah..." Trevon answered, "get me a fat pussy bar – they should be by the Baby Ruth's – a six-pack of titties, and a big bag of barbecue ass... you got all that?"

"Yeah, I got it." Tina said, opening the door laughing.

As she headed toward the store Trevon couldn't do nothing but shake his head. She walked in and had every man in the store mesmerized; they all did double takes and watched her out the corners of their eyes. She was so seductive, so beautiful, so sexy and walked like a stallion. She could put a man in a trance without even trying...

"Poor Dexter," Trevon mumbled to himself.

Tina returned and placed two cups of ice in the cup-holders before giving Trevon a pack of Newports and a lighter. She mixed the vodka and orange juice and handed Travon a cup. "I'd like to propose a toast," she said, holding up her cup. "To my baby...my best friend...my everything – cheers!"

They tapped cups and drank.

"Damn, I miss this shit," Trevon said, leaning back in his seat.

Tina pulled a pill bottle from her bag. She took a Xanax from the bottle and placed it in Trevon's mouth. Then she reached back in her bag and pulled out a blunt the size of a magic marker. She lit it and passed it to him.

"Welcome home, baby..." she said, as Trevon hit the blunt. "Are you ready to go back to Palm Beach?"

"I've been ready for the past three years," Trevon replied. "There's no place like home. There's no place like South Florida."

Tina rubbed Trevon's leg. "Well, I'm about to take you back..."

Trevon woke up just as they were passing a sign that read:

```
You are now
entering
PALM BEACH COUNTY
```

The sun was just starting to set, and the sky was awash with colors only found in South Florida: deep pinks, vibrant blues, radiant roses, and muted greens all swirled together on an aqua background...

"Damn, it feels good to see Palm Trees again," Trevon said, stretching his arms. "Where them Xanax at?"

"Look in my bag," Tina replied. Trevon found them and washed one down with some watered-down vodka and orange juice as Tina reached over and pinched his nose. "You want me to get you some yáyò? If you want it, you better get it now, 'cause when we get home, you're not leaving that house, Tre. So, you need to let me know what da lick read."

"Yeah..." Trevon said, lighting up a cigarette, "go ahead and put a handle on that."

"Hand me my cell phone."

Trevon gave Tina her phone. Afterward, he laid back, closed his eyes, and listened to Tina go to work:

"Hello? Dexter? Hey, boo-boo, how ya doin'? Yeah, I just got back from pickin' my cousin up..."

Cousin? Trevon thought. *Wow!*

"...can't tonight, baby. I have to take him to Miami to see our aunt... I'm sorry. I miss you too Dexter..."

Trevon looked at Tina smiling, and she rolled her eyes, as if to say, *he make me sick.*

"...matter-of-fact, why don't you meet me somewhere, so I can see you before we go to Miami...Where? Okay, I'll be there in 20 minutes...I'll see you then — oh, do you have some work...? Yeah, my cousin get down and he wanted some... You're so sweet, baby. See you in twenty."

Click.

"THAT'S-MY-DAWG!" Trevon exclaimed, sounding like

Smokey from *Friday*.

"I can't stand that bitch!" Tina said. "Talkin' to me like I'm his muthafuckin' child — ugly muthafucker!"

"Where he want you to meet him at?"

"At the convention center."

"At the convention center?!" Trevon exclaimed. "What damn convention center?!"

"A lot done changed since you've been gone, Tre... West Palm done blew up. It's downtown across the street from City Place. You wanna go walk through there? We could go to the Blue Martini or Wet Willie's and get some daiquiris. It's your night, baby, so we'll drink whatever you want."

"*Anything I want?*"

"Anything you want."

Trevon smiled. "They don't have what I want at the Blue Martini or Wet Willie's."

"Well, what do you want to drink, baby?"

"I wanna drink an orgasm," Trevon answered, "and I only know two places that serve good ones."

"Where?"

"The Blue Martina and Wet Coochies...Think we can swing by there?"

Tina looked at Trevon and smiled. "Yeah, we can do that... matter-of-fact, it just so happened that I know the owner, so I'ma make sure you get yo drink on real good..."

After they pulled into the convention center parking lot, Tina parked and called Dexter. "He'll be here in 10 minutes," she said. She leaned over and Trevon met her halfway, kissing her on the lips. Afterward, she gazed deeply into his eyes. "You're so handsome, Tre."

"No more than you're beautiful, princess," Trevon replied.

They stared at each other in silence.

Tina smiled, rubbed the side of Trevon's face, and brushed over his lips with her thumb. "I love your lips," she said. "Them shitz lethal. My pussy already tingling from just thinking about how good you're about to suck it — see..." Tina took Trevon's hand, leaned against the door, and pulled her G-string to the side as she spread her legs. When Trevon touched her she was wet...

Dripping wet.

It was the first time he felt pussy in three years. Tina was so moist. So warm. So slippery. He stroked his finger over the ultra-sensitive bud of

33

her clitoris, drawing it out, making her moan and arch her hips upward...

"See what you do to me, baby?" she asked seductively. "This yo pussy, Tre... this gon' always be yo pussy..." She was so wet her pussy smacked as Trevon rubbed it. "You hear that?" she asked. "This pussy callin' you..." Tina grabbed the back of Trevon's head, pulled him to her, then whispered in his ear, "It's saying, Tre... I want you, Tre...I need you, Tre..."

Tina pushed Trevon back in his seat.

Trevon smiled, knowing what was next. She snatched out his rock-hard dick and stroked it. Pre-cum oozed out and webbed her fingers.

"Now do you see that you do to me?" Trevon asked. "I'm not the only one that can make juices flow."

Tina smiled and licked the pre-cum off her fingers before swallowing half of Trevon's dick.

The phone rang.

"Hello...? All right." *Click.*

Tina looked at Trevon. "He's right down the street," she said, kissing Trevon's dick one last time before putting it back in his pants.

Seconds later, a white Hummer pulled up behind them blaring reggae music. "I'll be right back," Tina said.

Trevon looked through the rearview mirror and saw four men with long dreadlocks emerge from the Hummer. One walked up to Tina and gave her a hug while the other three stood nearby, searching the parking lot like secret service agents trying to spot a possible assassin.

They must be his goons, Trevon thought to himself. When he took a closer look at the one Tina was talking to, he said, "DAMN!" Tina said Dexter was ugly, but not that damn ugly; he made Shabba Ranks look like Usher.

Some more words were exchanged and Deter gave Tina a small brown paper bag. She hugged him, more words were exchanged, then she said, "Tre! Come'ere so you can meet Dexter."

"Shit!" Trevon said under his breath. "I don't wanna talk to this nigga." Reluctantly, he stepped out of the Acura and headed towards them. When he reached them, he got a bad vibe when he looked in Dexter's eyes, and from the way Dexter looked at him, Trevon could see the feeling was mutual.

They stared at each other for a short moment.

Trevon broke the ice: "What da lick read, dread?" he said, sticking out his hand.

Dexter shook it. "Wha ha um, my yute?" he replied with a heavy Jamaican accent.

"Can't call it..." Trevon said, "just happy to be home, you feel me?"

Dexter shook his head. "Yuh haffie be reel careful nowadays, my yute. Babylon dem waan lock up all da black mon dem and trow away da key, so chill, sén?"

"I am..." Trevon replied. "Thanks for the package, good lookin'."

"We need to get going," Tina cut in. "I'm not trying to be on that road all night..." She wrapped her arms around Dexter's neck. "You want some sugar before I go?"

"*Yeeess, gal,*" Dexter replied.

Tina grabbed Dexter by the back of his head and shoved her tongue in his mouth. While doing so, she opened her eyes to look at Trevon, who was standing behind Dexter, and winked at him.

Trevon laughed silently.

When Tina finished, she grabbed the sides of Dexter's face and licked across his lips. "How does that taste?" she asked afterward.

"So sweet, gal," Dexter replied, licking his lips.

"Sweet like sugar cane?" Tina asked.

"Sweeta den suga cane," Dexter said.

"Umm, that's the same thing I thought when I tasted it," Tina said sarcastically.

"Mi haffie get going," Dexter said, not catching on to what Tina was talking about. "Later, my yute, "he said to Trevon who was on his way back to the Acura.

"Later," Trevon hollered back.

Dexter and Tina exchanged a few more words while Trevon waited in the car. When she got back in the car, Trevon looked at her and she smiled. "What...?" she said. "I just wanted to get a second opinion. See, even Dexter think your dick is sweet."

"Nasty bitch," Trevon chuckled.

"That's okay, though..." Tina said. "I'm yo nasty bitch, and you love this nasty bitch..." she threw the bag Dexter gave her on Trevon's lap. He opened it and pulled out an ounce of weed and an eight-ball (3.5 grams) of cocaine.

"So, Dexter that dude, huh?" Trevon asked.

"Yeah, he's that dude... I seen inside of his safe once; I ain't never saw so much money in my life! And I already know what you are thinking... It's gonna be real hard 'cause he always have his peoples around."

"Naw..." Trevon replied, "just stick to the script and keep doing what you do, feel me? I need you to keep holmes close... I don't know why, but I got a bad premonition when I seen him, like I done seen dude somewhere before. I know I ain't trippin' because the way he looked at me..." Trevon looked out the window. "I know we know each other from somewhere, I just can't put my finger on it."

"Well, in the meantime," Tina said, as she pulled up her skirt and opened her legs, "while you're trying to put your finger on that, you needs to be putting your finger in this."

Trevon smiled. "That's a real good idea," he said, leaning over to take Tina up on her suggestion. He stuck two fingers deep inside of her while he sucked on her neck and ear. "Don't fuck around and crash now..." he whispered inside it.

●   ●   ●

Tina was renting a one-bedroom condominium in Royal Palm Beach, one of Palm Beach County's upscale communities. When they pulled up to the gate of the complex, Trevon's hand was covered with her juices. He had been fingering her while sucking on her neck for the past twenty minutes, and Tina was so ready to be sucked and fucked.

When they stopped in front of the security booth Trevon moved his hand, but Tina left her legs cocked wide open as she put the car in *park* and rolled the window down. The security guard, a tall, chubby white man in his late 30s, was on the phone writing something down. When he finished, he stepped out and said, "Caramel, howya doin' tonight, sweetheart?"

"Hey, Richard," Tina replied, turning off the car. "This is my friend, Tre. He just got in from out of town and he's gonna be staying for a while, so I need you to put his name on the visitor's list permanently."

Richard stepped off the curb, bent down, and looked at Trevon. "Hey."

"What da lick read?" Trevon replied.

Tina was still leaning back, with her legs wide open. Not only did Richard see a fat piece of pussy bulging out of her pink G-string, but he also saw a wet spot where her pussy hole was, running up along the print of her camel-toe, turning the light pink fabric dark pink in the center. He also saw Tina's pussy juices shimmering on her inner thighs...

Richards eye were glued.

"His name is Trevon Jenkins," Tina said with a big smile.

"Huh...?" Richard replied, looking lost.

"My friend... His name is Trevon Jenkins."

"Oh yeah..." Richard said. "How do you spell that?"

"T-R-E-V-O-N, last name, J-E-N-K-I-N-S."

Richard's eyes went right back in between Tina's legs after he put Trevon's name on the list. She looked at the wet spot and touched it with her middle finger. When she looked back at Richard, his eyes were still locked in on her wet, bulging pussy. "Richard, baby...? Heeellooo, up here," she said, trying to get his attention. "I'll see you at the club Monday night, all right?"

Richard didn't speak, he just shook his head, mouth wide open.

"Come'ere, Richard..." Tina said seductively, and Richard came like a trained dog. "Closer..." she ordered. "Closer Richard, it's not gonna bite you..."

Richard came closer and Tina used her left hand to pull her G-sting to the side, then used her right middle finger to rub her clit. "Hmmm, Richard, baby," she moaned, sticking two fingers deep inside of her. "You make sure you make it to the club Monday night, okay?"

Richard shook his head in a trance.

"Would you like a lil' somethin' to hold you over until then?" Tina asked.

Richard shook his head again.

"Come'ere then, Richard..." Richard stuck his head in the window and Tina rubbed her fingers across his lips. "You can suck it," she said teasingly.

Richard grabbed Tina's hand and sucked on her fingers like a newborn baby sucking on a bottle.

"This one is one me..." Tina said, cranking up the car, bringing the conversation to an end, "the next one is on you. See you at the club, Richard." Tina rolled up the window and Richard went inside to open the gate.

"Why you did that?" Trevon asked.

"Did what?" Tina answered innocently. "Richard is a regular customer of mines... That's a guaranteed three to four hundred just from him every Monday night. He pay a hundred dollars for a lap dance and all I have to do is stick my finger in my pussy and let him suck it."

"Damn, you had him hypnotized," Trevon chuckled.

They parked the car and took the elevator to the third floor. Tina unlocked the door, walked in, and Trevon followed. "Welcome home, baby," she said, turning on the lights.

Trevon looked around the living room. The condo was small, but real cozy and home-like. There was a black leather sofa with a matching love seat. There were gold post lamps on each side of the sofa, with a 52-

37

inch plasma TV hanging on the wall with a Sony stereo system sitting on a stand underneath; surround sound speakers were in each corner. There was a painting of two nude women making out on the opposite wall of the plasma.

"This is real nice," Trevon said. "This real tight work, baby."

"Come'ere, let me show you the bedroom," Tina said, pulling him by the hand. When they reached the bedroom, she turned on the lights and said, "Surprise!"

The first thing Trevon saw was his PlayStation that was hooked up to another plasma TV hanging on a wall. Tina had a huge king size Victorian four-post bed with a black comforter and black silk sheets. It was a dresser in one corner, and the chair that went with the rest of the living room set in the other corner by the bed.

Tina walked to the dresser. "The bottom two drawers are yours..." she said, taking out a pair of boxers and a tank-top and throwing them on the bed. "I'll take you to go get some clothes tomorrow." She wrapped her arms around Trevon's neck. "Do you like it?"

Trevon smiled, "I love it."

"Go jump in the shower and I'll go fix you a drink."

"Sound like a plan to me."

"Oh..." Tina said, going into the bathroom and returning with a small mirror and a razor blade. "I have some straws in the kitchen; you need to eat something before you start snortin' that shit."

"I did eat," Trevon said, matter-of-factly.

Tina put her hands on her hips. "What'choo ate, Tre?"

"I ate some Xanax...and I'm about to eat some pussy."

"You get on my nerves," Tina said, slapping Trevon across the head. "For real though, Tre. I want you to keep your weight on, you look good like that. You're all nice and chunky, make a bitch wanna eat you alive. Take these off..." Tina untied Trevon's shoes and slid them off. Afterward, she walked to the dresser, took her keys out of her bag, and walked into the closet.

"What'choo doin'?" he asked curiously.

"Nothin', baby..." Tina answered. "Just a little insurance."

Trevon jumped up and rushed to the closet. Just as he reached the door, he saw her closing the safe, locking her keys and his shoes inside. "What the fuck you did that for?"

"So, I won't have to fuck you up, nigga," Tina answered through clinched teeth. "Because if I wake up, and you're gone, that's yo ass, nigga! Palm Beach County ain't gon' be big enough for you and Fresh to hide in. I'm not playing with you, Tre. You're spending the whole weekend with me, so you can cancel whatever y'all had planned..." Tina wrapped her arms around Trevon's neck. "Look, Tre... we've been anticipating this day for a long time. I know you've been away for a while and you're anxious to catch up on lost time, but could you please do that on Monday?" She laid her head against Trevon's chest. "I just want it to be us this weekend, okay, baby?"

"That's cool," Trevon replied, "I don't have a problem with that. Shit, I had the same thing in mind."

"You did, baby?"

"Yeah, you know how many nights I sat up thinking about you? It would be an honor to spend the weekend with you. You ain't have to lock my shoes in the safe."

"You promise you're not gonna sneak off?" Tina asked suspiciously.

"Of course, I promise."

"Say it then."

"Say what?"

"Say you promise, nigga."

"I promise, nigga—*damn*! You feel better now?"

"Um hmm," Tina said, with a smile, "but them shoes still ain't coming out that safe. I know you, Trevon Jenkins. You can talk a cat off a fish truck, but you ain't about to run that shit here. Game recognize game, baby. You taught me how to run it, so when it's ran on me I can peep it..."

Tina pushed Trevon down on the bed. "I was gonna surprise you and have Casey come over."

"Who is Casey?" Trevon asked curiously.

Tina smiled. "My bitch."

"Why you ain't never say nothing about her?"

"Because it's not that serious," Tina replied. "I had to do what I had to do while you were gone. Every now and then I need to be held...and Casey has been there..." A devilish grin swept across Tina's face, "She got some good head, too."

"Better than mines?" Trevon asked suspiciously.

"No way. Casey was just holding me over until you got home." She started smiling again. "You're gonna be real proud of me. I want you to see how ya girl be putting it down."

"Oh yeah?" Trevon said with a grin.

"Um-hmm, later on we gon' give you a little freak show."

Trevon's face lit up. "That's what I'm talking about."

"There are two conditions though," Tina said, holding up two fingers. "One: you can't fuck her. Two: You can't eat her pussy. I don't mind if she suck your dick, but you ain't about to take my bitch with them

39

soup coolers," Tina said, pinching Trevon's lips.

"All I wanna do is watch."

Tina rubbed her hands together. "Oh, you gon' watch all right," she said, "You gon' like how I put the pick down."

"The pick?" What the fuck is 'The Pick'?" Trevon asked curiously.

A devious smile swept across Tina's face. "You wanna see The Pick?" She asked. "Are you sure you wanna see my dawg?"

"Yeah," Trevon chuckled.

"All right now...don't start hatin' when you see it..." Tina got up and went into the closet, closing the door behind her. Moments later, she yelled out, "Are you ready?" before bursting out the closet butt-ass naked, wearing Trevon's Miami Dolphins cap.

"Hell naw!" he said, laughing hysterically.

"Yeah, go ahead and hate," Tina said, stroking a 12-inch dildo that was strapped around her waist with a Velcro strap, with another strap connected to the waist strap, running down the crack of her ass, connecting to the nuts of the dildo.

Trevon was laughing so hard tears welled up in his eyes. "Come'ere," he said, "you need help, girl."

"I don't need help. I slang this muthafucker well," Tina said, pumping her hips, making the long dildo sway from side-to-side. She pushed Trevon on the bed, grabbed one of his legs, and cocked it back: "I take Casey like this...," then she started poking his crotch, "and I ask that bitch — WHO-PUSSY-IS-THIS-HUH?" Tina yelled loudly.

"Get the fuck off me, ole crazy-ass, girl!" Trevon said, trying to catch his breath.

I have her ass over this bed tryin' to run from this bitch." Tina said, sitting on Trevon's abdomen, with "The Pick" just inches from his face.

"Get that shit outta my face!" he demanded.

Tina yelled, "Shut up, nigga!" and slapped Trevon on the cheek with "The Pick," making a loud *smack* sound off.

"Stop bitch!" he said, wiping off his cheek. "Fuck wrong wit'choo? I don't know where that shit been at!"

"Be easy," Tina replied, "you know I keep my shit strapped up." She reached over, opened the nightstand drawer, and pulled out a Magnum XL condom. She opened it and rolled the condom down the long dildo.

Trevon rolled her over and kissed her on her forehead. "I love you, girl."

"I love you, too," Tina replied.

"You know you need help, right?" Trevon said, brushing hair away from her face.

"Naw...I'm straight, I don't need help."

"You got issues, baby?"

"Don't we all?"

Trevon smirked. "So, y'all be gettin' y'all freak on, huh?"

"Naw, it ain't even that type of party. I wear the pants around this bitch, so I be getting' my freak on..." Tina unstrapped "The Pick" and held it up. "Ain't nobody about to stick this big-ass shit up in me, tearin' up my muthafuckin' pussy. Are you fuckin' crazy? That's why I said you can't fuck Casey. You wouldn't want to fuck her anyways; I got that pussy wide open..." Tina started smiling, "I'm not trying to say you got a small dick, baby, but I done knocked the walls down in that pussy..." She grabbed Trevon's dick. "She ain't gonna feel this shit."

"You sure she ain't been knockin' the walls down in your pussy?" Trevon asked accusingly.

"Hell naw! I like getting my pussy sucked. Dicks come a dime a dozen, but good head is priceless..." Tina held up "The Pick." "Some bitches like this shit, but not everybody."

Trevon slapped "The Pick" on the floor. "One thing I know: a lie don't care who tell it."

"Oh, you think I'm lying?" Tina asked, reaching for Trevon's hand. She guided a finger inside of her. "Does that feel dug out?"

"Naw..." he said, "that don't feel like it's been dug out at all."

Tina flexed, and her walls closed around Trevon's finger. "This all the dick I need right here..." she said, pulling Trevon's out and sucking on it gently. "Now, I wish you would go get yo ass in the shower."

Tina opened the door and stuck her head in just as Trevon was about to get in the shower. She stood there for a moment, staring at him standing there stark naked with a semi-hard dick...

"Umm...I like, I like."

"Quit starin' at my dick," Trevon said, covering himself with his hands.

Tina threw a towel in his face. "It's mines, I can do whatever I want to it!"

"Wussup?"

"I just came in here to tell yo sexy ass I forgot to get soap, so you have to use my body wash," Tina said and slammed the door.

When Trevon stepped into the shower, he washed and sat there for what seemed like ages. He stood there under the hot water and thought. He thought about his son. He thought about Tina. He thought about his life. He thought about the last three years he'd spent in that concrete jungle they call prison...

Trevon had learned so much in those three years. He learned the virtue of patience. He prayed for wisdom. He searched for understanding. He learned that life was a succession of lessons that could only be learned by living. And living life was one thing he did to the fullest.

Trevon was home now, and the streets were calling him. "Patience..." he said to himself, "patience..."

The first thing Trevon saw when stepped out the bathroom was Tina lying against the headboard, legs wide open, rubbing the tip of a vibrator in a circular motion around her clitoris with one hand, and pinching her nipple with the other.

"It took you long enough," she said, looking straight ahead.

Trevon looked in the direction she was looking in and seen what had her attention. She was watching a porno flick on the TV hanging on the wall: Two women, one high yellow, the other midnight black, with the pinkest pussy he had ever seen. They were in the sixty-nine, and black was on top, winding her hips, grinding her pussy on Red's mouth. Red's legs were cocked back, and Black was sucking her pussy like a true vet, sticking about three inches of tongue in Red's ass...

"Damn, that shit looks so real," Trevon said, walking to the plasma and touching the screen.

"Because it is real, you fool." Tina replied.

"Not the porno, you freak... I'm talkin' about the picture; it's like you can stick your hand in and rub their pussies."

"That's why it's called a 'plasma TV' — duhh... You have a lot of catching up to do..." Tina got up and went into the bathroom. She reached under the sink, pulled out a douche, and turned around. "I got you set up on the nightstand. Be ready when I come out; I want that dick primed up." She screwed the nozzle on the douche and licked it from the bottom to the top before closing the door.

Trevon smiled when he looked on the nightstand. Tina fixed him a vodka and orange juice and placed a Xanax next to the glass. She had 10 even lines of cocaine line up on the mirror she brought out of the bathroom earlier, with a straw lying in the middle, and there was a Newport lying in the ashtray, with a lighter lying next to the mirror.

Trevon sat in the chair, popped the Xanax, and picked up the mirror. He put the straw to his nose and inhaled, sniffing the white crystalized powder. He laid his head back and exhaled, letting it drain down his throat. He leaned back over the mirror, inhaling two lines in each nostril before placing the mirror back on the nightstand. Trevon picked up the Newport. He lit it, pulled on it, and let the smoke fill his lungs. He laid his head back on the chair as the cocaine numbed his face. It drained down his throat. He tingled as the sensation flowed through his veins and spread throughout his entire body: his chest, his arms, his legs, his feet, and blood rushed to his dick as that sensation touched his groin.

When he looked at the TV, the images on it intensified the sensation; seeing Black and Red eat each other out really aroused him. Trevon took off his boxers and began stroking himself. He sat there smoking a Newport butt-ass naked, watching two beautiful women make out, looking like a baby with a big dick. He wanted Tina so bad he was about ready to go snatch her out the shower...

"Patience..." he said to himself, "patience."

●　　　●　　　●

Trevon looked like a different man when Tina came out of the bathroom. The way he looked at her sent chills through her body. His eyes were usually soft and gentle; at that moment, they were wild and unsettled. Tina looked over to the night stand and noticed that half the lines she'd lined up were gone. She wore only a G-string and a black silk robe tied close with a sash.

The outline of her nipples strained through the thin fabric. She untied the sash, arched her back, and the robe slipped off her shoulders.

"Why are you lookin' at me with that look?" she asked.

"With what look?" Trevon replied, coolly.

"With that 'I'm 'bout to beat that pussy up' look."

"Because I am about to beat that pussy up...right after I eat that pussy up — how you gon' keep Tre waitin' like that?"

Tina poked out her bottom lip. "I'm sorry, baby," she said, kneeling in front of the chair Trevon was sitting in, "don't be mad at me..." she grabbed his shaft, about to wrap her lips around the head of his dick...

Trevon stopped her and kissed her passionately. "It's your turn now, baby," he said. "Stand up and let me look at you."

Tina stood and looked at Trevon a short moment before she did a sexy three-sixty. "You like?"

"Naw..." he replied, "I love. Turn around." Tina turned, and Trevon grabbed her hips and pulled her toward him, kissing her ass cheeks one-by-one. He cupped her buttocks and drew them apart before licking the rim of her ass. Instinctively, Tina's sphincter tightened and

43

relaxed as Trevon's tongue penetrated her, wiggling like a wet worm.

"Ooh, baby, damn," she purred.

Trevon stood, licked up the curve of Tina's spine, and sucked on the back of her neck.

Tina turned around and kissed Trevon passionately before pushing him back into the chair. She straddled her legs around him, tossing her long hair to the side, moaning as Trevon cupped her breast in his hands, molding them gently. He placed her nipples in his mouth one-by-one, sucking them gently, turning them into hard little nubs.

The area between Tina's legs was throbbing, aching, and wet. Trevon's hand eased between her legs. He rubbed her clitoris. Tina moaned, arching her back as his finger entered her wet womb.

"Oh, Tre..." she whispered, bending down to kiss him, probing the inside of his mouth with her tongue.

"Stand up," Trevon ordered. Tina stood, and he tore off her G-string, popping the string around the waist. After doing so, he turned her around and gently sat her down in the chair. He kneeled in front of her and spread her legs.

"I've been waiting for this for so long, Tre." Tina cooed, as she leaned back in the chair.

Trevon grabbed Tina's legs and pulled her to the edge of the chair. He teased her, licking around her vulva and clitoris, coming within centimeters of touching it with his tongue. Then he stuck his tongue deep inside of her, then around the clit again, making sure he didn't touch it. He sucked on her lips, stuck his tongue deep inside of her, then licked around her clit again...

Tina's nail dug into the chair as Trevon neglected that spot she needed licked the most.

Trevon used his thumbs to peel the pink, wet flesh away from her clitoris and blew cool air on it. Tina's body twisted and heaved as he freaked her.

"Umm, suck it, baby," she begged. "I can't take it no more. Please suck it," she pleaded, and Trevon did. He wrapped his lips around her clit and sucked while the tip of his tongue flickered across it. "Oh-my-gawd," Tina moaned as her body jerked upward, her head falling back into the soft cushion of the chair. She placed her hand on the back of Trevon's head, wanting the feeling to go on forever.

Tina's legs started trembling, and Trevon said, "Don't cum yet, baby; I'm just getting started." He wiggled his tongue deep inside of her, his lips making a slurping sound as he sucked the juices out.

"What are you doing to me...?" Tina whispered.

Trevon pulled her to her feet and kissed her passionately. Tina kissed him back, sucking her juices off his lips as he turned her around and laid her on the bed. He kneeled on his knees while Tina laid on the edge of the bed, with her feet resting on his shoulders. He used his index fingers to spread her labia, drawing out her clit in such a way that it looked as if it were circumcised. He licked up and down, and side-to-side with amazing speed. The way he used his tongue was almost mechanical, driving Tina into absolute madness.

Trevon made her feel like he was a part of her body; he knew how to lick, where to lick, when to suck, when to suck and lick at the same time, while doing all of this, he stuck his thumbs inside of her and rubbed the walls of her pussy...

Tina's body had never felt so much pleasure.

She was perspiring but had done absolutely nothing to be sweating. Trevon worked her with his tongue; it felt as if he was sucking the life force out of her body with his lips. Tina was breathless, her heart raced, and her body was trembling, on the verge of an orgasm. She grabbed her knees and pulled them back as far as she could to eliminate some of the shaking in her legs.

A tingling sensation invaded her body and she started gasping for air, trying to catch her breath as that sensation found its way to her abdomen. As Trevon sucked her clitoris, he sucked that sensation from her abdomen, slowly making it come down, touching all her female organs: her fallopian tubes, her ovaries, her uterus, her cervix...

A warm flood of ecstasy dripped down the walls of her pussy.

"Oh-my-gawd, baby! Please-don't-stop!" Tina moaned as she squeezed her breast, her nails digging into her flesh. Her body shook convulsively, and the orgasm came down like a flood. She turned her head sideways and moaned, "I'm cumming, baby," through clenched teeth.

Trevon felt her pussy pulsating on his bottom lip. "Mmmh, does that feel good, baby?" he asked seductively, his head moving around in circles, rubbing his lips all over her pussy, sucking out cum hungrily.

"Yes...oh yes," Tina purred.

Seconds later, she tried to pull away when the climax was finished, but Trevon kept sucking like a wild animal. He stood and grabbed the back of Tina's knees and pushed them back, putting her in the buck. "Tre, stop!" she exclaimed.

Trevon ignored her request, making sound effects as he sucked: "Slurrrrrp! Mmmmmmh! Ummmmmmh! Slurrrrrp! Hmmmmmmh!"

"TRE, STOP!" Tina yelled, trying to kick out, but couldn't because he had all his weight pinned down on her. "STOP, TRE! BABY, PLEEEASE!" she begged with tears in her eyes.

Trevon let her go and she balled up in a fetal position, trembling and sweating. He sat beside her and started laughing, wiping her cum off his mouth. "I told you I was gonna eat that pussy up, didn't I?" he said, placing his hand on her arm.

"STOP!" Tina yelled, pushing his hand away. "Don't goddamnit touch me!"

Trevon grabbed her arm and turned her over on her back. "It's like that now?" he asked with a smirk.

"That shit ain't funny, Tre! You could've killed me!"

Trevon burst out laughing. "I'm sorry, boo-boo," he said, wiping the sweat off Tina's face.

"Don't touch me — I'm not playing with you, Tre!"

Trevon used a thumb to wipe the tears from Tina's eyes. "What'choo cryin' for, girl?" he asked, trying not to laugh.

"Because that shit tickle, nigga!" Tina exclaimed before slapping Trevon across the chest. "Why you did that shit, Tre? That shit ain't funny! You done fucked up a perfectly good orgasm!"

"I told you I was sorry — *damn!* I got carried away... That pussy was tasting like a pork chop, and when you started cummin', it tasted even better...like a smothered pork chop."

Tina burst out laughing. "You're so damn stupid! You make me sick! Get off me — move!" She pushed him, and he leaned over and stuck his tongue in her mouth. Tina accepted it, grabbing the sides of his face. She gazed deeply into Trevon's eyes...

Her body was trembling.

Trevon began kissing her again, sticking two fingers deep inside of her. "You ready for some wood, now?"

"Umm hmm, I surely am."

Trevon spread Tina's legs and got in between them. "I'ma man of my word..." he said. "Didn't I tell you that I was gonna eat that pussy up?"

"Yes, baby."

"Did I not eat that pussy up?"

"Yes...and you ate this pussy up real good, too."

"What I told you I was gonna do after I ate that pussy up?"

"You said, you were gonna beat this pussy up."

"Are you ready...?" Trevon asked, placing his hands on Tina's knees, pushing her legs back...

They were still trembling.

There was a light *smack* as her lips parted wetly to welcome Trevon in. Tina's clitoris and labia were swollen and puckered like a rosebud. She was so wet and ached deep inside, wanting to feel Trevon plunge into her. He rubbed the head of his dick around her vulva, teasing her, making her wind her hips, trying to push herself onto him.

Trevon laid down on top of Tina and she gasped as the head of his dick penetrated her. Still, he teased her, only plunging in about two inches deep. Her hips were winding harder, wanting to feel him inside of her.

Trevon began a gentle back and forth movement, gripping her shoulders, looking Tina in the eyes. "Mmmh, baby," she moaned, her hips moving rhythmically with his as he plunged in deeper and deeper. Trevon's hips recoiled, his ass tightened, and he pushed deeper until Tina's inner resistance was gone...

Trevon made love to her for what seemed like an eternity.

So slow. So gentle. Caressing her, kissing her, and she felt every inch of him as he rocked back and forth inside of her, each stroke bringing her closer and closer to another climax. Tina grabbed Trevon's ass, grinding herself as deeply on to him as she could. She matched his thrust with slow upward lunges. Their bellies slapped together in a wet rhythm. Trevon's pelvic bone smacked against Tina's thighs. Her moans mingled with the moans of the women on TV, and the slurping sound of hard dick beating wet pussy mingled with the headboard banging against the wall.

The pulses of Tina's second orgasm began and her pussy creamed Trevon's shaft. She grabbed the back of his head and dug her nails into his neck.

"Oooh, don't stop, Tre," she moaned. Trevon's body convulsed, and she felt his warm semen gush deep inside of her, and at the same time, her orgasm came down: the feeling of both of their fluids being released inside of her made her eyes roll back in her head.

Trevon sank down on top of Tina, every muscle trembling, his heart pounding hard against her breast. She could feel him getting softer inside of her as her thighs trembled.

Trevon pulled out and laid beside Tina. His dick was shiny with her wetness; the inside of her thighs was wet and slick, glistening with pussy juices and cum. Their bodies gleamed with perspiration. Tina's face was flushed, her breast heaving as she rolled over to lay in Trevon's arms...

"I love you, Tre," she said, sincerely.

"I love you, too, baby."

They held each other, sweaty, emptied, and drained...

"Tre?"

"Yes, princess?"

"Please don't leave me again..." Tina said, as a tear fell on Trevon's chest. "I wouldn't be able to take it. I'll go crazy, baby."

"I'm gonna do everything in my power not to," Trevon replied, wiping the tears off Tina's face.

"You promise, Tre?"

"Yeah."

"Say it then."

"Say what?"

"*Say you promise, nigga!*"

"I promise, nigga — *damn*! You happy now?"

"Yeah..." Tina replied, as she squeezed him, nestling her head on his chest, "if you keep your promise."

They fell asleep holding each other, once again feeling complete...

"Jenkins! Hey Jenkins!" the deputy yelled.

"Huh? What?" Trevon said, reentering reality, emerging out of his daydream.

"Snap out of it," the deputy said, "you have an attorney visit..."

Love at first Sight

As Trevon was being escorted to the attorney visiting room, he said a silent prayer, hoping the public defender was there to tell him something good. Usually, it took four to six weeks before the case file made it downtown to the public defender's office, then another two to three weeks before the public defender even had a chance to look over the file to see what kind of plea the prosecutor would offer.

Trevon had a good feeling that it was good news being that he was only locked up two weeks. Nine times out of ten, the P.D. was probably there to offer him a plea bargain, because plea bargains were the only thing "public pretenders" were good for.

Damn! I hope this muthafucker ain't come up here to offer me some bullshit–ass plea, Trevon thought to himself. He had too much shit on his mind and really didn't feel like acting a fool today. Although, if that was the case, he'd already made up in his mind that he was going to curse his or her ass out and tell 'em to kick rocks...

"Aye, these cuffs too tight, dude!" Trevon said to the deputy that was escorting him.

"Sounds like a personal problem," the deputy replied. "If you hadn't cursed the judge out, you wouldn't have to be escorted in handcuffs, now would you? You've been classified as a security risk, so deal with it, Jenkins! You made your bed — now lay in it!"

"You get off on this shit, huh, white boy?" Trevon asked nastily. "I bet you can't wait to go home and tell ya fat-ass wife how you cut the circulation off on a nigga wrist!"

"Whatever."

"It's the truth."

"I could care less about you and your wrist, boy!"

"*Boy?*" Trevon chuckled. "I got your boy, hillbilly,"

"I got your hillbilly, porch monkey."

"I got your porch monkey—"

"Shut the fuck up, Jenkins!"

"Fuck wrong wit'choo?" Trevon fired back. "I'ma grown-ass man! How the fuck you gon' tell a grown-ass man to shut up?"

49

"Keep talking and you're gonna get what you are looking for, Jenkins!"

"You just bumpin' ya gums, cracker! You ain't gon' fuck with me — not by yourself anyways. Take that badge off and let's get in the paint so I can show you what da lick read—Fuck Boy!"

The deputy grabbed the handcuffs and squeezed them tighter.

"Aaaahh—you muthafucker!" Trevon howled in pain.

The deputy looked at Trevon and smiled. "When we get to this attorney visiting room and I remove these cuffs, please, do something stupid; we gon' beat yo black-ass until you play dead!"

"Yeah," Trevon chuckled, "I like how you use your pronouns. I see you specified the plural 'we', meaning more than one, and that's your best bet, because if you would've used the singular terms 'I' or 'me', meaning by yourself — I'll beat the breaks off yo ass, peckerwood."

"Oh, you're smart ain't you, boy?" the deputy replied sarcastically. "Apparently you ain't too smart because you keep bringing your dumb-ass back to jail. As long as you keep coming back, I'll always have a job; I make good money babysitting you state babies..." The deputy laughed hysterically.

Trevon looked at the deputy's ear while he giggled. It took everything he had to restrain himself from doing a Mike Tyson on his ass and spitting his ear in his face afterward...

Trevon couldn't even respond because it was the truth, and you already know what they say about the truth...

Yeah, that shit hurt like a mufucker.

"I ain't no goddamn state baby," was all Trevon could come back with.

When they reached the attorney visiting room, the deputy removed the hand cuffs slowly. After they were off Trevon rubbed his wrist as they stared at each other for a moment before Trevon flinched at the deputy and said, "BOO!"

The deputy jumped back and reached for his pepper spray as Trevon burst out laughing.

"Look at yo bitch-ass," Trevon said, trying to catch his breath. "You shook like a mufucker — with your scary-ass!"

"Sit your stupid-ass down, Jenkins, before I slap these cuffs back on your ass!"

Reluctantly, Trevon sat down, knowing he was in a no-win situation.

The deputy turned to leave.

"Bitch!" Trevon spat as he walked out the door.

Five minutes later, Trevon's attorney arrived. The woman that walked through the door caught him completely off guard; on a scale of one to ten, she transcended the ten and stood at the 99.9 mark.

Her beauty was hypnotizing, and her body... her body was intoxicating, so unbelievable, like the concept of the Big Bang Theory; acceptable on a profound level, but in reality, beyond human understanding.

She didn't look like she was conceived and born into the world like normal human beings. She looked more like she was created in a laboratory by some mad scientist that was a loyal subscriber to *KING* magazine.

There wasn't a name for her complexion, but if he had to come up with one, he would say she was the color of mocha latte with a splash of cream, that went perfect with her long golden hair. She stood at about 5'5", with the perfect sized breast (a handful), and a waist so small that if he wrapped his hands around it, his fingers would've practically touched each other. Her hips curved perfectly into her firm, plump thighs, and she had the prettiest toes a pair of feet could have.

When she turned to close the door, Trevon's eyes popped out of their sockets — DAAAMN! he said to himself; this woman had the chunkiest booty he'd ever seen.

Trevon felt himself getting hard as he sat there processing all her attributes, storing them in his memory bank, because as soon as he got back to his cell, he was going to have a talk with Mary Palmer and beg her to give him another chance...

"Hello, Mr. Jenkins," she said, as she sat across from Trevon.

"Hello," he replied, spellbound.

She opened her briefcase and pulled out a folder. "My name is Ms. Baker and I will be representing you for the charges you're in custody for."

"That was fast," Trevon said.

"What was fast?" Ms. Baker asked.

"You coming to see me."

She smiled, "For the amount of money you're paying us, I ought to be."

"The amount I'm paying you? What amount?"

"Twenty thousand dollars."

"Twenty thousand dollars?!" Trevon exclaimed. "Since when does a public defender cost twenty thousand dollars?"

"I'm not a public defender, Mr. Jenkins. I'm a private attorney, and as of yesterday, I'm your private attorney."

"I don't understand..." Trevon said, looking confused. "I didn't hire you, and I sure as hell don't have twenty stacks to retain you."

"Well, someone did," Ms. Baker said, opening a folder, "because the retainer has been paid in full..." She pulled a card from the folder and slid it across the table.

Trevon picked it up and looked at it.

The card read:

Fetterman & Associates
We The People, For The People
Protecting Your Rights

Monique Baker	Office: (561) 687-2116
Attorney at Law	FAX: (561) 889-3158
Florida Bar	

"Monique," Trevon said to himself.

"I just came by to ask you a few questions," Monique said, looking Trevon in the eyes. "Before I do, I want you to know that anything you tell me is privileged. That means it stays between you and I, but I need to know the truth..." She pulled a pen and pad from her briefcase.

Trevon was still confused, trying to absorb everything he'd just heard. He had a hundred and one questions but lost all focus of them as he looked into Monique's eyes; they were soft and gentle, giving her face an angelic appearance.

She had him mesmerized.

Trevon knew, at that moment, he wanted this woman. There were no ifs, ands, or buts, he was going to do whatever it took to get her.

"Why are you looking at me like that?" Monique asked curiously.

Trevon smiled. "Because you're the most beautiful creature I've ever seen."

His response caught Monique off guard, but at the same time, it brought a smile to her face.

"Well, thank you...," she said, picking up the pen, "umm, where was I?"

"You were on the part about needing to know the truth," Trevon answered, casually.

"Yeah, that part..." Monique replied, smiling harder now. "Well, I'm waiting..."

Trevon took a deep breath before he began: "There's nothing much to tell Ms. Baker. The car wasn't mine, and I had no idea the gun was in there."

"What about the money?"

"No idea."

Monique looked at Trevon suspiciously, "Mr. Jenkins...please, let me get something clear: I am very good at what I do. I may not have been doing it as long as some lawyers, but I haven't lost any of the sixteen trials I've been in. That's why Mr. Fetterman assigned me to your case... But I can't help you if you're not honest with me. Do you understand that?"

"Yeah," Trevon answered, "What do you want me to tell you? A lie? That wasn't my gun or money. I know you've seen my past criminal history and think I'm guilty as hell, but I assure you, Monique—"

"Please, I would prefer you call me Ms. Baker," Monique corrected.

Trevon smiled.

Monique returned the smile.

"I'm sorry," he said, apologetically, "but I assure you -Ms. Baker- that I'm not the monster you think I am. Over the years, I've been..." Trevon looked up in the air as if he were looking for the right words to say. "I've been a victim of circumstances...unfortunate circumstances. I'm telling you the truth; that wasn't my gun or money."

"Well, whose gun and money was it?"

"Don't know."

"Whose car was it?"

"A friend."

"How long did you have it?"

"A few hours."

"Are you employed?"

"Yes."

"Where?"

"I do independent construction work." He lied, not wanting to bring attention to Joey and the restaurant.

"How long have you been a resident of Palm Beach County?"

"17 years."

Monique wrote down a few more things before saying, "I have good news, and I have bad news... The good news is that I spoke to your parole officer yesterday and he said he won't be filing for a community control violation being that you only had two days left...He also spoke very highly of you."

Trevon smiled. "Did he?"

"Yes, he did. Highly enough to come to your bond hearing and speak on your behalf."

"My bond hearing?"

"Yes, your bond hearing — that's the bad news. I'm going to get

53

you a bond, but the problem is your past criminal history. There's a good chance the judge will set a very high bond."

"I guess that's better than no bond at all."

"What kind of bond do you think you'll be able to make?"

Trevon shrugged his shoulders, "I don't know, about $20,000 or $30,000 paying 10%."

"I can't promise that it'll be that low. We'll just have to keep our fingers crossed."

"When is the hearing?"

"The day after tomorrow," Monique answered, putting her belongings back in the briefcase. "9:00am, we're going before Judge Berman; he's pretty fair. Like I said, we have to keep our fingers crossed..." Monique stood up. "It was nice meeting you, Mr. Jenkins."

"Same here," Trevon replied, reaching for her hand.

Monique extended hers and they shook. "I'll see you Tuesday morning..." With that said, she turned and walked out.

●   ●   ●

Trevon was in such a euphoric state after he left Monique that he didn't even feel like chastising the deputy as he escorted him back to his cell.

Trevon looked over at him as they walked down the hallway...

This muthafucker called me a state baby, he thought to himself. On second thought, maybe he did feel like chastising the deputy...

"Aye, I wanna apologize for bringing your wife into our conversation earlier," Trevon said sincerely. "That's my bad—I was dead wrong."

"Um hmm," the deputy replied, looking at Trevon suspiciously.

"For real, dude! That was fucked up on my behalf. I'll sleep a little better tonight knowing you accepted my apology."

The deputy looked at Trevon and Trevon looked back at him, batting his eyes, making an *"aw-shucks"* face. "Apology accepted," he said. "No harm done."

"No harm intended," Trevon replied reassuringly. "I know you must really love her."

"Yes-I-do," the deputy stated with pride.

There was a short silence...

"So..." Trevon said, breaking the silence, "how long you and your sister been married?"

"You-black-sonofabitch!" the deputy said through-clenched teeth, squeezing the cuffs on Trevon's wrist until they wouldn't close any more.

"Aaaaagh!" Trevon howled in pain. "You muthafucker!"

●   ●   ●

Hours later, Trevon laid in his bunk bed thinking about Monique and Tina as nasty images clouded his mind: the two of them naked, kissing and caressing each other's body, begging him to join in.

"Maybe the fantasy could become reality if you play cards right?" he muttered to himself.

Things were definitely changing for the better. It was a good chance he was getting out Tuesday. There was no doubt in his mind that Fresh and Tina put the money up to retain Monique, but where in the hell did they get $20,000?

Trevon laid there with a big-ass smile on his face, thanking God for Tina. He closed his eyes and began to think about her, drifting back to the day after he got out of prison...

Back down Memory Lane

Ten Months Earlier -

Tina woke up the next morning in Trevon's arms feeling whole again. Her head was rested on his chest with her leg wrapped around his lower body and her arm wrapped around his torso as she watched him silently. Admiringly, she studied his profile: His lips, his cheek bones, his strong jawline, and the little dimple on the tip of his nose.

His eyes were open, and he was staring at the ceiling, thinking about Lord knows what. "Good morning, princess," he said, his eyes still focused on the ceiling.

Tina cupped her hand over her mouth, trying to conceal her morning breath, smiling as she looked at him. "Did I wear that ass out last night?" she asked playfully.

Trevon leaned over and kissed her on the eye. "Naw..." he said, turning over and spreading her legs, "matter-of-fact, I want some more of that good pussy."

"Hold on, Tre," Tina said, trying to push him off, "I need to go wash up. I was too tired to do it last night."

"I don't care."

"But I do! All yo' damn sperm drippin' out of me. That shit feels nasty, Tre—*move*!"

Trevon leaned back and looked between Tina's legs: there was a big wet spot in the center of the silk sheet that started turning crusty, and his semen was oozing out of her vagina and smeared all over the inside of her plump thighs. He pointed between her legs and said, "Ewww! Yeah, you need to go wash up."

Tina smiled, "Why don't you lick me clean," she said playfully.

"Giiirl, stop!"

"Why not? It's yours."

"Well, now it's yours—go in there and clean it up."

"Don't complain now," Tina said as she got up. "If you would've pulled out you wouldn't have to worry about your nut drippin' all over the place..." She got up and looked at her sheets. "Damn! Look at my silk sheets, Tre! Them shitz all fucked up!"

"Well, then wash 'em," Trevon replied, before locking his fingers behind his head.

Tina rolled her eyes and walked into the bathroom with her legs spread, looking like a duck.

"Quack! Quack! Quack!" Trevon teased.

"Keep it up, Tre...you gon' fuck right around and get me pregnant cummin' in me like you crazy."

"Stop da blood-clot cryin'," Trevon said, trying to sound like a Jamaican. "If you would've got your lazy-ass up last night and wiped off, nut wouldn't be drippin' all over the place."

"You wore me out last night, Tre," Tina said, getting back in the bed, straddling her legs around Trevon. "You put it down last night, baby — true story..." She reached between her legs and began stroking Trevon, getting him hard. "You want some more of this good pussy?" she asked, leaning to the side and putting him inside of her. She rocked back and forth, taking him in inch-by-inch. When he was all the way inside of her, she started winding her hips as she contracted the muscles in her vagina. "Is this pussy good to you, baby? She asked teasingly. "You like how I make it squeeze that dick?"

"Goddamn, Tina," Trevon said through clenched teeth. "Yes, baby, yes!"

"This my dick, nigga!" Tina hissed. "My dick—do you hear me?"

"Yes, baby," Trevon moaned.

"Say it then! Say it!"

"This yo d—" the cordless phone rang.

"Shit!" Tina exclaimed. "That ain't nobody but Fresh punk-ass!"

"Well...answer it," Trevon said, sitting up.

"HELL NO! FUCK FRESH!" Tina said, pushing Trevon back down. "I'm 'bout to catch me a nut! Fuck wrong wit'choo?"

"Just see what he want," Trevon insisted.

Reluctantly, Tina grabbed the phone and answered it: "What, Fuck nigga?"

"Rise and shine, BEOUCH!" Fresh replied. "Get'cho ass up and go spit them babies out. Why the fuck you ain't call me when y'all got back last night?"

"It's 9:30 in the morning, Fresh! What the fuck you want?"

"BITCH! You know what I want! I want you to stay of Broadway...give the other hoes a chance to make money — they gosta eat, too."

"*You got me fucked up!*" Tina screeched. "You ain't never see or hear about Tee sellin' pussy on sum muthafuckin' Broadway. You must got me mixed up with that footdragon you fuckin' with."

"*Footdragon?*" Fresh said defensively. "You gots my boo fucked up, crumbsnatching ass bitch!"

"*Crumbsnatcher?*" Tina quipped back. "Naw, you gots me fucked up! Tee don't snatch no muthafuckin' crumbs, FUCK BOY! Tee be snatchin' a nigga whole bank account—yeah, the rent money and all—I gosta have that too. I done broke up more happy homes than crack cocaine. I'm straight nigga. I got my own shit, my bank account fat, and I don't have to depend on nan nigga—unlike your BOO! She's the one around here suckin' dick, depending on your trick-ass to pay her rent. This Tee, nigga! Who the fuck you think you talkin' to? I'ma true player—that's what I do—I play these niggas. Once upon a time, you used to be a player, too. Now ya 'BOO', gotcha pockets in a chokehold. Matter-of-fact, you still are a player, 'cause you just played yourself callin' Tee a crumbsnatcher, PUSSY-ASS-NIGGA! Now what the fuck you want, Fresh? I'm trying to get some dick, and you're fuckin' up my shit!"

"You know what I want, BITCH! Put my dawg on the phone!"

"Did I stu-stu-stutter, muthafucker? Did I not just say we were in the middle of fucking?"

"I don't give a fuck if you were suckin' Bill Clinton's dick, Monica Lewinsky. Put my dawg on the phone."

"Yeah, I'll be all that. But I wasn't when them niggas put that thang on your ass and you was laid up in St. Mary's, cryin' like a lil bitch, beggin' me to bring yo punk-ass somethin' to eat."

"Damn, Tina," Fresh said emotionally, "why you had to go there?"

"Cause you're getting on my nerves, Fresh," Tina said in a calmer voice. "Now ain't the time to be playing. You're fuckin' up my shit."

"Damn, my bad, sis. You catchin' feelings and shit; it's not that serious."

"Look, I'm sorry about bringing up that situation about you getting shot," Tina said sincerely. "That's my bad, okay?"

"It's all good..." Fresh replied. "I'll be over there in an hour, so call up to the security gate and put my name on the list."

"All right."

"For real, Tina. Call up there now, 'cause if them flashlight cops give me a hard time again, I'ma act a fool out there."

"Go ahead; they gon' lock your black-ass up. You know these crackers don't play out here."

"Call up there, Tina!"

"A'ight, nigga — *damn*!"

"Bye...crumbsnatcher!" *Click.*

"Lil punk ass muthafucker," Tina said under her breath as she clicked over to call the security gate.

Trevon looked up at her, smiling with pride. He taught her well. She had a fly-ass mouth and didn't think twice to use it when someone stepped out of bounds.

"What?" she asked after hanging up the phone, putting Trevon back inside of her.

"Somebody need to wash your mouth out with soap."

"I get it from your slick-talkin'-ass," Tina said, rocking back and forth on top of him.

"That shit turn me on," Trevon replied, throwing the dick back to her.

"And you need to talk to Fresh when he come over here. He's been on the bullshit, running around here like he damn O-dog."

"I've heard..." Trevon replied. "I'll talk to..."

"Shhh," Tina said, covering Trevon's mouth with her hand, focusing on an orgasm. "You're talkin' too much right about now. Unless you're talkin' about getting this pussy, I don't want to hear it." Tina leaned back and grabbed Trevon's legs so she could change positions. She unfolded her legs and positioned her feet under Trevon's shoulders while leaning back on her hands, using her arms to rock her body back and forth.

Trevon placed his hands on the inner part of Tina's thighs. He used one thumb to peel the flesh away from her clitoris, and the other to rub her clitoris in a circular motion, watching his shaft slide in and out, glistering with her wetness.

"Mmmmh, baby," Tina moaned, only taking in about four inches. At the angle she was sitting, she was in the perfect position, grindin' herself on Trevon, making the head of his dick rub the top wall of her pussy, hitting her G-spot dead on.

Trevon tried to pull her to him, wanting to go in deeper.

"Don't go in deep," she said. "You're hittin' my spot like this. Let me catch my nut then you can do what you do..." She started grinding harder as Trevon pumped his hips fast, short stroking upward, pounding the head of his dick into her G-spot, setting her pussy on fire.

Trevon smiled when Tina's body began to tremble, knowing she was on the verge of a climax. Seconds later, her body convulsed, and she cried out. The friction turned Tina's orgasm into a foamy cream as it flowed down Trevon's shaft. Wrung out, Tina folded her legs back under her and laid on top of Trevon, breathless.

"That was quick," he chuckled.

"You was hitting my spot, nigga." Tina replied, trying to catch her breath.

"You might as well get'cho ass up," Trevon said, grabbing the globes of her ass, "It's my turn now."

"What'choo talkin' bout? Issa wrap," Tina said jokingly. "I played you, nigga. I'm about to go to sleep."

"So now I gotta take the pussy?"

"I'm just playin', baby...you know I'ma break you off a lil somethin'." While Trevon was still inside of her, Tina turned and faced the opposite direction.

Tina looked back at Trevon. "You like that, baby?" she asked, winding her hips slowly. "You want me to go faster?"

"Um hmm," Trevon moaned.

"Spank me then," she demanded, and Trevon slapped her ass cheek—*SMACK!* "Ooh, baby," she purred, speeding up. "You want me to go faster?" *SMACK!* "Hmm, like that?" *SMACK!* Tina leaned forward and started throwing her pussy as fast and hard as she could as Trevon pulled her by her hips while he pumped his...

Thirty minutes later, they were in the same position and pouring with sweat. Tina was riding Trevon so hard a crack was in the wall from the headboard banging against it. She was working on her third orgasm, and both her ass cheeks were red and welted up from Trevon slapping them for the past half hour.

"My knees hurt, Tre! Hurry up and cu-" *SMACK!*

"Shhh!" Trevon said, after slapping Tina's ass viciously. "I'm about to cum," he said, trying to grip her sweaty, slippery ass.

"My stomach, Tre! Hurry up and—" *SMACK!*

"Shhh!" he hissed, after slapping her ass again. "Don't stop! I'm cummin'!"

"You said that 20 minutes ago, Tre! My knees hu—" *SMACK!*

"Shhh!" Trevon said, plunging in as deep as he could, hitting Tina's cervix. The bed shook as warm semen flooded deep inside of her.

"This yo muthafuckin' pussy, Tre..." Tina said, exhausted and wore out.

"I know it is..." Trevon replied, out of breath. "Now get'cho ass off me."

"I can't move...my knees done locked up."

A few seconds later, Tina managed to gain enough energy to get off Trevon and flop down at the foot of the bed when they heard banging on the front door: BAM! BAM! BAM! BAM! "PALM BEACH COUNTY SHERIFF'S DEPARTMENT!" Fresh yelled, while banging. "WE HAVE A WARRANT FOR TREVON JENKINS! OPEN THIS

GODDAMN DOOR BEFORE I KICK THIS MUTHAFUCKER DOWN!"

"Oh, hell naw! Tina exclaimed. "I know that nigga ain't out there beatin' on my shit like he crazy! Go get'cha homeboy, Tre, before I wet his ass up."

Trevon slipped on his boxers and walked to the front door laughing. When he opened it, Fresh was standing there smiling from ear-to-ear, holding a cigar and a bottle of Hen-dog (Hennessy).

It had been three years since he'd last seen him, but he hadn't changed any. He stood about three inches shorter than Trevon, with a butter pecan complexion. He had straight, even white teeth, and sported a low hair cut which revealed a head full of waves that was now covered with a navy blue fitted New York Yankees cap that went with his navy-blue T-shirt and baggy jeans.

They stood there looking like innocent childhood friends. To the people that didn't know them, neither Trevon nor Fresh looked like killers; that was a deadly mistake in identity that many made.

Trevon meet Fresh six years earlier in 2000. Back then, he was known as 'Nicholas.' Nicholas was from the fearsome Vandeveer projects in the Flatbush section of Brooklyn and was quick to let everyone know of his affiliation with the Bloods.

His mother sent him to Florida to stay with his father because he was knee deep in the bullshit of gang life in New York...

Little did she know, she was kicking her son out of the frying pan into the fire...

His father couldn't handle him, so he ended up kicking him out. Therefore, Nicholas broke in houses and cars, stealing whatever he could to put money in his pockets.

Trevon used to see him around the neighborhood hustling and would buy almost everything Nicholas came to him with. Not because he needed it, but because he respected how he hustled and wasn't afraid to get money. He still remembered the first time he spoke to him after he sold him a radio...

"Where you from, dirty?" Trevon asked.

"BK, Flatbush, nigga." Nicholas stated with pride.

"Why are you always rockin' that red bandanna? You in a gang or somethin'?"

"This rag represent my set," Nicholas said, throwing up the B.

"I respect that, lil homie, but you needs to slow down. I understand you're from New York and all — not saying New York soft or anything — but y'all be coming down here acting like Florida slow or

61

somethin'. This shit ain't nothin' like the NYC. This is the F-L-A; it's some real killers down here, and these niggas don't care nothin' about what color you're representing. The only color we see down here is green, you feel me? Niggas come down here and get missing quick-like, so don't think 'cause you're from Flatbush you can come down here with an 'S' on your chest, breakin' in people shit. I done seen niggas get killed for less."

"I hear you, son, but I gosta eat."

"You call stealin' CD players and TVs eatin'? See, that's what I mean: the only color that matters is green. All that other shit is irrelevant."

"You got a better idea?"

Trevon smiled. "You might not be ready to get down how I get down, bug. I play for keeps, don't take no hostages."

"I ain't never been shook, son," Nicholas replied earnestly. "I need to get money in the worse way, so I'm ready for whatever."

"One day, I'll take you on a real lick. Until then, quit fuckin' with all that petty shit before you get yourself killed..."

A couple of days later, Trevon was sitting in his car, snorting a small pile of cocaine off his hand when Nicholas jumped in on the passenger's side unexpected. Trevon picked up the .45 that was lying on his lap, cocked the hammer back, and pointed it at Nicholas, ready to squeeze the trigger.

"Fuck wrong wit'choo?!" he exclaimed. "See! That's the shit I was talkin' 'bout! You almost got'cha head buss on the house!"

"Be easy," Nicholas replied, nervously, looking at the .45 and bag of coke Trevon was holding.

"Be easy?!" Trevon said, looking around paranoid while wiping off his nose. "Fuck you mean *'be easy*? You just scared the shit out of me. Man, you done blew my muthafuckin' high with that bullshit!"

"I got something for you, son," Nicholas said, holding up a red bookbag.

Trevon smelled what it was before he opened it. He looked inside and saw four pounds of Crip (hydroponic grown marijuana) and an Ingram MAC-10.

"Where you got this shit from, bug? Trevon asked curiously.

"I broke in dread crib and got his ass."

"Over in Lake Crystal?"

"Yeah."

"You tell anybody else?"

"Hell naw! Who I look like, Larry Lunch Meat?"

"Good, keep it that way," Trevon said before going into deep thought. "Look," he said, going into his pockets, "all I have is five hundred. I'ma give you two-fifty now, and we gon' jump this reefer and come up..." He looked at Nicholas a short moment. "Stay the fuck out of Lake Crystal. You hear me? Them dreads ain't nothin' to be fucked with. If they find out you got'em, they gon' want blood."

"A'ight, son, but check this: they got like thirty or forty more pounds up in there, in the closet. I just grabbed these four pounds from out the kitchen."

"Don't fuck with me, lil nigga."

"I swear on stacks, son! They got booku weed up in there. I only took four pounds because how the fuck I was supposed to carry all them trees?"

Trevon sat in deep thought a short moment. "We gon' let shit cool off, a'ight?"

"A'ight," Nicholas replied, looking at the bag of coke Trevon was holding. "Let me hit that shit."

"How old are you, bug?" Trevon asked before dumping a small pile on his hand and sniffing it.

"I'm eighteen," Nicholas answered, "I'm grown. How old are you?"

"I'm twenty-two but I've been there and done that," Trevon replied, cleaning off his nose. "You ever done this shit before?" he asked, checking his nose in the mirror.

"Hell yeah!" Nicholas answered.

Trevon looked at him suspiciously for a moment before passing him in bag.

"I'm hungry, son," Nicholas said, "them dreads got mad weed up in there. I'm ready to eat them niggas food..."

Weeks later, Trevon and Nicholas had out West on smash. Everybody and they momma was coming to cop some of the fat dime bags Crippy they were selling. Somehow, word had gotten out that Nicholas was the one who broke in dread's house, because everyone knew that B&Es were Nicholas' M.O.

One evening, two days before the fourth of July, a black Expedition pulled up in front of the apartment building Trevon and Nicholas sold weed out of. Trevon reached under his shirt and cocked the hammer back on the .45 as three Jamaicans got out, one of them carrying an AK-47. Another one sat in the back seat looking at Trevon and shaking his head.

"What y'all got going on?" Trevon asked, standing up. "Y'all can't come around here with that chopper like that — y'all making the spot hot."

"Weh yuh ah do, eh?" one of the Jamaicans said. "Mi ah look fa da yute dey call Nicholas...you see him?"

63

"Naw..." Trevon replied, praying Nicholas didn't come out the apartment. "never heard of him."

"Ah blood-clot lie yuh ah tell, pussy hole," the Jamaican spat as the other cocked the assault rifle, pointing it at Trevon.

"Fuck you," Trevon retorted, "you goat eatin' muthafucker! You fuckin' with a real nigga — it's on and poppin', bitch!"

"Nah, fuck yuh, Yankee bwoy! Yuh tell da bwoy Nicholas him tink say him can run? Ah load mi go load mi gun. Tell him he ah dead mon walking, yuh ear? DEAD!" With that said, they got back in the Expedition and left.

Seconds later, Nicholas stepped out the house holding the MAC-10. "How the fuck they knew it was me?" he asked nervously.

"Did you tell anyone?"

"Not a soul!"

"I don't know then, maybe someone saw you. I know one thing: when they see you, it's on and poppin'. You're in the major leagues now, bug. You ready to earn some stripes?"

"No doubt, son. I been told you I was ready."

"I hope so, cause its war and we 'bout to bomb first..."

Two days later, on the fourth of July, Trevon and Fresh were sitting in a stolen car in front of the Jamaicans' apartment. Both wearing black sneakers, pants, hooded sweatshirts, gloves and ski-masks that were pulled half-way down...

"You ready, bug?" Trevon asked. "If you're not up for this shit, now is the time to say so. These dreads ain't fucking playin', you hear me? If you slip one time, they gon' buss yo muthafuckin' head. I need to know I can depend on you to pop off."

"I got you, son," Nicholas replied. "That's my word, B."

"Good, just stick to the script. Do I need to go over it again?"

"Naw, I got it down packed."

"Let's get it like Drac, then."

"*Get it like Drac*?" Nicholas said, looking puzzled. "What the fuck that mean?"

"You don't know what get it like Drac mean?" Trevon asked cocking the .45.

"If I did, I wouldn't be asking," Nicholas replied sarcastically.

"You know who Drac is, don'tcha?"

"Naw."

"Dracula, nigga...You know how Dracula get it, don'tcha?"

"How?"

"In blood, nigga!"

Nicholas smiled and shook his head. "I like that shit, son..." he said, cocking the MAC-10 and pulling down his mask. "Let's go get it in blood."

Minutes later, they were at the back window, cutting through the glass with a glass cutter. Once inside, they could hear several different voices and reggae music playing from somewhere in the apartment.

"You ready, bug?" Trevon whispered, and Nicholas shook his head.

They opened the bedroom door and stepped into the living room. Trevon was pointing the .45 at the three Jamaicans sitting at the table eating while Fresh aimed the MAC-10 down the hallway covering Trevon's back.

Trevon put his index finger to his lips. "Shhh," he hissed. "If one of you fuck niggas so much as breath too hard—I'ma let you have it. Y'all understand what the fuck I'm saying?"

"Wha da blood-clot problem, bwoy?" one of the Jamaicans said in disbelief. "Yuh know who da fuck—" SMACK! Trevon slapped him above his temple with the barrel of the .45 and blood trickled down his face.

"Did I stutter, muthafucker?" Trevon said, pulling him by his dreadlocks and snatching his head back. "I said, don't say-a-mutha-fuckin-word..." Trevon looked at all three of the Jamaicans one-by-one, making a mental note of the one that pointed the AK at him earlier. "Y'all lay down on the floor and lock your hands behind them nappy-ass dreadlocks."

All three complied.

Trevon gave Nicholas the .45 and pulled a roll of duct tape from the pocket of his sweatshirt. One-by-one, he taped their hands behind their backs. After doing so he grabbed the .45 from Nicholas and said, "Dome-check they ass if they move."

Trevon searched the apartment room-by-room; the whole place smelled like high grade hydroponic marijuana. When he got to the last room, just like Nicholas said, the closet was stacked with one-pound bales of Crip. "Booya!" he said to himself before taking two heavy duty trash bags from his back pockets and filling them.

"We're in business, bug," he said, dragging the trash bags into the living room.

"Yuh ah get weh yuh waan, bwoy?" the Jamaican said icily. "Mi have ah nuff of da fuckery! Yuh tink say yuh can just cum in ear an tief London gunja? Yuh ah dead mon! Yuh ear? Ah dead mon! Yuh pussy-clot head ah London chop off when he—" WHAM!

"Shut the fuck up, bitch!" Trevon said, kicking the Jamaican in the mouth. "London ain't gon' fuck wit' me! Fuck wrong wit'choo?!" Trevon pulled up his ski mask and pulled the Jamaican's head back, so they could be face-to-face. "Look at me muthafucker! Didn't I tell you, y'all fucked up pullin' that chopper on me?"

"Twahh!" the Jamaican spat blood in Trevon's face.

Trevon laughed. "You must know you're about to get yo fuckin' head buss," he said, wiping the spit off his face. He stood up and stood over the other two Jamaicans and shot them in the back of the head one-by-one: *Pop! Pop!*

"You said you was lookin' fa da bwoy, Nicholas," Trevon said to the last Jamaican, pulling the ski mask off Nicholas' face. "Well, here he go..." Trevon took the MAC-10 from Nicholas and handed him the .45, but he hesitated before taking it, looking at the two dead Jamaicans lying face down in a pool of blood. "HANDLE YOUR MUTHAFUCKIN' BUSINESS!" Trevon yelled. "Fuck wrong wit'choo?! I'm going to the car. If you ain't there by the time I get there—I'm outta here! Leave this nigga living if you want to; you can bet yo ass, when they run down on you, it's gonna be a wrap!" Trevon grabbed one of the trash bags and turned to walk out. Before he reached the door, he heard *Pop! Pop! Pop!*

Trevon turned around and saw Nicholas standing over his victim as his body shook from the first stages of death.

"You good?"

Nicholas looked at Trevon in a daze and shook his head. "Ye-yeah."

Trevon shook his head as well. "A'ight...let's go get this money..."

They rode in silence for the first five minutes as Nicholas stared out the window in a daze...

"You did good tonight, bug," Trevon said, breaking the silence. "You got some stripes; yous'a killer now, lil nigga."

Nicholas looked at Trevon with an evil smile. "That shit felt good, son," he said, looking at the .45 like it was a precious jewel.

"Wipe that biscuit down," Trevon said, handing Nicholas a rag and a can of WD-40, "and spray it down with the WD-40... This is your first lesson in murdernomics, bug. Killin' is a science — just like forensics — and just like any other science, it's laws and rules to this shit. Always remember: I don't care how much you may love a strap, after you do dirt with it, it gotta go — and always spray it down with something oil-based, so them crackers can't lift any prints off it just in case they do find it at the bottom of the canal..."

Nicholas did as he was told.

Trevon looked over at him. "We gosta come up with a new name for you, too," he said as Nicholas sprayed and wiped the .45 down, "that

Nicholas shit too corny. You're never gonna be who you were before...this a fresh start for you..." Trevon looked at Nicholas again "...Fresh...how you like that, bug? Fresh."

"Fresh..." Nicholas said, shaking his head. "I love that shit, son... Young muthafuckin' Fresh..."

Nicholas Anderson was now a bonafide head busser. July 4th, 2000 was the night that Young Fresh the killer was born, and Trevon would later regret giving birth to him.

Six years later, here he was, standing in front of him with that same evil smile. "Look at you," Fresh said, handing Trevon the bottle of Hen-dog, "you done got all swole up and shit. You're rockin' a bald head now, huh? He said, rubbing Trevon's bald head.

"It's not by choice, dirty." Trevon replied. "My shit started getting thin up there, so I just cut it all off."

"What the fuck you sweatin' like that for?" Fresh asked as he stepped through the door.

"Tina...been in there tappin' that ass."

"You look like you been in Dee-Bo's pigeon coop all night; you're sweating like a Hebrew slave," Fresh said as they walked to the bedroom. When they walked in, Tina was drenched with sweat, balled up at the foot of the bed, naked and uncovered. The room looked like a hurricane hit it: the mattress was on the box spring crooked. The blanket, sheet, and pillows were thrown all over the floor, and the air reeked of sex. "Goddamn, it smells like budussy up in this bitch!" Fresh said, as he entered the room.

"Why the fuck was you out there beatin' on my door like that, Fresh?" Tina yelled without moving. Both of her ass cheeks were cherry red and had Trevon's hand print imprinted on them.

"Damn, son!" Fresh exclaimed when he saw them. "You really was tappin' that ass, huh?"

"You thought I was playin'?" Trevon said before getting in the shower.

"You get on my nerves, Tina, but I ain't even about to front, you're finer than a mufucker." Fresh said, slapping Tina's sweaty, sore ass cheek.

"Stop, Fresh!" she yelled, still unable to move. "That shit hurts!"

"Don't yell at me, bitch!" Fresh yelled back. "You ain't yell at Tre when he was in here beatin' yo ass like Ike Turner."

"You ain't Tre, muthafucker!"

"You needs to let a nigga like me get up in that ass," Fresh said, sitting in the chair by the bed, pulling out a small bag of weed and an even

67

smaller baggie of cocaine.

"You couldn't handle this pussy, lil boy. You wouldn't know what to do with it if it came with instructions."

"I don't want none of that shit anyways; that pussy poison. I done heard rumors about you. They say you have niggas lookin' for you with a flashlight in the daytime. If you got pussy that good, I don't want no part of it. You never was to fuck Young Fresh up..." Fresh looked on the nightstand and saw the left-over coke on the mirror Trevon didn't snort the night before. He picked it up, shoved his face into it, and snorted until it was all gone. When he was finished, he laid back in the chair with his lips and the tip of his nose covered with cocaine residue.

Tina sucked her teeth. "Y'all get on my nerves with that shit... Bunch of damn junkies."

"Hush, bitch!" Fresh said, cocaine residue still on his face. "What the fuck are you? Lying up there butt-ass naked, balled up sweatin', lookin' like you're fiendin' for another shot of dick...yous'a junkie, too — a dick junkie."

"That's okay, though," Tina said defensively, "a bitch can be all that... Pass me the blanket, Fresh."

"No! Fuck wrong wit'cho arms?"

"Please, Fresh," Tina pleaded, "I can't move."

"Sorry. No-can-do. I'ma junkie, remember?" Fresh replied as he broke down the cigar so he could roll up a dirty (weed laced with cocaine).

Trevon came out of the bathroom and put on the same clothes he had on the day before. "I see you helped yourself to my paint (cocaine)," he said, jokingly.

"Be easy," Fresh replied, holding up the bag he brought, "you know I got you covered, homeboy."

"You need to eat somethin' before you start getting high, Tre," Tina said. "You haven't ate anything since you've been out."

"I'm not about to get high," Trevon replied, "I gotta go see my parole officer... I need to get my shoes out of the safe."

"YOU PROMISED YOU WASN'T GOING NOWHERE, "

"I told you I had to go see my P.O.—*damn*! And I promised I wasn't gonna sneak off...I'm not sneaking off; I'm tellin' you I'm leaving."

"I'll take you, then. Just let me take a nap first."

"Go ahead, I'll be back by the time you wake up."

"No, you won't!" Tina yelled, still lying in the same position she'd been in for the past twenty minutes. "Y'all gon' be gone all fuckin' day! You're so full of shit, Tre! Haul ass—get the fuck on!"

"I need my shoes."

"Come'ere..." Tina whispered the combination to the safe in

Trevon's ear.

Trevon smiled when he opened the safe. Tina came a long way; she really had her shit together. There was four or five thousand in there along with a zip lock bag full of Xanax that was sitting on top of a chrome snubbed-nose .357. "Get some money so you can get me something to eat!" Tina yelled from the bedroom.

Trevon grabbed a $100 bill, his shoes, and closed the safe. "What'choo want to eat, baby?" he asked, stepping out the closet.

"Get me a dinner from the Jamaican Restaurant...Go to *Oxtail's* by *Video Ave.* on Military Trail."

"I know where Oxtail's at. I haven't been locked up that long... What kind of dinner do you want?"

"Brown stew chicken with rice, peas, and cabbage...and a champagne soda...and a beef patty...and some cocoa bread...and tell them don't—"

"Cook your cabbage hard," Trevon said, finishing Tina's sentence. "You like it crunchy—I know, I know. Anything else, massa?"

"Yeah..." Tina said matter-of-factly. "Cover me up and give me a kiss..." After tucking Tina in, Trevon and Fresh were on their way...

"I see you done turned into a real Floridian," Trevon said, getting into Fresh's car. He had a purple '76' Chevy Caprice sitting on 26-inch gold spoked rims.

"I got tired of niggas looking down on me when they rode by," Fresh replied. "Made me feel like a peon...shit done changed since you've been gone, son; niggas ain't rollin' twenties no more."

"So, what's good in the hood?" Tre asked as Fresh pulled off.

"Shit crazy, son," Fresh answered. "The feds got Palm Beach County on smash. It's a lot of new cliques, a lot of gun-play been going on. The Latin Kings done got mad deep; Spanish Cobras blowin' up, too. Then the Haitians got a clique called San Castle. Tina's cousin, Papa Doc, supposed to be the H.N.I.C. Them boys ain't fuckin' around, they're about that trigger-play all day, you feel me? Then it's O.F.L.—Out For Loot — you remember, Chauncey?"

"Lil punk-ass Chauncey?"

"Lil punk-ass Chauncey ain't Lil punk-ass Chauncey no mo'... O.F.L. is his clique and them niggas doing some real head bussin'. That's why the feds are all over the place. Them niggas from San Castle and them niggas from O.F.L. on some new shit called *Facebook*, taking pictures with ski masks and choppers-n-shit. And check this, some other niggas done made a DVD called *Gangsters and Thugs: Palm Beach County After*

69

Dark. Them niggas selling them shitz on the fuckin' internet. That shit was all on *CNN* and the *World News*. They on the DVD cookin' up dope, doing drive-bys, fighting and all other types of shit. They got the spot hot, son. It's zero tolerance about them assault rifles now. They giving niggas a thousand years for them shitz."

"Yeah, I heard."

"Well then you heard right — oh yeah!" Fresh said excitedly. "You know that dude David Copperfield, the magician? They robbed his ass when he came to do a show, down at City Place. These niggas done went crazy in Palm Beach."

"What's up with them niggas that shot you?"

"I don't know exactly who shot me," Fresh answered. "I think it's one of them O.F.L. niggas, but I'm not for sure."

"What was it about?"

"Money...they got a trap out west not far from our trap..."

"*Our trap?*"

"Yeah, our trap... It ain't nothin' major, though. We sell a lil weed, and I was jumpin' beans (ecstasy) until my ex-connect got popped. I sell Xannies, too, whenever Tina ain't tryin' to rape me with them high-ass prices."

Trevon looked at Fresh and smiled, "You're doing your thang, huh?"

"It pays the bills, you feel me? Plus I'm able to feed Da Grimlinz."

"Da Grimlinz?" Trevon said, looking puzzled. "Who're Da Grimlinz?"

Fresh looked at Trevon and smiled. "Your new clique, homeboy... Look, Tre, I know how you are about cliques and gangs, but shit done got crazy, son. We need reinforcements with all these new cliques coming into the picture. We ain't nothing major, it's only eight of us including you and me. After you see your P.O., we'll swing by the trap, so you can meet the troops."

"Where these niggas from?" Trevon asked suspiciously. "Who are they?"

"Be easy," Fresh replied, "I handpicked these niggas myself. They ain't buss no heads yet, but I know they got it in 'em. One of them is my cousin Wooda, came down from New York last year. He's Blood, too; we're from the same set. And I already know what you're about to say—Da Grimlinz is not a gang. We're a clique, a family. I still remember what you told me the first time we met: the only color that matters is green, remember?"

"Yeah," Trevon answered, "I remember."

"So, that's the color we represent," Fresh said, holding up a money green bandanna. "We're a get money clique. That's what it's all about, gettin' money and bussin' heads. Everything else is irrelevant; we're not about gang bangin'."

"I hope so, Fresh. I ain't trying to go back to prison for no bullshit."

Fresh smiled. "So, whattup wit'choo, gangster? I know you were in there going ham, bussin' heads left and right."

"Actually, I wasn't..." Trevon said, matter-of-factly. "Ain't nothin' gangster about that shit, Fresh. I lost, homie—them crackers took three years of my life, three years I could never get back. I was way at the top of Florida hearing about you shootin' up shit down here like you're Billy The Kid. You need to tighten up and get your priorities straight, Fresh. Hurtin' somebody ain't nothin' to be braggin' about."

"I know you ain't talkin'!" Fresh snapped. "What happened to bomb first? Kill or be killed? You turned me up, now you're tellin' me I'm making too much noise? You did this—not me! Shit was all good when you was out here burnin' niggas, right?"

"I never bragged about it, Fresh. Play with fire you get burned; I never burnt anyone that didn't deserve it, and even then I wasn't proud of it..."

There was silence.

"Look. lil bruh, all I'm trying to say is that prison helped me grow up. I don't see things the way I used to. Just because a nigga go to the pen, or get shot, or kill somebody, it don't mean they're real—anybody can kill somebody! Now the question is, can you turn a negative into a positive? Do you possess the ability to acknowledge your mistakes, learn from 'em, and correct them? Now that's my definition of real—that's being gangster! You need to understand that shit, Fresh. I'm not going back to prison for no bullshit. I got big plans, homeboy; I'm tryin'a cop fifty acres on Mars..."

Fresh drove in silence, looking straight ahead with an angry expression on his face.

"...I'm getting older, Fresh. Please understand where I'm coming from..."

"You know what I want you to understand?!" Fresh howled. "I want you to understand that I came to pick my homeboy up today, then you showed the fuck up! Who the fuck are you? I don't know you! Yous'a impersonator! Frontin' like you're Trevon Jenkins! You ain't Tre, nigga! Where my dawg at? I ain't even tryin' to hear that shit you're talkin'. Yous'a head busser, that shit gon always be in your blood..." Fresh was almost in tears. "How the fuck you gon' turn your back on me, Tre? I

71

thought you would've been proud of me. Proud of what I started... Nigga, Da Grimlinz is your clique! All I used to do was talk about you, how you're the realest nigga alive. Them niggas can't wait to meet you—now you're on this cornball shit! What's good, Tre?"

"I never said anything about turning my back on you, and I am proud of you. I'ma always be there for you, you're like blood, nigga..."

Fresh's face straightened up as he looked at Trevon. "I ain't even trying to hear that shit you're talkin' son. You're still shell shocked from prison. Them crackers done rehabilitated yo ass, but you'll be back to yourself in no time, trust me, homie..." He passed Trevon the blunt he rolled. "I rolled it just how you like it, homeboy—dirty, dirty, heavy on the paint..."

Twenty minutes later, they were sitting in the lobby waiting for Trevon to be seen by his parole officer.

"You sure they ain't gon' piss ya today?" Fresh asked.

"Naw," Trevon answered, "they ain't gon' do that until the second visit..." He looked at Fresh. "I got a question: why you ain't never come see me?"

Fresh took a deep breath. "I told Tina not to tell you until you got out, but I know she done told you already...That nigga Chris was fuckin' Desiree while you were locked up. I couldn't come see you and look you in your face knowing that and not tell you. I didn't want to tell you nothin' until you got out 'cause I didn't want you in there stressin' that shit knowing you can't do nothin' about it."

"Yeah, Tina told me about that."

"I swear, that bitch mouth run like water..." Fresh said, closing the magazine he was reading. "Yeah, holmes was runnin' around poppin', tellin' everyone how he had your baby moms in the Boston Crab. That shit had me fish grease hot, son. Wanted to wet that nigga ass up, but I know he's your best friend, so I decided to let you put a handle on it."

"*Used to be best friend*," Trevon corrected. "You did the right thing, bug. Chris gon' get his in due time."

"Jenkins!" the parole office called, standing in the doorway. He was a black man in his early 40's who looked exactly like George Jefferson.

For the next 10 minutes, they talked about Trevon's transition back into the community. He asked Trevon several questions: the address where he would be residing? Had he used any drugs (funny question)? What were his plans for employment? Etc...

He also informed Trevon that he would be stopping, unannounced, by the address he'd given to check on him. He also informed Trevon of his 7pm curfew, and told him he needed to get a job

ASAP, then Trevon was on his way...

"This gon' be a long 10 months," Trevon said, as he and Fresh rode to the trap. "Dude act like he don't like me. He gon' violate my ass the first time I slip."

"It ain't nothin' but 10 months," Fresh replied, "it'll be over before you know it. We gon' make sure you eat. As soon as you're off, it's on and poppin'.'"

They turned on Stacy Street and pulled into the Brandywine apartment complex. "Welcome home," Fresh said, turning off the car. He got out and look around angrily.

"Fuck wrong wit'choo?" Trevon asked curiously.

"I done told them niggas about this shit once," Fresh said, storming to the front door. He unlocked it, slung it open and yelled, "Officer on deck!"

The six men in the apartment, all rocking money green bandannas, jumped to their feet before Fresh finished what he was saying. Trevon stepped in behind Fresh and scanned the place. It looked like any other trap: it was clouded with weed smoke. There were two semi-automatic handguns lying on the floor along with a riot-pump shotgun. There was a sofa, two chairs, and a coffee table full of dime bags of weed. There was also a stereo that was blasting a Soulja Slim song, and a PlayStation 3 that was hooked up to a big screen TV that was showing the Madden 2006 game they were in the middle of playing; two of them still had the controllers to the PlayStation in their hands.

"The last time I checked this was a trap — not a fuckin' arcade!" Fresh yelled, turning off the radio. "Why ain't nobody outside on point?" he asked, looking at each of them one-by-one. "This ain't Chuck-E-Cheese, nigga! This the spot! How the fuck we're supposed to make money when y'all niggas in here playin' video games?"

Everyone just sat there looking high and stupid. All six, with the exception of one, looked older then Fresh, but it was obvious that Fresh was in charge; Trevon looked on with pride as Fresh barked at the troops.

Fresh turned around and looked at Trevon. "This is Spike," he said, pointing to his mentor, "the head fuckin' Grimlin...Tre meet your offspring..." All of them rushed Trevon, greeting him with handshakes and daps, all speaking at one time. All Trevon could make out were a series of, "Whattup?" "What's good?" "We done heard so much." "We won't let you down," and "Just give us the word."

As Trevon looked into the eyes of the six standing before him, he saw fire and mischief. The six standing before him were ready to prove themselves, and there was no doubt in Trevon's mind that they were ready to do whatever to show they were worthy.

Maybe Fresh was right, Trevon thought to himself, *maybe Da Grimlinz ain't such a bad idea after all...*

"At ease!" Fresh yelled, bringing the troops to silence. "This is Wooda..." he said, pointing to his cousin from New York. They called him Wooda because he was always saying, "I wish he *wooda* did this, or, I wish she *wooda* did that, or, I *wooda* beat that nigga ass if he tried me like that, or, I *wooda* slapped that bitch if she tried me like that—get the picture?"

Fresh pointed to the next troop. "That's my nigga, Ooh-Wee." And *Ooh-Wee* were the exact words that came to Trevon's mind when he saw him; yes, he was just that ugly, so he earned his name honestly. "That's Teddy," Fresh said, pointing to the biggest one of the group, who was 6'4" and 320 pounds. "That's Bam," A short pretty boy. "That's Jug." A big-headed Jamaican with short dreadlocks. "And, that's Slim." Tall and skinny and appeared to be the youngest one of the group. "Teddy, Slim, Bam, and Jug—y'all go get on point. Y'all two stay put..." Fresh said, looking at Ooh-Wee and Wooda. "What the fuck is wrong wit'choo niggas?" he asked, after the others were gone. "Y'all supposed to be setting examples for the others. I chose y'all to be in charge while I'm gone for a reason."

Ooh-Wee and Wooda spoke at once: "I'm sorry, dawg." "It won't happen again."

Fresh looked at them in silence for a moment. "It needs to be at least two people outside on point at all times. Y'all figure it out, come up with shifts and rotate every two or three hours."

"A'ight," they both answered in unison.

"K-den," Fresh said, "we're about to bounce. Get them niggas in here and get right."

"Let me see your phone," Trevon said when they got in the car. Fresh passed it to him and he punched in the number and hit the call button: "Hello? Desiree?"

"You're just now callin'?" Desiree replied, nastily. "Your son been asking about you since yesterday. When are you coming to see him?"

"I'm about to come pick him up now."

"AND TAKE HIM WHERE?!"

"That's my son! He came from my nuts! I don't have to explain where I'm taking him! He's spending the weekend with me - that's all you need to know!"

"I don't want my son around that bitch, Tre!"

"You've got some nerve, Desiree..." Trevon said, dourly. "I didn't want my son around Chris while you were fucking him."

"I never had Lil Tre around Chr—" Desiree cut short what she was saying. "Look Tre... I'm sorry about what happened, okay? Please don't keep throwin' that shit up in my face. What happened between me and Chris was a big mistake. I'm sorry, Tre. I'm so sorry. Please believe me... I'll see you when you get here." *Click.*

Trevon and Desiree were high-school sweethearts. He, her, and Chris all stayed in the same neighborhood and everyone used to think that he and Chris were brothers because they looked so much alike. They could have passed for twins, the only difference between the two was Chris had a mouth full of gold teeth and Trevon had none.

The two were inseparable, they were the best of friends; it wasn't nothin' they did without each other. When Trevon heard about the affair between Chris and Desiree, he couldn't believe it. He already knew she was fuckin' around for years, but he had no idea it was with his best friend.

Desiree was never home and would always drop Lil Tre off at her mother's so she could go club hopping with her home-girls and her cousin, Big Wanda. Trevon never paid it any attention because he was doing his own thing. So, whenever she came home late, he would act dumb—if he was there—just like she would act dumb, both knowing that the other had been fucking around.

They had an unspoken mutual agreement: you do your thing, and I'll do mines. Lil Tre was the only reason they were together. Desiree knew all about the other women Trevon was messing with but never said a word...

Until Tina came along.

It was something about Tina that made Desiree snap. She hated Tina with a passion. When Trevon would spend the night with Tina, she would answer his phone while he was asleep and chastise Desiree before hanging up on her, which led to Desiree kicking Trevon out. Truth be told, Trevon still loved Desiree, and always would. She gave him something more precious than his own life: his son. How could he ever hate her? She was the mother of his child, and for that reason, Desiree would always own a piece of his heart.

Besides her infidelities and club hopping, Desiree was a good woman and a good mother. She took care of their son, spoiling him to death. There wasn't anything Lil Tre wanted that Lil Tre didn't get. Desiree was independent and worked hard for what she wanted; Trevon praised her for that. No matter what she did, Trevon had to forgive and forget. Lil Tre was seven-years old, so that meant they still had 11 years left on their 18-year contract.

"Go out to the Raw," Trevon said to Fresh, after hanging up with Desiree.

•   •   •

Riviera Beach was the slum of the slum of Palm Beach County. Some called it "Rawviera," some called it "Da Raw," but when it all boiled down, it was all the same.

Shoot-outs were a regular routine for the residents of Riviera Beach; like the newspaper being delivered; or the ice cream truck coming through - get the picture? Yeah, it's-really-that-serious! And you thought Palm Beach was all about the rich and famous, huh...?

Nah-huh.

Riviera Beach earned its nickname because just about everyone that lived within the city limits were on eight-balls. No, not eight-balls of malt liquor, but eight balls of raw cocaine, and if they didn't use it, they sold it.

Rawviera was a breeding ground for real niggas. It didn't matter how soft someone was, after spending a week in "Da Raw," they're coming out game tight, which is why Trevon wanted to get his son away from there ASAP. He didn't want his son raised in that type of environment.

Desiree shared a house in the Monroe Heights housing development with her cousin, Big Wanda. Big Wanda was 300 +, which is why they called her "Big Wanda". She took no shit and had knocked out more dudes than Floyd Mayweather.

When Trevon and Fresh pulled up in Desiree's driveway, they saw Big Wanda sitting on the front porch cleaning collard greens. Aside from being big, Big Wanda had a beautiful face that clashed with her ugly attitude and her slick-ass mouth: "It's about time you came to see your son, fuck nigga!" she spat at Trevon as he got out of the car.

"Where I'm from, 'fuck nigga' are fightin' words," he retorted.

"Where you from, *fuck nigga*?"

"Palm Beach County, *fat bitch*! Where you from?"

"I'm from a small town called fresh off a fuck nigga ass," Big Wanda said, standing up and kicking off her shoes, looking like she was ready to charge, "and you're making me homesick."

"Bitch, you lucky you're my son's aunt..."

"*Or what?!*" Big Wanda demanded, smashing her fist in the palm of her hand.

"Man, throw that bitch a turkey leg," Fresh said, jumping behind

Trevon.

At that moment, Big Wanda's four-year-old son, Keshawn, burst out the front door crying: *"Aaaaaaagh!"*

"What's wrong wit'choo boy?" Big Wanda asked, grabbing him by the arm.

"HIM-HIT-ME!" Keshawn whined.

"Who hit you?"

"Lil Treeee!"

"While you're out here fuckin' with me, you needs to be teachin' that lil nigga how to talk," Trevon said in the midst of laughing, "talkin' 'bout some *'him-hit-meee!'* he said, trying to sound like Keshawn. "That's the same shit Bernie Mac was talkin' about: them no talkin'-ass, bad-ass kids."

"My churen ain't bad," Wanda said, defensively. "I got good churen!"

"'No wonder shawdy can't talk," Trevon said, laughing harder now, "you can't dammit talk... talkin' 'bout some damn *'churen.'* It's not churen, it's pronounced children, *chil-dren.* It's two easy syllables, stupid muthafucker. And how you got good children? I could've sworn I seen shawdy right there in that movie, *Children of the Corn,*" Trevon said, pointing to Keshawn.

Fresh burst out laughing.

Big Wanda charged at both of them, chasing them around the car. After several minutes, she gave up, out of breath. "I'ma... I'ma... I'ma fuck... I'ma fuck y'all up... When I catch y'all!" Big Wanda yelled, gasping for air.

"Damn, Big Wanda!" Trevon replied. "We ain't do shit to you! You started fuckin' with us first!"

"You was picking on my baby!"

"I'm sorry, Wanda—*damn!"*

"Tell my baby you're sorry!"

"*Him* don't want no apology," Fresh said, sarcastically, still trying to make fun of Keshawn. "*Him* okay, ain't you, Keshawn?" he asked the little boy.

"Chill out nigga," Trevon said, laughing hysterically, "or *her* gon' kick yo ass."

"TELL MY BABY YOU'RE SORRY!" Big Wanda yelled.

"Okay, okay," Trevon said. "We're sorry, Keshawn," they both said in unison.

"Now give my baby some money so he can get somethin' from the ice cream truck."

77

Fresh went in his pocket and peeled off a $5 bill from his bank roll and gave it to Keshawn.

Desiree stepped through the front door. She was 100% full blooded Floridian hood rat. She was 5' 7", red, and had a body like the rapper, Trina. She had her hair braided in micro dots that hung down to her ass and was wearing a baby blue cut off Baby Phat shirt, and coochie shorts so short her pussy lips were practically hanging out.

Damn, she's lookin' so good, Trevon thought to himself. *This bitch know what the fuck she doing!*

Desiree knew Trevon liked microdots, and that coochie shorts broke him down like kryptonite broke down Superman. "Hey, Tre," she said, seductively.

"Hey," Trevon replied, looking at her like a three-piece chicken dinner.

"Well, are you gonna come inside and see your son? He's been asking about you all week..." They stepped inside, and Desiree yelled, "Lil Tre! Guess who's—"

"Daaaaddyyyy!" Lil Tre exclaimed, running out the room and jumping into Trevon's arms. Lil Tre was the spitting image of his father. Looking at him in Trevon's arms was like watching *Austin Powers* and seeing Dr. Evil hold Mini-Me. It's so strange how genetics work. They had not seen each other in three years, yet, they were so genetically intertwined they were almost dressed alike. Ironically, Lil Tre had on all white Reebok Classics, a pair of white Dickie shorts, and a white tee with a tank-top underneath and a white Miami Dolphins starter cap. So, Lil Tre didn't only inherit his father's looks, he inherited his father's style, attitude, and ways as well.

This is why mothers are so skeptical to let their children play with Lil Tre. He was a natural-born ringleader; if something happened in the neighborhood, or in school, you can bet your last dollar Lil Tre had something to do with it. Even the older children looked up to him because he was so manipulative.

One time, his teacher caught him selling candy in class (for the third time) and made him stay after school for detention. During the detention, not only did Lil Tre talk the teacher into giving him his candy back, he also talked her into buying a few pieces as well. So, like everyone else, she too was wrapped around Lil Tre's finger.

To be seven years old, Lil Tre had better game than the average man. He was bad as hell, but you couldn't help but fall in love with him.

"Damn, daddy! Your necklace so icy—can I wear it?" Lil Tre asked, pulling the chain over Trevon's head before he had a chance to answer. "I'm spending the weekend wit'choo, right?"

"Yeah," Trevon answered, putting his son down.

"Uncle Fresh!" Lil Tre yelled, running over to Fresh and giving him dap before putting his hands on his hips, leaning back and saying, "You're looking like a Black Jesus at The Last Supper right about now," looking Fresh up and down from head-to-toe.

"What's that supposed to mean, bug?" Fresh ask curiously.

"That mean break bread wit'cha boy, nicca," Lil Tre answered, holding his hand out.

Fresh couldn't do nothing but laugh and go in his pockets. They say game is to be sold, not told. He had to break bread for the line he'd just shot at him; he was definitely going to use it later. Fresh peeled off a $20 bill and placed it in Lil Tre's hand. "There you go, bug."

Lil' Tre took the bill and held it up to the light, checking the authenticity, making sure it wasn't a dummy, before throwing it in his pocket and shooting his hand back out, waving his fingers back and forth. "What I'm supposed to do with twenty dollars? I said break bread, not bread crumbs. Gas sky high nowadays—you know Bush got the game messed up."

"You don't drive," Fresh replied, "so you don't have to worry about gas."

"No, I don't, but a little boy got other needs, Uncle Fresh, you feel me?"

Fresh laughed, peeled off another $20 bill, and placed it in Lil Tre's hand.

"Yeah, now that's what da lick read," Lil Tre said, holding the bill up to the light. "Ma, you got my bag packed?" he asked his mother.

"Yeah, it's on my bed."

"Hey, Travis!" Lil Tre yelled, and moments later, a boy that looked to be 13 or 14 appeared. "Turn my PlayStation off and wrap up my controllers," Lil Tre ordered. "I'm going with my ole boy for the weekend, so y'all gotta kick rocks."

"All right, Lil Tre," the boy said. "When are you coming back?"

Lil Tre's face balled up as he looked back and forth from his father to Fresh before looking back at the boy like he was stupid. "Didn't I just say I was gonna be gone for the weekend? Damn!"

"Oh..." The boy replied dumbly, "that's right."

After Lil Tre got all his stuff together and kicked his friend out, they were out the door...

"Take care of my baby," Desiree said as Trevon leaned against the car.

"I will."

"You look good, Tre."

"I know."

"I know you're not going to believe this, but I've been really missin' you."

"You're right, I don't believe it."

"Well I do, Trevon Jenkins."

"Um-hmm."

"We need to sit down and talk whenever you get a chance, okay?" Desiree said, wrapping her arms around Trevon's neck. He hugged her back, pulling her close to him. She felt his dick jump as it started to get hard, poking her in the stomach. She grabbed it and said, "When you coming to get this pussy?"

"Don't do this, Desiree," Trevon said, pushing her hand away.

"I need you, Tre..." she whispered, "to feel you inside of me. My pussy getting wet from just being near you."

"Is that what you told Chris?"

"No! I told you what happened between me and Chris was a mistake. I'm—"

"You did some triflin' shit, Dee! You broke a code of honor: family and friends are off limits. I would never stoop that low and sleep with one of your friends. That's like a commandment, a law, and you broke that shit. You're lucky I ain't O.J. y'all ass, left both of y'all ass stanker than a bitch around this muthafucker. I forgive you, Dee... but I'll never be able to forget. You crossed a line; it ain't no coming back from what you did."

"I'm so sorry, Tre," Desiree said, tears welling up in her eyes.

Trevon's heart began to ache. He wanted to grab her so bad and comfort her and tell her that everything was okay, that they can start all over and forget about the past...

But he couldn't.

Desiree had broken a code that was punishable by death. As bad as he wanted to make love to her, he couldn't just give in that easy...

"I gotta go, Dee..." Trevon said before getting in the car. "I'll call you when I get a chance..."

They picked up Tina's food and went back to Royal Palm Beach so Fresh could drop them off. When Tre and Lil Tre walked into the bedroom, Tina was still balled up at the foot of the bed snoring.

"Tina!" Lil Tre exclaimed, jumping in the bed and hugging her.

"Hey, baby!" Tina said, trying to hug him and keep herself covered at the same time. She hadn't been up to do anything since Trevon left earlier. "You done got so big, boy! You look just like yo damn daddy!"

"Lil Tre, go watch TV in the living room so Tina can get dressed," Trevon said. "Damn, girl! You been sleep all this time?" he asked, after little Tre was gone.

Tina got up and stretched. "I'm tired, negro... You wore me out, baby. Let me jump in the shower right quick." Her legs wobbled as she took her first few steps. She was weak-kneed and ached deep inside her body (the side effects of good head followed by some good dick). Tina thought about what Fresh said when he called her a dick junkie...

Mmmmh, how right he was, because she was hooked on Trevon Jenkins.

When Tina got out the shower and stepped into the bedroom, she saw Trevon lying on the bed with his fingers laced behind his head, staring at the ceiling. He put fresh sheets on the bed and cleaned up the room.

"Thank you for cleaning up, baby," she said, lying on top of him naked.

"All right now," Trevon said, grabbing the globes of her ass.

"We can't do nothin' tonight, Tre. My pussy sore..." Trevon's dick was starting to rise as she spoke. When she felt it, she jumped up. "I'm not playin' with you, Tre! You got my whole body aching."

"You don't even want no head?" Trevon asked, teasingly.

Tina stood in deep thought for a moment before smiling. "You know I want some head, negro—but that's it, deal?"

"Deal."

"Get that money from out of the safe," Tina said, putting on panties and a bra, "I put it up so you can get some clothes."

"Thank you, princess," Trevon replied, "I really appreciate everything."

"I know you would do it for me," Tina said, giving Trevon a wink.

Tina, Tre and Lil Tre had a wonderful time. They went shopping, filling the back seat and the trunk of the Acura with toys, clothes, and shoes. Tina took Trevon to SYMS to get him sized up and dropped $1,500 on a tailored 3-piece Armani suit and $350 on a pair of Italian leather Armani shoes for his job interviews.

They went out to eat and rented movies from *Video Avenue* before returning home. Trevon was so thankful that God blessed him with such a good woman.

Tina treated Lil Tre like he was her own, spoiling him the same way his mother did. She loved Lil Tre, and for that, Trevon loved her even more. There was no way he could ever show his gratitude for all she had done.

They laid in the bed and watch DVDs for the rest of the night. After the last one, they left Lil Tre in the bedroom and throwed a blanket and two pillows on the floor in the living room...

"Thanks for everything," Trevon said as Tina laid in his arms.

"Don't thank me," she replied, pulling off her panties, "that shit wasn't free."

Trevon smiled. "Well, how can I repay you?"

"I'm feindin'..." Tina said, pulling Trevon by the neck and shoving his face into her pussy, "I need another fix..."

Twenty minutes later, Trevon came up wiping Tina's cum off his mouth. She laid beside him, her whole body trembling and glistening with sweat, balled up in the usual fetal position she always got in after Trevon had sucked the life out of her body.

A "fix" is exactly what he gave her. He took her on a high that was better than any drug, and made her body feel and do things she never knew was possible. The way he used his tongue was intoxicating; Trevon Jenkins was an addictive drug and Tina felt like an addict as she laid balled up, shaking and sweating...

"*Hold me, baby,*" she pleaded, as she backed up against him.

●   ●   ●

The next morning, they woke up and went out to breakfast before going down to Hollywood, Florida to spend the day at Boomers. They played video games, laser tag, took pictures, and rode the go-karts before leaving.

When they got back to West Palm Beach, they stopped by Publix to pick up a few things so Trevon could cook dinner. Once they got home, Trevon went straight into the kitchen so he could get started while Tina and Lil Tre sat in the living room watching videos on BET...

"I'll suck your titties for five dollars," Lil Tre whispered to Tina.

"*What boy?!*"

"I said I'll suck your titties for five dollars," Lil Tre repeated.

"No, nigga!" Tina said, putting him in the head lock playfully.

"Why?" he asked. "You pay my daddy to suck your titties."

"No-I-don't!" Tina said, defensively.

"Stop lying!" Lil Tre screeched. "I heard y'all last night talking 'bout some '*ooh baby, suck it. Ooh suck it like that, don't stop, Ooh, that feels good'*," Lil Tre said, doing his best impression of what he heard Tina say the night before.

"Your daddy wasn't sucking my titties," Tina said, reassuringly.

"What was he suckin' then?"

"None of your business! I'ma tell your daddy—Tre!"

"Wussup?" Trevon said, stepping out the kitchen.

"Guess what your bad-ass son just said to me," Tina said, trying her best not to laugh.

"What?"

"He said he'll suck my titties for—"

"*No I didn't!*" Lil Tre exclaimed, smiling from ear-to-ear. "Stop lying on me, Tina!"

"I'm lying, Lil Tre?"

"Yeah!"

"Okay, you wanted five dollars to suck my titties... if you tell the truth, I'll give you twenty dollars."

"*Put it in my hand,*" Lil Tre said, holding his hand out.

Tina grabbed her Coach bag, pulled out two $10 bills, and placed them in Lil Tre's hand.

"Yeah, I said it," he said, looking at his father with a straight face. "I just played you, Tina," he said, looking back at Tina. "Yo dumb-ass could have gotten both of your titties sucked for only five dollars, but since you want to snitch on Lil Tre, it just cost you twenty dollars—that's ten dollars a titty—Lil Tre just came up!" Lil Tre said, holding up the bills.

Trevon was laughing so hard he had tears in his eyes.

"That shit ain't funny, Tre!" Tina screamed at him, "That's why he's so bad! You be encouraging him to do shit like that when you laugh at him!"

Lil Tre pulled out a big wad of 1s, 5s, 10s and 20-dollar bills and added the two $10 bills Tina had given him to the collection.

Tina's eyes popped out of her sockets. *"Where you get all that money from Lil Tre?"*

Lil Tre's head bounced back and forth from his father to Tina. "*Damn!* Who you is? The IRS?"

Tina put her hands on her hips. "Do I look like the damn IRS?"

"What'choo trying to audit Lil Tre for then? I don't need you countin' my dollars. You needs to go back to work so you can make that money for Lil Tre, so Lil Tre can count yo dollars."

Tina sat there with her mouth wide open, not believing what she was hearing come out of Lil Tre's slick-ass mouth. He was so sharp to be only 7 years old. "Wasn't nobody trying to count your dollars, boy!"

"Yeah you was," Lil Tre said as he flipped through his bankroll. "Don't *ever* ask Lil Tre about his paper—even my momma knows better than that." "Come'ere, nigga," Tina said, grabbing Lil Tre and hugging him. "You get on my nerves wit'cho slick-ass mouth, but I love you though..." She looked at Trevon standing behind them smiling. "This boy so much like you it's scary," she said as Trevon hugged them both, amazed how mature his son had gotten. Lil Tre was only 7 years old, but sharper than a razor blade.

They dropped Lil Tre off when the weekend was over. Trevon knocked on the door and Desiree answered it. She looked in the car where Tina was sitting and slowly mouthed the word "*bitch*" silently, making sure Tina saw her. In return, Tina stuck up her middle finger, wiggled it around and mouthed the words "*fuck you*". Then Desiree mouthed the words "*I'ma beat yo ass*" as she smashed her fist into the palm of her hand. Then Tina raised her hand, palm outward, and mouthed the word "*whatever*".

"Are y'all through now?" Trevon asked, stepping in between them, cutting off their view. "Why y'all gotta act like that?"

"Well, don't bring that bitch to my house then," Desiree said, rolling her neck.

Trevon shook his head. "I'll call you later, Dee," he said, walking to the car.

On the way home, they stopped by the Quick Stop and Trevon bought a copy of the *Palm Beach Post*. He spent the evening scanning the job section of the classifieds and made a list of potential employers before going to bed and accommodating Tina with another "*fix.*"

The next morning, he woke up and got into the shower before putting on his new Armani suit. "Damn, you're lookin' so good, baby," Tina said jubilantly as Trevon stepped into the living room. "Sheiit! I'll give yo ass a job; you can work for me," she said, wrapping her arms around his neck and inhaling the Sean John cologne he'd just put on.

"You really like it?" Trevon inquired sheepishly.

"Boy, you know you look good!"

"*I knoooow,*" Trevon said conceitedly.

"You look like you just stepped out of a fashion magazine," Tina said. "Wherever you go, they're going to hire you on the spot. Especially if it's a female."

"I hope you're right."

"Trust me, you're going to be successful on your journey today..."

Trevon took the car and started out on his mission. He started with the first name on his list: an Italian restaurant called Amici on the island of Palm Beach.

Once there, he was given an application and was told to have a seat at the bar to fill it out. He answered all the questions as truthfully as he could, but got stuck on one particular question: Have you ever been convicted of a felony? *Yes. Why lie?* He thought. His parole officer had to contact them anyways to verify his employment.

After he was finished, he gave his application to a waitress and she told him to have a seat while she went to get the GM (general manager). Minutes later the GM came from the kitchen holding Trevon's application...

"Hello, Mr. Jenkins. I'm Joey Rosario, the GM," he said, holding out his hand to greet Trevon. He was definitely Italian. He was in his late twenties, slim, and had black curly hair, with an intelligent face and strong Sicilian features. "You have really neat handwriting," Joey complimented, and for the next 10 minutes he discussed their needs at Amici. How busy they were and the hours that needed to be worked. He asked Trevon what he was looking for and his plans for the future, and listened attentively as Trevon began shooting game, telling him everything he wanted to hear. Then he told Trevon about how they hired so many people, and how they left because they couldn't handle the pressure and how much of a loss it was to invest all that time and training in someone for them to just up and leave. "Is this something you would be interested in for the time being," Joey asked, "or are you looking for a long-term commitment?"

"Definitely long-term," Trevon answered.

"If I hired and trained you, could I depend on you to commit yourself to Amici or will you up and leave like everyone else when the pressure hits?" Joey asked, leaning back in his chair, waiting for Trevon's response.

"That's like building a production plant to produce one automobile..." Trevon answered. "That's craziness, Mr. Rosario. One hand washes the other. If you give me a chance, I give my word that I will be diligent and dependable... They say pressure burst pipes; my pipes have never leaked, better yet burst."

"I like that," Joey said, producing a big smile. He picked up the application and scanned it a moment. "You said you've been convicted of a felony."

Damn! Trevon thought to himself. *There it goes!* "Yes," he replied. "Look, Mr. Rosario, there's no reason for me to lie because if you hire me, my parole officer is going to tell you anyways... A few years ago, I got into an altercation with someone that ended up with me assaulting them with a gun. I've changed, I repaid my debt to society. Please, Mr. Rosario I need this—"

"You're hired," Joey said, cutting Trevon off.

"*What?*" Trevon said in disbelief.

"I said, you're hired," Joey repeated. "We all make mistakes, Mr. Jenkins. From the conversation we just had, I can see that you're very intelligent and you possess great potential..." He stood and grabbed Trevon's application. "I need you on the three to eleven shift. Is fourteen dollars an hour good for you?"

"That's perfect," Trevon answered, trying to conceal his excitement.

"Can you start tomorrow?"

"I'll be here at two forty-five."

"I'll see you then..."

Trevon called Tina as soon as he got in the car. "You're not gonna believe this shit, Tina," he said, trying to sound disappointed.

"What happened, baby?" Tina asked sympathetically.

"I GOT A JOB!" Trevon yelled. "Fourteen dollars an hour!"

"I'm so proud of you! Didn't I tell you that you were going to be alright?"

"I'll be home soon. Let me take care of something right quick, alright?"

"Okay, baby." *Click.*

Trevon sat in deep thought for a few minutes. Things were changing for the better. He loved Fresh with all his heart but couldn't afford to get caught up in anything dealing with Da Grimlinz. He trusted Fresh's judgment, but he still had to put up a wall between him and the bullshit.

Ten minutes later, Trevon was inside Walmart. After purchasing what he needed, he was on his way. When he pulled up in front of the trap, Jug, Teddy, and Wooda were outside on point.

"Damn, Tre! Where you going all dressed up lookin' like Niggeraccie and shit?" Teddy asked jokingly.

"Y'all come inside," Trevon replied, "we're about to have a pow-wow."

Once inside, Trevon turned off the radio as everyone sat down. He placed the Walmart bag on the table and pulled out a chessboard set. They all looked at each other puzzled, wondering what Trevon had in mind. "I'm snatching rank," he said, looking at Ooh-Wee and Wooda.

"For what?" Ooh-Wee asked. "What we do?"

"Nothing," Trevon answered, "it's nothing personal. Fresh did a good job organizing this shit, but y'all need to learn what organization mean. It's about to be a chain of command. The first one to beat me will fall in rank behind Fresh as Captain, the next one a lieutenant, the rest of y'all will be grunts."

"I don't know how to play chess," Wooda whined.

"Shut the fuck-up!" Fresh barked. "You ain't know how to play Madden when you first played it but you learned!"

"Like I said," Trevon continued, "it's about to be a chain of command. Meaning grunts have no business discussing anything with Fresh and I. Any and everything will be relayed to your superior - which would be the lieutenant - and it will be sent up the chain..."

Trevon spent the next hour teaching the basics of the game: how to set up, how each piece could and couldn't move, how to castle, offense and defense.

"You'll be ranked according to your ability to think," Trevon said before leaving, "according to your ability to use your head and analyze shit. Y'all have one week to practice. After that, each of you will have one chance per day to play me until the ranks are filled, understood?"

The weeks that followed were wonderful. Trevon studied the menu from Amici thoroughly and became an excellent chef. Joey was very pleased, pleased enough to give Trevon a raise. So, after only six weeks, he was making $15.50 an hour.

Ironically, Teddy beat Trevon the first game they played, earning the rank of captain; Ooh-Wee fell in as the lieutenant.

"Y'all learned a new skill..." Trevon said to the clique after the ranks had been filled. "The same way y'all analyzed this game to beat me, y'all need to analyze life. I'm trying to teach y'all how to stay one step ahead of the game, that's why I wanted y'all to learn how to play this one..." Trevon said, pointing to the chessboard. "It teaches you how to use your head, how to analyze shit before you make a move. I promise you all, if you take the fundamental structure of this game and use it with the skills you learned from playing it, you'll be able to conquer any obstacle life throws at you... I'm giving y'all something more precious than money... I'm giving y'all knowledge..."

They all sat looking at their General, shaking their heads, absorbing what he was saying. They had a new found respect for Trevon. In the months that followed, Da Grimlinz became more and more organized, each taking their rank seriously. Trevon was amazed at how fast they picked up on what he was trying to do and was proud of the organization that formed between them; they were starting to use their heads. He tested them all and they passed, as did time...

Nine months had passed, and Trevon had only one more left

until he was done with his community control. One evening before Trevon went to work, Mr. Bryant, Trevon's parole officer, stopped by unexpected.

"Hello," Tina said after answering the door.

"He-hello," Mr. Bryant replied, spellbound by the sight of Tina in her silk robe. She was completely naked underneath and her nipples were piercing through the thin fabric. "I-I-um-I'm Mr. Bryant," he said getting choked up on his words, "Mr. Jenkins' parole officer. Is he in?"

"Oh..." Tina replied, stepping to the side, "come in and have a seat. I'm Tre's friend, Caramel. He'll be right out, he just got in the shower."

"That's no problem, I can wait."

"Would you like something to eat while you wait?" Tina asked as she sat across from him. "I just got finished cooking."

"No, thank you," Mr. Bryant answered, undressing Tina with his eyes. "Are you Trevon's girlfriend?"

"Oh no! We're just friends," Tina answered with a big smile, sitting back and spreading her legs wide open so Mr. Bryant could get a good view of what he was trying to see. He looked up in disbelief after he saw Tina wasn't wearing any panties. "Are you sure you don't want anything to eat?" she asked teasingly, rubbing her finger in the pink flesh between her legs. "Because you sure look hungry, and I got plenty for you to eat..."

When Trevon came out of the bedroom, he was caught off guard by Mr. Bryant's presence. Tina was leaning against the arm of the sofa smiling devilishly, and Mr. Bryant was standing beside her, wiping off his mouth with a bulge in from of his pants. Trevon quickly put two and two together and smiled before saying, "Mr. Bryant, hey, how ya doing?"

"Hey..." Mr. Bryant replied nervously.

"I see you met Caramel..." Trevon said, reaching for Mr. Bryant's hand to shake it. Afterward, he looked at Tina and said, "*Bad girl!*" pointing his finger at her like she was a dog that pissed on the floor.

"Mr. Bryant is staying for dinner, Tre," Tina said matter-of-factly, "aren't you Mr. Bryant?"

"Ye-yeah," he answered, not knowing what to say.

"Well..." Trevon said, heading for the door, "I have to get to work. Tina, be good now."

"I will," she chuckled as Trevon left.

He stuck his head back in the door seconds later, just as Mr. Bryant was shoving his face back in between Tina's legs. "Enjoy the meal," he said sarcastically. Trevon didn't know how Mr. Bryant was going to explain to his wife the decline in their checking and savings accounts because they were definitely about to take a huge plunge fucking with Tina Baptiste.

Later that night, it was a hectic rush hour at Amici and Joey was running around like a madman. Trevon sensed that there was something different about him; his senses told him right.

When the customers started to leave and things started to slow down, Joey came to Trevon and commended him for a job well done. That's when Trevon saw the reason Joey had been running around the place like a chicken with its head cut off: Joey had cocaine residue on his nose and his eyes were dilated.

"Your nose is dirty," Trevon chuckled.

"What?" Joey replied, not catching on to what Trevon was talking about.

"Your nose..." Trevon repeated, "you got coke on your nose."

Joey wiped his nose, looking around nervously. "It's not coke."

"Yeah, yeah, yeah, and today ain't Friday. Come on, I got something for you..." Trevon said, walking out the back door.

Joey followed him to Tina's Acura.

"Jump in," Trevon said, disarming the alarm. When they were inside Trevon said, "It's cool, Joey. Your secret is safe with me. I get down too, see..." Trevon pulled out of pill bottle full of Xanax with a small glassine baggie of cocaine.

Joey smiled. "Thanks for pulling me to the side. My father would've fuckin' killed me if he would've seen that shit on my face."

"Your father?" Trevon said, looking confused. "How would your father have seen it on your face? Did he come in to have dinner?"

"Fuck no! He owns the place!"

"You mean Frank?"

"Yeah, you didn't Frank was my father?"

"Naw," Trevon answered, "I haven't even seen him yet, he's always up in his office."

"That's a first; everyone knows my father. I thought everything would change when we move down here to Florida. We were better off in Jersey."

Something clicked in Trevon's' head and the pieces of the puzzle started falling in place. Words and names started jumping from his memory bank:

FRANK-ROSARIO-MURDER-JERSEY-MOB-UNDERBOSS

Then it hit him: "Oh, shit!" he exclaimed. "I don't know why I ain't peep this shit earlier. Frank is Frank Rosario—y'all mobbed up!"

"You really didn't know who we were?"

"Nah, I swear! I've been so caught up in my own shit, I never paid it no attention. That's why you hired me so fast after I told you I pistol-whipped a dude. Shit, Frank makes me look like Harry Potter. I remember hearing all about y'all a couple years ago. Frank beat the Feds in some murder and racketeering charges. I knew something was up when I used to see them Cubans come through the back door all the time. I just brushed it off 'cause it was none of my business..." And Trevon was right. Frank Rosario was in the restaurant and real estate business. For those who were stupid enough to inquire, Frank was also into more colorful businesses, too. He owns several brothels throughout South Florida that were disguised as massage parlors and tanning salons. He was also into extortion, counterfeiting, loan sharking, gambling, and murder-for-hire. "I don't believe this shit," Trevon said, "I got Frank Rosario's son in my car."

"Believe it, Tre," Joey chuckled.

"Oh, here," Trevon said, remembering why they were out there, "take this," he said, handing Joey a Xanax...

"What's this?"

"A Xannie... if you take 'em while you're snortin' coke, it'll take away the obnoxiousness that comes with the high. Meaning you'll get the cocaine high but without the paranoia and shakes, and your eyes won't get all big, like how they were tonight."

"Sounds good to me," Joey said before swallowing one.

The next day Joey caught Trevon as soon as he walked through the door. "Hey Tre! Come outside, I need to talk to you..." he said walking out the door. "That Xannie was the shit. Can you get more?"

Trevon smiled. "Yeah, come on..." They got in the Acura and Trevon pulled out the pill bottle. He took his little baggie of cocaine out of the bottle and gave it to Joey. "It's about forty in there," he said.

"How much you want for 'em?"

"It's on the house this time. If you want more, they're three dollars apiece."

Joey's face lit up. "I got something for you too, bro," he said, pulling out of a wad of 20 and 50-dollar bills, passing one to Trevon.

Trevon pushed the bill back. "I told you the Xannies were on the house."

"Naw, take it," Joey insisted.

Trevon took the bill.

"Look at it," Joey ordered.

Trevon looked at the bill. "Yeah... and what?" he asked.

"You know what you're holding?"

"Yeah a twenty dollar bill."

Joey started laughing. "Wrong bro! You're holding some of the best counterfeit money in the world."

"Get the fuck out of here," Trevon said, turning on the interior light to examine the bill; it looked, felt, and smelled like real money. It even had the security thread running vertically up one side with *"USA TWENTY"* engraved in it, and the hologram picture of Andrew Jackson.

"They're so good they can even pass the money pen test. The only way to tell them apart from the real is to burn 'em."

"Meaning?"

"They burn like a fuse."

Trevon thought for a short moment. "How much are they going for?"

"Fifty for every hundred, but for you, I'll do thirty. And for chrissakes Tre, can't nobody know about this. I'm dealing with Victor Pagan behind my father's back."

"Who's Victor Pagan?"

"Remember when you said you see Cubans in and out of the back of the restaurant all the time?"

"Yeah."

"That's Victor and his peoples. They're from Miami, supposed to be plugged in with one of the Mexican cartels. Been doing business with my father for years. That's where I get my coke from. If my father finds out—forgeddaboudit—he'll fuckin' flip! He doesn't want me in the business, wants me to run the restaurant—fuck that!"

"Your secret is safe with me," Trevon reassured him.

"I really like you, Tre. You turned out to be all right"

"Sheiit, you did, too."

Joey smiled, opened the pill bottle, and popped a Xanax. "I need you to keep these coming."

"I got you, homie," Trevon replied.

●   ●   ●

Things went on as usual for the next 3 weeks, until Joey pulled Trevon to the side looking distressed. "Tre, I need you to do something for me," he pleaded, ushering Trevon out of the door. "Look, I have to meet some of Victor's people in an hour."

"And?"

"I can't leave! My father has been on my ass about running the place. I can't leave for a long period of time, he'll miss me. Eddie, Frank's

91

bodyguard, can't leave either, he'll miss him, too. If he finds out Eddie has been in on my dealings with Victor, forgeddaboudit! You and Eddie are the only two I can trust. Eddie can't leave—that leaves you... I'll give you five thousand in counterfeit for doing it."

Trevon looked at Joey in silence for a short moment. "I got a question Joey...you said if Frank finds out Eddie has been in on your dealings with Victor—forgeddaboudit... What exactly does 'forgeddaboudit' mean?"

"That means he'll have Eddie whacked."

"And what do you think will happen to my black-ass if Frank finds out I've been helping you?"

"Whacked," Joey answered truthfully.

There was another short silence. "Five thousand in counterfeit, huh?" Trevon said. "How can I refuse that?"

"Good, you got a piece?"

"What the *fuck* I need a gun at work for, Joey? What am I about to pick up? What I need a gun for?"

"Eddie's gonna give you fifty thousand in counterfeit. Give that to Victor's people and they're going to give you twenty thousand in real bills and a quarter kilo of coke. I'll call them and let them know you're coming, capisci? Wait in your car and I'll have Eddie bring you the money and a piece just in case you need it..." Joey wrote down the address to where Trevon had to go. Moments later, Eddie appeared at the Acura holding a brown paper bag.

"For you," he said, handing Trevon the bag, "the piece is in there with the money. Joey said call him if there's any problems." With that said, Eddie left.

Trevon opened the bag. There was an envelope and a .380 semi-automatic inside. He pulled out the envelope and opened it: $5,000 in counterfeit money, all in $20 and $50 bills. Trevon pulled the .380 out of the bag and looked down at the $50,000; even though the money was fake, it was still a pretty sight.

There was a note on top of the money. It read: $50,000 in fake, $20,000 in real in return along with you know what... J. "We're in business, Fresh," Trevon mumble to himself.

Before meeting Victor's people, Trevon stopped by the trap to drop off the dummy bills so Fresh could swap them out with real money as they made sales. After doing so, he headed to his destination when out of the blue, he saw blue; blue and white lights flashing in his rear-view mirror. "Shit!" he exclaimed.

A sheriff's deputy pulled him over and ran his name, which came back possibly armed and dangerous, which led to the search of the vehicle, which led to the discovery of the money and gun, which led to Trevon's arrest...

Now here he was, lying in a bunk inside the Palm Beach County jail, hoping that Monique would be able to get him out the day after tomorrow. *What the fuck I'ma tell Joey?* he thought to himself. He hoped Joey would understand.

Only time will tell, he thought. How right he was because only time would tell...

And the Game was Told

October 1st, 2007 the present

> Love is not some affectionate,
> sentimental emotion. Love is
> trust, understanding, and
> intelligence, which in return
> brings compassion...
>
> Steven Brown

I wish they would hurry up! Tina thought to herself as she sat in the visitation lobby of the Palm Beach County jail. She'd been there for the past hour, waiting to see Trevon. She hadn't seen or heard from him in almost three weeks and was starting to get worried. She missed him so much and prayed that Monique Baker would be able to get him a bond when he went to his bond hearing tomorrow. If so, she was getting her baby out no matter what the amount was. She didn't care who she had to fuck, or who's dick she had to suck, her boo is coming home.

After an hour and 45 minutes, she sat in a room, waiting for Trevon to come in. She didn't go with the rest of the visitors though. For some reason, Trevon was in confinement, so he didn't get visits with the rest of the general population, which was fine with her because they had the room all to themselves. She didn't know why he had to always act a fool. Regardless... Trevon was still her baby, no matter what he did.

Finally, the lock popped, the door opened and Trevon walked through it, handcuffed, being escorted by a deputy that looked like he wanted to kill her baby. She couldn't hear what was being said because the two-inch glass separated them, but she knew some foul words were being exchanged before the deputy took off the handcuffs.

Once they were off, Trevon and the deputy stood nose-to-nose and she was able to make out the words *"state baby"* and *"peckerwood"* because they yelled them as loud as they could. After a few more seconds of staring each other down, the deputy turned to leave. When Trevon sat down, Tina picked up the phone and placed her hand on the glass.

Trevon placed his hand where hers was and silently mouthed the words *"I miss you"* as he picked up the phone. Tears welled up in Tina's eyes. "Why haven't you called?" she asked as she wiped one from her cheek.

"I'm in lockdown," Trevon answered, "so I'm only allowed to call my attorney."

"I'm not even about to ask while you're in there," Tina chuckled.

"I cursed the judge out."

Tina smiled. "That's my baby."

"Sorry 'bout getting your car towed."

"It's okay. They held it for a week, tearing it apart and searching it, but I got it back... Look, I don't trust these phones, so I need you to peep game."

"Shoot."

"When they called me and told me they had my car, and what they found in it, I didn't know what to do. I waited four days for you to call, but you never did. I remember what you told me about that situation and who was supposed to make that situation jump off. I didn't know what to do, so I called that person (she was referring to Joey), and told him what was going on... Please don't be mad at me, Tre."

"I'm not, you did the right thing. I'm glad you did call."

Tina smiled. "He said that everything was all good and that he hoped you wasn't mad at him. He said that he was worried about you because he hadn't heard from you and his peoples hadn't either—whatever that meant. Anyways, he told me to find out what it would cost for an attorney, and to come pick up the money after I did. He's real good people's, Tre, 'cause when I found one, he gave me all the money to pay her off, no questions asked... I got you a real good lawyer, baby."

"I know, she came to see me yesterday."

A big smile swept across Tina's face as she shook her head. "She's finer than a mufucker, ain't she?"

"That she is."

"I knew you would like her. I sure would like to put 'The Pick' on her."

"You just might get your wish," Trevon replied. "I'ma get at shawdy."

"I don't think you going to be able to do it, Tre. I know your game tight and all but I don't think Monique gon' go for it."

"What'choo want to put on it?" Trevon asked casually.

"Head on command for a month."

"Deal."

"You got thirty days."

"Naw," Trevon said, "she ain't even want me to call her by her first name. Shawdy real uptight, real prissy."

"I'll go one better... I'll give you sixty days from tomorrow.

"Why tomorrow?"

"Because you're coming home tomorrow."

"How are you so sure about that?"

"Because I know how good Monique is—she's Dexter's lawyer, too. She just got him out on a trafficking charge about two months ago. She got his ass out on bond ASAP, so I know she gon' be able to do something with your case."

"I hope so..."

There was a short silence as Trevon gazed into Tina's eyes.

"Tre?"

"Yes, princess."

"I've been meaning to ask you something."

"Shoot."

"Why?" Tina asked.

"Why what, Tina?"

"Why me? Why did you invest so much in me? I was seventeen, Tre. Young, dumb, and had nothing to offer you. Out of all the women in the world, why did you choose to mold me?"

Trevon took a deep breath. "Do you still remember the things I told you the day I gave you the game, Tina?"

"Every word of it," Tina answered, "if I hadn't, I wouldn't be where I am today, Tre. The things you told me that day have been engraved in my heart, in my mind, to this day it keeps me going. That's what I live by, how could I ever forget?"

Trevon smiled. "So you remember the part about how hateful a woman can be?"

"Yes."

"I left out the other part to that because I didn't feel like it was necessary for you to hear it then..."

"Please tell me, Tre."

Trevon looked into Tina's eyes, thinking about the first time he saw her. Time had flown so fast; he couldn't believe it had been six years. He cherished every day, every moment he'd spent with her.

"Tina, I'ma explain to you the best way I know how so you'll understand what I'm trying to say..." Trevon looked up in deep thought before speaking again. "A woman... a woman is like a flower. She's fragile... She's delicate, she needs certain elements to grow. Water. Sun. Air... These are the elements a flower needs to grow, and when given these elements, it'll radiate whatever it absorbs and blossom into something beautiful. But without those elements, it'll wither up and become something ugly... A woman is no different. Love. Understanding. Affection... These are the elements that a woman needs to blossom. When she absorbs these elements, she radiates something beautiful... What I'm trying to say is, the same way a woman can hate you, she can love you. Once a woman absorbs the element she needs, the love and loyalty she radiates is so genuine, so precious, so beautiful. Like I told you before: you were a flower that was bound to blossom regardless of what—I just gave you what you needed to grow. My thesis must be right because your love and loyalty has been unconditional throughout the years you've been in my life. I don't know what I would do without you—"

"You'll never have to find out," Tina said. "I'ma always be here for you, Tre."

The lights flickered, indicating the visit was over.

Tina placed her hand on the glass as Trevon did the same. "I'll be here to pick you up tomorrow," she said as tears welled up her eyes.

One fell from Trevon's, leaving a rivulet on his cheek. "I'll be here waiting..."

Tina beat her steering wheel when she got back in her car, crying uncontrollably. She laid her head against the headrest and stared at Gun Club (the county jail). She hated this place, and as she sat there staring at it, it felt like déjà vu all over again. Here she was, sitting in the same parking lot, looking at the same building, feeling the same way. She closed her eyes and found herself drifting back in time...

Tina Baptiste was born May 25th, 1984. She was the only child born to her Haitian father, Gene Baptiste, and her Dominican mother, Rita Cortes.

Tina's father was killed when she was a baby, so she had no memories of him. The memories she did possess were of all the different men her mother brought home. She remembered the sound of the headboard banging against the wall. She remembered the sound of the mattress squeaking. She remembered the moaning. She remembered the heavy breathing. She remembered her mother and her mother's boyfriends yelling in Spanish and broken English...

"Fuck me! C'mon—fuck me harder!"

"Dios Mio! I'm trying!"

"Give it to me! Cogeme!"

Rita used to be one of the most beautiful women in the Dominican Republic, but like the seasons, Rita's time came and went.

97

Although Rita was no longer beautiful, she possessed something that kept men coming back: sucking and fucking were her two and only talents, and she utilized them hoping to regain some of the attention she received when she was in her prime.

Rita showed little Tina no affection and gave her no love and would blame her every time one of her boyfriends would leave: "I hate you!" she would tell Tina. "You little puta! I wish you were never born! I should've flushed you down the toilet..."

They came to America to stay with Tina's uncle and cousin when she was 10. They stayed in Miami for a year before moving to West Palm Beach. Tina hated this country when she first got here. She spoke both, Spanish and Creole, but spoke no English. She was teased so much that by the age of 12, she spoke English so well you would've never known of her Haitian and Dominican bloodline unless she told you.

Even after Tina learned to speak English she still didn't have many friends. She had always been different and was antisocial when she was around other children. Tina was a good child, but the one element she needed most was missing: love.

Tina remembered Carlos, her mother's boyfriend at the time. She remembered her 13th birthday, and the words he said to her...

"Hola, mami. Today es ju birthday," he said with a strong Spanish accent. "Look at ju... Ju have grown to become so beautiful..."

No one had ever called Tina beautiful, so Carlos' words had really flattered her. Afterward, she stood in front of the mirror and stared at herself...

Am I really beautiful? she thought. Her reflection showed a young woman with a round face, curly, jet black hair, almond brown eyes, caramel skin, and full lips. And if Tina's face fell short of being beautiful, which it didn't, her body made up for it. At 13, Tina had the body of a grown-ass woman, with round, firm breasts, a narrow waist, a plump ass, thick thighs, and hips that moved intuitively. Tina started putting on makeup and would go out of her way to be noticed by Carlos so he could flatter her with more sweet comments. And that's exactly what he did, and Tina loved the attention he gave her, not knowing that it would all soon change...

Two weeks after her 13th birthday, Tina got out of the shower and walked into her bedroom to find Carlos lying in her bed naked. She stood there not knowing what to do, watching Carlos' limp dick as it began to rise. The sight of him lying there naked aroused something in Tina and the area between her legs begin to tingle and moisten. She untied the towel she had wrapped around her and let it fall to the floor, exposing her nude, firm body.

"Si, mami," Carlos said as he sat up, "come to me."

All Tina knew is that she wanted to please Carlos; she didn't want the attention he'd given her to ever stop.

"Come on, mami, put ju mouth on it," he said, grabbing the back of Tina's head and forcing himself into her mouth. "Aieee mami!" he exclaimed as Tina's teeth scraped the head of his dick. "Ju never do deez before?" he asked afterward.

Tina shook her head no.

"Ahh, ju ah virgin, si?"

Tina shook her head yes.

Carlos smiled. "Come on, lie down, mami..."

Tina laid down and the events that took place next would be remembered for the rest of her life...

Her first time with a man, the day she lost her virginity, the one thing every woman remembers.

Tina had heard stories from the other girls at school; how pleasurable their experiences were; how good it felt; how they would never forget. Out of all the things she heard, it was one thing she would be able to agree with and it wasn't the pleasure...

She would never forget.

She would never forget the deranged look in Carlos' eyes as he spread her legs. She would never forget how he spat on his fingers and shoved them inside of her. She would never forget the excruciating pain she felt as Carlos' dick penetrated her, ripping her tender, virgin flesh. She would never forget the feeling of Carlos' thick shaft stretching her insides. She would never forget how Carlos cocked her legs back and fucked her viciously. She would never forget how she beat on Carlos' chest, screaming in pain: *"Carlos, please stop! You're hurting meeee!"*

"Callate, punta!" he yelled back as he pounded her insides.

She would never forget how she laid there looking up at the ceiling with tears in her eyes, praying that he would hurry. She would never forget how Carlos pulled out and ejaculated on her. She would never forget the feeling of his warm semen gushing on her stomach and thighs. She would never forget how Carlos got up and used the towel to wipe off his bloody dick before throwing it in her face and telling her to wipe off. She would never forget how she laid there crying on her bloody sheets. She would never forget how nasty she felt as she wiped Carlos' sticky semen off of her, or how he tore her tender flesh, or how bad it burned when she urinated. It all lasted it no longer than five minutes, but it seemed more like five hours. Tina would never forget any of these things...

Never.

These events took place for the next three months while Rita was at work. Then things changed. Carlos started coming to her room while her mother was there, sometimes even while Rita was awake in the next room, knowing what Carlos was doing to her daughter. He would sell Rita and Tina dreams about moving them to Puerto Rico, so Rita would let him have his way with her daughter. It had gotten to the point where Tina would sleep naked and keep a towel by the bed to wipe off Carlos' semen, and at times, she needed a towel to spit the semen into. When he would come to her room and she would just roll over and spread her legs, wishing he would hurry and do what he came to do.

When all of her classmates left school, they went home to loving families. Tina, on the other hand, went home to suck Carlos' dick and get fucked. But like all of the rest, Carlos left Rita high and dry.

Tina was no stranger to sexual activities by her 9th-grade year. At the age of 14, Tina's body was more developed than all the 12th-grade girls, therefore for attracting all the 12th-grade boys.

Because of Rita, Tina had really thought that a woman was supposed to give herself to a man. She never understood the fundamentals of love, nor the fundamentals of making love. From the tender age of 13, all she knew how to do was get fucked, and that's exactly what she did throughout her high school years, earning a "slut" reputation.

Tina had numerous boyfriends. All of them the same; all of them said they loved her; all of them made promises; all of them fucked her...

All of them left their promises unfulfilled.

Yet, Tina would open her legs to let the next one in. When it all boiled down it was just a fuck. Tina really didn't see what women got out of it. She just felt like it was something she was obligated to do.

The rumors had gotten so bad by her senior year that she dropped out of school...

That's when Eric, Rita's new boyfriend moved in, and like with Carlos, Rita gave her daughter to him as a sacrificial lamb.

Eric was a wannabe pimp/heroin junkie from Tennessee, therefore, he was a smooth talker. He told Tina everything she wanted to hear: How beautiful and sexy she was, and how he can make her rich with a body like hers. He had told her all about pimpin' and hoein' and took her shopping. He bought her a cell phone, dresses, and lingerie, not knowing it was all for his benefit. Every night she was in a different drug dealer's bed while Eric sat in the living room getting high. After she was finished, he will give her $20, sometimes $30, not knowing he was getting between $120 to $150, sometimes $200 for every trick she turned. At 17, the money she was making was good. Besides, she had a job at McDonald's...

She had no idea how big of a fool she was.

Nevertheless, Tina liked Eric more than Carlos because she didn't have to worry about him coming to her room at night to suck his dick the way Carlos did. Eric was too busy sticking needles in his arm, therefore he had no time to stick his dick in her, which was fine with Tina because she was really starting to despise dick, as well as men. She was starting to believe they were all the same. Her opinion soon changed, just like her life had, the night she met one particular man in the summer of 2001 while at work...

"Welcome to McDonald's. May I take your order?" Tina said into the headset while standing at the register at the drive-thru window.

"Yeah, let me get ahh... a three-piece dinner with a biscuit and coleslaw, and... another three-piece dinner with macaroni and cheese and potato wedges. And make one of them dinners crispy and one original— you got that?"

"I'm sorry, sir," Tina said, laughing at the asshole out at the menu, "but this is McDonald's, not KFC. We don't serve chicken dinners."

"Well, then let me get two number ones with Orange Hi-C's, *pleeaassee!*" the man said sarcastically.

"Your total is nine eighty-seven. Drive around to the first window, please."

Moments later, the inside of McDonald's was blaring with Triple J, an underground rapper from Riviera Beach. The man Tina was just talking to was three cars back, but the system in his Chevy Caprice was so powerful it sounded as if he was sitting at the window. The song "Yankee Man" came on and two of Tina's co-workers (hoodrats) left their registers to come to the drive-thru window to see who was playing Triple J.

"Oooh—that's my shit, girl!" Tawanna said, dropping down low and scrubbing the ground as Tina and Shameaka did the same.

*"Giiirl—*look at that there!" Shameaka said as the car pulled up to the window.

"Damn he look good!" Tawanna exclaimed, pushing Tina out the way.

"Y'all get back to work!" Mr. Kent, the manager yelled. "This ain't the damn Soul Train! Customers up there waiting while y'all back here shaking y'alls ass!"

After Mr. Kent left, Tina continued to dance as the mystery man turned the music down with an angry expression on his face. *"Oh, hell naw!"* he said, putting the car in park.

"What's the problem, sir?" Tina asked, looking confused.

"Where's your manager?" the customer demanded, crawling out

the car window and into the drive-thru window looking angry and serious.

Tina didn't know what to think. She thought he was about to complain about the way she was dancing. "What's the problem, sir?" she asked pitifully.

"I don't appreciate this shit," he answered, backing Tina into the corner.

"You don't appreciate what, sir?"

He grabbed Tina's hand and kissed her knuckles. "I don't appreciate how they got you throwed back here in the drive-thru window. As beautiful as you are, they're supposed to have you up front attracting and mesmerizing the customers. But I guess I can't complain..." He paused to look at her name tag. "...Tina, 'cause if you were up front, you wouldn't be back here right now attracting and mesmerizing me..."

Tina looked up and saw that all her coworkers and the customers were smiling admiringly at her and the man that just crawled through the drive-thru window. He put her on top of the world. Tina knew he was spitting game, but the way he spat it set her heart on fire. She didn't too much care for light skinned men, but this one was an exception. He was tall and had beautiful light brown eyes, high cheekbones, plump lips, and the cutest nose that had a little dimple on the tip of it. "Thank you," Tina said bashfully.

The stranger unhooked the cell phone that was clamped to Tina's belt. "Check me out, shawdy," he said, programming his number into her phone. "My name is Trevon, but my peoples called me Tre..."

"Heeeey Treeee!" Tawanna hoodrat-ass yelled from the front register, waving her hand like she was trying to flag a cab.

"Look here, Tina," Trevon chuckled. "I'm not the type of dude that's gon' ask you if you got a man... I'm not the type of dude that's gon' ask you for your number either. However, I am the type of dude that will give you mines... 'cause if you do got a man, I'm the type of dude you can call when things ain't going so well with your relationship, you feel me shawdy?"

Tina couldn't speak; all she could do was shake her head. She had met a lot of men and heard a lot of game, but this man was different. At that moment, she knew she was in the presence of a true player....

"My number is right there," Trevon said, holding up the phone and pointing to the screen, "programmed under Tre..."

"What the hell you doing back here?" Mr. Kent asked as he stepped out of the office. "Look at that line out there, Tina! And you can't—"

"It's cool, burger boy," Trevon said, cutting Mr. Kent off. "I'm about to go."

"Well then get the hell out!" Mr. Kent yelled angrily.

Trevon's friend stuck his head in the window, looking like a pit bull ready to attack. "You better watch yo muthafuckin' mouth, bitch!"

"Everything cool, bug," Trevon said. "Ain't it, burger boy?"

Mr. Kent shifted nervously. "I'm gonna call the police if y'all don't—"

"Oh no—not the police!" Trevon's friend exclaimed, and everyone burst out laughing.

Trevon slid back out the window like a thief in the night, and a thief in the night was exactly what he was because he had just stolen Tina's heart and mind. He put the car in *DRIVE* and blew Tina a kiss before driving to the pickup window to get his food. All of Tina's coworkers crowded the window as Tawanna gave Trevon his food and drinks.

Tina was so spellbound that she'd forgotten to get the money for Trevor's order. She was in a daze for the rest of the night. Trevon had such a powerful aura that his presence could be felt hours later.

When Tina cashed out of the end of her shift her drawer was short $65.32. She had no explanation for her mistakes, so she got fired right along with Tawanna and Shameaka who got fired for leaving the front register and customers waiting.

When Tina got home she told Eric she didn't feel good because she didn't feel like being bothered. She was starting to get tired of his shit. He was starting to get possessive and controlling, demanding that she turned tricks. It was to the point where he had something lined up every night she got off work. But this night, she flat out told him she wasn't doing anything and went to bed, tossing and turning, thinking about Trevon. She fought the urge to call him. She didn't want him to think she was too desperate...

So, she waited a few days to call.

Tina was in the living room of a drug dealer's house while Eric was in the bedroom discussing business. The drug dealers brother (an ugly muthafucker with short dreadlocks) was sitting next to her, squeezing his crotch as he underdressed her with his eyes...

"Why do you keep staring at me like that?" Tina asked irritably.

"Because," the boy replied, "you're finer than a mufucker, bitch."

"Well...I wish you would stop. You act like you ain't never seen..."

Eric came out of the room and nodded at Tina. "Let's get this money..."

Tina felt nauseous when she stepped into the bedroom. She saw several roaches crawling on the walls. It was dirty and hot; the air was humid and smelled like dirty laundry. The man she was about to fuck (even uglier than his brother in the living room) was just sitting on the edge of the bed with his shirt off. Sweat shimmered on his skin as he looked at Tina with the same perverted look his brother displayed moments earlier. He stood up and pulled down his boxers.

Tina's eyes fell to his crotch. *"Oh hell naw!"* she said. He had the biggest dick she'd ever seen. "I'm not about to do nothing with you! You must be out your damn mind."

"Girl quit trippin'! I ain't about to hurt you."

"I don't care!" Tina snapped. *"Ain't no way in hell! You might as well go in there and get your money back!"*

The man sucked his teeth and put on his boxers before storming out of the room to go get Eric.

Tina sat on the bed, naked. Waiting for him to come in. The room was hot. She had already begun to perspire and hadn't even done anything yet. There was a fan on the dresser that swayed back and forth, teasing her with flashes of cool air, cooling the sweat that coated her body.

"What the fuck is your problem, bitch?" Eric asked as he stepped into the room.

Tina could tell that he had just finished shooting up from the way his eyes were rolling.

"His dick too big, Eric!" Tina whined. "Ain't no way in hell!"

"And what'choo mean *'go get your money back'?* You don't get no refund back on pussy! *Bitch*, this ain't Walmart! Fuck wrong with'choo?"

"Eric, I can't—"

"Tina, you can—and you are—gonna get this money, you hear me? If you're 'bout that life, then start livin' it like you are. If you gon' let somethin' like this stop you from getting money, then you're not ready for this lifestyle. You think you're gonna be young and pretty forever? You better get it while the getting' is good. I don't care if you get pregnant... Bitch, you better kill the baby and sell the blood..."

Tina thought for a moment, watching the fan sway back and forth. "Okay," she said, "tell him to come on, and hurry up—I'm ready to go."

Moments later, the man had Tina's legs spread, sticking two fingers deep inside of her as he stroked himself. She watched in amazement as he grew bigger and bigger. When he was fully erect he leaned down to penetrate her.

"What are you doing?" Tina asked, sitting up and pushing him off of her.

"Fuck you mean, *'what am I doing'?* I'm about to fuck the air out of yo ass."

"You gosta put a condom on..."

"I ain't got nothin', bitch!"

"I don't give a fuck—you ain't bout to run up in me raw!"

Reluctantly, he got up and got a condom from the dresser drawer. Tina watched as he rolled it down his shaft, stretching it to capacity, only covering two-thirds of his dick. After he was finished, he spread Tina's legs open and spat in her pussy, using the head of his dick to smear the saliva around her vulva. She moaned in pain as he rocked back and forth, stuffing his dick inside of her, forcing the walls of her vagina to spread until all her inner resistance was gone.

"Don't go in that deep!" Tina screech as he hit her cervix. "You're hurting me!"

"Shut up, bitch!" he quipped. "I just paid two hundred for this pussy—I'm about to air your ass out..." He grabbed both of Tina's legs, forced them back, and pumped his hips. He pumped so hard that every time he thrust into her, his long shaft bent when the head of his dick smashed into her cervix. After 10 minutes, Tina's insides were numb. She couldn't breathe; the air was hot and stale. Both, she and the pervert were pouring with sweat. It dripped off his chin and chest into Tina's eyes and mouth. He stroked as fast and hard as he could, making the headboard bang against the wall with each thrust: *Bam! Bam! Bam!* was all that could be heard in the living room where Eric and the brother sat laughing.

Between having her legs cocked back and yelling, Tina was so hot and tired she just laid there staring at the ceiling with tears in her eyes. She was so turned off her vagina had completely dried up, so the pervert had to stop every few minutes to spit in it for lubrication.

After 30 minutes of torture, he pulled out, pulled the condom off, and stood over Tina, stroking his shaft, shooting his cum all over her. Tina turned her face sideways as warm semen was being shot all over it. "*Damn*, you got some good pussy," he said, slapping his dick on Tina's cheek. Afterward, he put on his boxers, picked up a dirty shirt, and threw it in Tina's face. "Wipe off with that," he said before walking out of the room.

Tina balled up on the bed and cried, hating men, hating herself, hating life. "*Oh God, please help meeee,*" she whispered, wiping sweat and semen from her body.

The brother walked into the room. "You ready for round two?"

"It ain't a round two!" Tina yelled. "I'm leaving!" she said as she got dressed.

Eric came storming into the room: "You ain't going nowhere until you finish, bitch!"

"My stomach hurts, Eric! I can't—" *SMACK!*

Eric slapped Tina with enough force to send her flying backward on the bed. "I'm getting sick and tired of all that goddamn whining bitch!"

he said as he stood over her. "Now either you gon' *suck,* or you gon' *fuck!* Whichever you choose to do is up to you, but you will do one or the other, bitch! Do you understand me?"

Terrified, Tina shook her head as she held her cheek.

Eric smiled. "Good... now let's get this muthafuckin' money, hoe..."

Tina sat on the edge of the bed and moments later the brother walked back into the room, squeezing his crotch the way he was when he was in the living room earlier. He stood in front of her and she got up and walked to the drawer where she'd seen the first pervert go to get a condom. She sat back on the edge of the bed, grabbed his limp dick, and stroked it until it was erect. Once it was, she rolled the condom on and rock her head back and forth as she sucked and jacked his dick in unison...

"Yeah, suck that dick, bitch," he moaned, grabbing a handful of Tina's hair and pulling her head as he pumped his hips, shoving his dick into her mouth. Moments later, he too snatched the condom off and shot cum on Tina's face. She tried to turn her head, but he snatched her hair and turned her face back to him as he shot semen on it. It dripped off like slime, oozing down her shirt and skirt. He rubbed the head of his dick on Tina's lips as he stroked his shaft, squeezing out the last bit of his orgasm, smearing it all over Tina's face before walking out of the room smiling.

Tina cried as she wiped off, listening to the three of them out in the living room laughing at her. She was too ashamed to face them, so she sat on the edge of the bed crying, with her face buried in her hands. She could still smell the pervert's odor on her; she felt nasty and sticky from the perspiration and dried semen that clung to her like a second layer of skin.

Eric walked into the room smiling. "Now that wasn't so bad, was it?"

Tina looked at him with fire and tears in her eyes. "I'm ready to go, Eric. Please, take me home."

"We'll leave when I say so," Eric replied, throwing money on the floor in front of her. Tina picked it up and looked at it in disbelief "forty dollars? *Are you fucking serious?*"

"Bitch, you're lucky you're getting that with all that goddam whining!"

"He paid you two-hu—" *SMACK!*

Eric slapped Tina again. "*Bitch*—don't you ever get in my pockets!"

"Keep this shit, junky-ass nigga!" Tina yelled, throwing the money back and running out the door.

"You'll be back, bitch!" Eric yelled back. "How the fuck yo' stupid ass gon' get back to West Palm...?"

Tina sat on a curve four blocks away from the house. She sat there crying, not knowing what to do. She was a long way from home, had no money, or no one to call. She felt dirty and ashamed. She wanted to die and started thinking of ways to kill herself. The most hurtful part about that was that if she did, nobody would have even given a fuck; she didn't even have nobody to come to her funeral.

Tina reached into her purse, pulled out her phone, and started going through her contacts. When she came across Tre's name she thought: *I might as well call. I can't stoop any lower than I already have tonight. So what if he found out I'ma whore...*

"You made the call—it's your thirty-five cent—*speak*," Trevon stated after answering the phone.

"*Hello? Tre?*" Tina replied with a sniffle.

"Who is this?"

"*Th-this is Tina,*" Tina answered, getting choked up on her words.

"What's wrong, shawdy?" Trevon asked in a more serious tone.

"*Ca-can you-pick-me-up?*"

"Where are you?"

"*In Del-Delray...*" Tina blew her nose. "*Can-can you come—get me?*"

"I'm getting on I-95 now," Trevon answered. "Where at in Delray...?"

Trevon and his friend pulled up to the curb where Tina was sitting. She got in the back seat and Trevon pulled into a nearby gas station. "Fresh, let me talk to shawdy right quick," he said to his friend. "Come up here and talk to me, girl," he said after Fresh got out.

Trevon's nostrils flared when Tina got in the front seat. He could smell the unmistakable scent of pussy—recently fucked pussy. The odor was overpowering; wet, sweaty, and musky. He saw the dried-up cum stains on her shirt and skirt and knew right away that she had just been mutted. Her eyes were swollen as well as her cheek, and her eyeliner and lipstick were smeared.

"What's going on, Tina?" Trevon asked, reaching for her hand.

"*No-nothing,*" Tina answered, "*just take me home, please.*"

Trevon squeezed Tina's hand. "Look at me..."

Tina continued to look out the window in a daze.

"Look at me!" Trevon snapped.

Tina complied.

"I might be a lot of things," Trevon began, "but I ain't never been a fool. I can help you, shawdy, but you have to help yourself first. You need

107

to let me know what da lick read, 'cause I can't help you if I don't know what's going on, you feel me?"

Tina shook her head as she shifted on the front seat. Every time she moved, Trevon got a whiff of the wet, fishy odor that came from between her legs.

"I want you to understand something..." Trevon continued. "There's nothin' you can tell me that's gonna make me look down on you— *nothin*! I kind of got an idea of what's going on, but I want to hear it from you raw and uncut, you hear me?"

Tears welled up in Tina's eyes; she blinked, and one fell.

"I'm here if you want me to be..." Trevon said, reaching out his hand, palm upward. "Take my hand...let me help you."

Tina looked at Trevon's hand for a short moment before reaching for it. She grabbed it and squeezed it tight as she broke down, telling him everything word for word. Trevon listened attentively as she explained what happened. The more she spoke, the harder and blacker his soft, brown eyes became. After she was finished, Trevon had one question: "Where these niggas at now...?"

They parked down the street from the house Tina had not too long ago walked out of. When they reached the house, Trevon and Fresh stood to the side as Tina knocked on the door tap: *Tap. Tap. Tap.*

"I told you that bitch would be back," she heard Eric say.

The first trick Tina slept with peeped out of the window and smiled before but opening the door. "I'm glad you came back," he said, squeezing his dick, "'cause I want some more of that good pu—"

Trevon pushed him back into the house as Fresh pulled out a big chrome revolver.

"*What the fuck*?!" Eric said, jumping to his feet. "*Bitch*! What the fuck you bring these niggas here for?" he continued, not caring about what Fresh was holding in his hand. "If y'all know what's good for ya, y'all better leave while y'all still have a chance! I'm Big E, nigga—*are y'all fuckin' crazy?*"

"*Am I crazy?*" Trevon asked casually, closing the door behind him. "*Am I crazy?*" he asked again, reaching into his pocket and pulling out a small glassine bag of white powder. He dumped a pile in the groove between his thumb and index finger, held it up to his nose, and inhaled. "*Am I crazy...?*" he asked again, repeating the process, only this time he held his hand to Fresh's nose and the cocaine disappeared with a loud snuff. "*Am I crazy?*" he asked for the fourth time as he wiped his nose. "If I wasn't crazy, I am now, muthafucker..." *Click-Click.*

Fresh cocked the hammer back on the revolver and the metallic sound of the cogs locking the cylinder in place pierced the air.

"Look..." Eric said nervously, "I don't know what this bitch told—"

"SHUT THE FUCK UP!" Fresh yelled. "GO SIT THE FUCK DOWN—ALL Y'ALL!"

Trevon took the pistol from Fresh and walked to the sofa where the brothers were sitting. "I'ma ask you this one *muthafuckin'* time," he said poking one of them on the forehead with the barrel of the revolver, "then I'ma buss yo *muthafuckin'* head if I don't get the right *muthafuckin'* answer—do you understand me?"

The trick nodded nervously.

"Where the *muthafuckin'* money and dope at?"

"In the kitchen, in the drawer by the sink," he answered without hesitation.

Fresh pulled out a roll of duct tape and taped their hands and feet. Afterward, he walked into the kitchen and returned with two zip lock bags, one full of money, the other heroin.

Trevon looked at Tina. "Go in the room and get whatever you wiped off with and wrap it up in the sheets y'all were laying on—get the pillowcases, too."

Tina did as she was told as Eric sat on the sofa shaking like a hamster in a pet store. "Look at this nigga, son," Fresh said, pointing at Eric. "He's shaking like a stripper—you scared, son?"

Tina returned and dropped the sheet with everything in it on the floor. Fresh pulled out a can of WD-40 and shook it as he made his way into the room Tina had just walked out of.

"So, yous'a pimp, huh?" Trevon asked Eric who just sat there speechless. "ANSWER ME WHEN I TALK TO YOU!" he yelled, making Tina jump.

"Ye-yeah," Eric answered.

"*A muthafuckin' pimp*," Trevon chuckled. "Aye, Fresh, we got a pimp here, homie."

"Get the fuck out of here," Fresh replied, stepping out of the room. "I ain't never met a real pimp before. Yous'a pimp, son?"

Eric was speechless—*SMACK!*

Trevon slapped the dog shit out of him. "My homeboy asked you a question, pimp!"

"Ye-yeah," Eric answered nervously.

Trevon smiled. "You know the definition of a true pimp?"

Eric shook his head no—*SMACK!*

"Speak up, pimp!"

"*I-I-I don't know*," Eric answered with tears in his eyes.

"How the fuck yous'a pimp, country-ass nigga, and you don't know what pimpin' is all about?"

Eric shrugged his shoulders—*SMACK!*

"*I-I-don't know,*" he answered with the quickness.

"A true pimp get money by all means..." Trevon said, standing over Eric, "even if that mean he has to sell himself—you ain't know that, pimp?"

"Na-naw," Eric said hesitantly.

"You're not a pimp," Trevon said, poking Eric in the head with the barrel of the gun. "Yous'a bitch—my muthafuckin' bitch! Do you understand me—" *SMACK!*

"*Ye-yeah,*" Eric answered quickly.

"Say it—" *SMACK!*

"*I-I'm yo bitch.*"

Trevon looked at Tina. "Take off your skirt and panties."

Tina looked back at Trevon and frowned.

"I SAID TAKE 'EM OFF!" he yelled, and Tina did as she was told as Trevon took off his jacket, so she could cover herself with it. "Put these on, bitch!" he said, throwing Tina's skirt and panties in Eric's face.

Eric picked them up and stared at them—*SMACK!*

"I said put'em on, bitch! And when I lift that skirt up, I don't want to see nothin' but camel toe, bitch-ass nigga. You better have that shit tucked good too, 'cause if I see any dick or balls, I'm blowin' them shitz off!"

Eric did as he was instructed as the brothers looked on fearfully, not knowing what was in store for them. Fresh looked on laughing while a fire began to burn inside of Tina. She thought about Carlos and all the other men that lied to and abused her. She watched as Eric put her panties on and tucked his dick between his legs. Trevon was degrading him the same way he degraded her...

But it wasn't enough.

SMACK! "Tuck that shit some more, bitch-ass nigga! I thought I told you I ain't wanna see nothin' but camel toe when I lift that skirt up."

Fresh laughed hysterically as Eric attempted to tuck his dick in Tina's panties. It was a pitiful sight to see such a thing, but at the same time, it gave Tina a sense of satisfaction.

Trevon pulled the skirt up. "What'choo think, Fresh?"

"Yeah," Fresh chuckled, "he's lookin' like a real bitch-ass nigga right about now."

Trevon grabbed Eric by the neck and walked him to the brothers. "Look at what I got for y'all trick-ass niggas..." He pressed the barrel of the revolver to the back of Eric's head and he kneeled down to his knees in front of them.

Eric looked up at Trevon with tears I his eyes. "Please..." he began to beg, "don't make me—" *SMACK!*

"You gon' *suck*, or you gon' *fuck*," Tina said after slapping Eric, "which one you choose to do is up to you, but you will do one or the other—BITCH! Do you understand me?"

Eric looked at Tina, incredulously—*SMACK!*

"*Ye-yeah*," he answered.

"Good... now get my muthafuckin' money, hoe," Tina said, reciting the exact words he'd spoken earlier.

Trevon cocked the revolver. "Don't make me tell you again, bitch."

Eric pulled down the trick's pants, pulled out his dick, and began to work his suck muscle.

"Swallow it, muthafucker!" Tina yelled, pushing the back of Eric's head, making the trick's dick shoot down his throat, which made Eric gag and throw up on the trick's lap, which made Fresh laugh so hard he began to choke. The fire that was burning inside of Tina burned out of control. She picked up the liquor bottle that was sitting on the table and smashed it into the back of Eric's head, knocking him unconscious. She used the broken bottle to stab the brothers in their crotches: "I HATE YOU MUTHAFUCKERS! I HATE YOU! I HATE ALL YOU MUTHAFUCKERS!" she yelled at the top of her voice, the brothers' painful moons muffled by the duct tape.

Trevon grabbed Tina and wrapped his arms around her.

"*Oh God, please help meee!*" She howled in pain as she shook in Trevon's arms. "*Please—help—meeee!*"

After a short moment, Trevon pulled away and pried the broken, bloody liquor bottle from Tina's hand and threw it in the sheet with the rest of the evidence before looking at Fresh a long moment. Then he wrapped his arm around Tina and they walked out the door, leaving Fresh behind...

When they got in the car, Trevon pulled the armrest up for Tina so she could ball up on the front seat. His heart ached for her as she laid on his lap crying and trembling. Tears welled up in his eyes and one fell, dropping on Tina's cheek as he rubbed her beautiful face. He didn't know Tina, but her emotions—the pain, the anger, the fear, the hate—were all so overwhelming he could literally feel it as it radiated off of her. She reminded him of a wounded bird, flopping around on the ground, trying to flop its broken wing. That's when he decided to take her under his wing and to never let what just happened, happen ever again...

"It's okay..." Trevon whispered, "Tre's here now. I'm not going to let nothing happen to you ever again, you hear me?"

Tina shook her head and squeezed Trevon tight.

At that moment, Fresh open the door and got in the backseat. No words were exchanged; they just stared at each other and Fresh nodded his head before handing Trevon the gun...

"Can you stay with me tonight?" Tina asked when they pulled up in front of her house.

"I can't tonight, shawdy," Trevon answered. "I've got some things to take care of. You don't have to worry about nothing, though. That nigga E is the least of your worries—I promise. You got my number; call me if you anything, or if you just want to talk."

"When am I going to see you again?" Tina asked pitifully.

Trevon smiled. "Call me tomorrow, a'ight..."

●   ●   ●

Tina woke up the next morning and called Trevon only to find out that her phone has been disconnected. Eric always paid the bill, so she'd lost track of what time of the month it was supposed to be paid. Tina didn't know what to do; she had no money, and now, no job.

Her next check is going to be short $65.32 because of the money she had to pay back for her drawer being short. Plus, she had a $450.00 tennis bracelet on layaway with a $175 balance that was due in 3 days or she would lose the $275 she'd already paid. Reluctantly, Tina got dressed and walk to the payphone down the street...

"Hello? Tre?"

"Who is this?"

"Tina."

"Wussup, shawdy? What number are you callin' me from?"

"It's a payphone..."

"Why are you calling from a pay phone?"

"Because my phone got turned off and I don't have the money to—"

"I'll be there in a hot minute to pick you up and we'll go get it turned back on, all right?"

"All right, Tre... Thanks."

An hour later, Trevon pulled up and blew the horn just as Tina was getting out of the shower. She peeped out the door with a towel wrapped around her. "Come inside, I have to get dressed..."

When Trevon walked through the front door, the eyes of hundreds of plastic and porcelain saints stared at him. Sentries standing guard at the crossroads of Catholicism and the dark spiritual realm known as "voodoo".

The saints were everywhere: on the counters, on shelves, in pictures, and on every table, surrounded by dozens of different colored candles that were also covered with the saint's faces.

When Trevon looked closer at the crowded shelves, he'd seen jars of brightly colored powders and liquids labeled with funny names: love potion, lammou douce; confusion powder; sadmi ceca.

"What's all this shit?" he asked.

"It's my mother's," Tina answered. "She practices obea."

"Obea?"

"Yeah, obea—y'all Americans call it 'voodoo'."

"Y'all Americans? What the hell are you?"

"Dominican and Haitian."

"Get the fuck out of here! You're an island girl?"

"Yeah," Tina chuckled.

"You talk and act like you're American."

"Y'all done rubbed off on me."

"What does your mother do with this stuff?"

"They're Iwas," Tina answered, "or should I say spirits... Back in the slavery days, the Africans of Haiti weren't allowed to practice their pagan religion, so they disguised their Iwas—or spirits—as Roman Catholic Saints... It's a process called 'syncretism'. Images of Catholic Saints are used to represent various spirits—'mysteries' is the term we use in Haiti."

"Mysteries?"

"Yeah, mysteries."

"So, y'all worship saints?" Trevon asked curiously.

"Not exactly... vodouisants believe that there is one God—referred to as 'Bon Dieu'—which means 'Good God' in Creole... Bon Dieu is very distant from his creation though. So it's the mysteries or angels that the Vodouisants turn to for help; they serve God but worship the spirits...different spirits... that come from different families that share a surname like Ogou, or Ezili, or Azaka, or Ghede. For instance, Ezili is a family, and Ezili Freda and Ezili Dantor are two individual spirits in that family. Everyone is said to have spirits, and each person is considered to have a special relationship with one particular spirit who is said to 'own their head'."

"*Well, I don't,*" Trevon answered defensively. "Don't nobody own my muthafuckin' head but me."

"Yes, you do," Tina giggled, "you just don't realize it. Where do you think the term 'guardian angel' comes from?"

"What's this shit?" Trevon asked, pointing to the powders and candles.

"For talking to the spirits," Tina answered. "You could burn a Ghede candle to bring good fortune or use the powders to bring confusion in an enemy's life or use them to mix and make a love potion."

"What's that?" Trevon asked, pointing to a statue of a black Madonna.

"The Goddess Erzuli," Tina answered.

"And why holmes keep lookin' at me like that?" Trevon asked nervously, pointing to a five-foot statue of a skeletal figure.

"He's not looking at you, boy," Tina answered defensively.

"Yes, he is—watch..." Trevon walked back and forth in front of the statue. "*See!* Everywhere I go his muthafuckin' eyes follow! What the fuck is that?"

"Gheda..." Tina answered, "the god of death."

Trevon's skin began to crawl as he thought about what Tina said moments earlier, about how they had hidden their spirits inside the saints and statues. "Hurry up and get dressed," he said as he made his way out the front door, "I'll wait for you in the car."

Trevon observed Tina as she walked to the car. She looked like she was about to take a stroll on Broadway. She had on a short, tight-fitting skirt, a spaghetti string tube top, and open-toed pumps. She also had on an excessive amount of make-up: bright red lipstick, dark eyeliner, fake eyelashes, and way too much eyeshadow.

Trevon shook his head because there was no need for any of it. Tina was oblivious to her beauty; it seemed as if she were trying to hide it. There was something so mystical about her. Not only her looks but the way she moved, the way her hips swayed when she walked; she was completely clueless about the potential she possessed.

Trevon purposefully had out his bankroll when Tina got in the car. "How much is your phone bill?" he asked as he folded the wad of money and stuffed it in his pocket.

"I don't know," Tina answered, looking at the bulge in Trevon's pocket, "I never paid it, Eric did."

After they paid the phone bill, they stopped by T.G.I. Friday's to have lunch. Tina told Trevon her life story, then about how she'd lost her job and needed the money to get her tennis bracelet out of lay-a-way. In return, Trevon told her a bunch of bullshit: that he was a drug-dealer, that he had two houses and big money...

Tina believed every word of it.

"Check this out, shawdy," Trevon said after they got in the car. "You said you needed the money to get your tennis bracelet, right?"

Tina nodded her head.

"Well, then we can help each other out. I got a couple of homeboys at the Six (Motel Six) and they're on deck, you feel me? I know you can make three or four hundred easy, and you ain't got to worry about no bullshit; my homeboys good peoples."

"Are you gonna stay with me?"

"Naw... but all you gosta do is call me when you're finished, and I'll be right there to pick you up."

Tina sat there in silence, not knowing what to say. She didn't want to disappoint Trevon, but she didn't feel like selling no more pussy either. Then she thought about the wad of money Trevon had in his pocket and made her decision: "Okay, I'll do it."

"I'll go in with you, so I can introduce you," Trevon said when they pulled into the motel parking lot. He gave Tina the key to the door when they reached the room...

She unlocked it and walked into an empty room.

"Where are they?" Tina asked, turning around to look at Trevon. As soon as she did, she saw the palm of Trevon's hand as he grabbed her by the face. Relentlessly, he pushed poor Tina so hard she flew halfway across the room before hitting the floor and sliding across the other half.

"FUCK WRONG WIT'CHOO, STUPID-ASS GIRL?!" Trevon yelled, closing the door behind him.

Tina remained on the floor looking fearful.

"GET THE FUCK UP!" Trevon demanded.

Tina got up and Trevon grabbed her by the face and pushed her down again. "What's wrong with you, Tre?!" she asked, her eyes welling up with tears.

"SHUT THE FUCK UP!" Trevon yelled. "GET YOUR STUPID-ASS UP!"

Tina got up and Trevon pushed her down again.

"Tre, please sto—"

"I SAID SHUT THE FUCK UP!"

Tina got up and backed up against the sink fearfully as Trevon walked up on her. "Tre, please stop, you're scaring me," she said, tears falling from her eyes.

115

"SHUT THE FUCK UP!" Trevon yelled. "If you're scared, that's good, 'cause that's exactly what I'm trying to do! What was going through your head, Tina?"

"I-I-I thought yo—"

"You thought what? You thought 'cause you seen this everything was all good...?" Trevon pulled out the bankroll he had earlier. "Take it!" he said, shoving the money in Tina's hand. "Look at it!"

Tina did and flipped through five $20 bills that were folded over one hundred fifty $1 bills. Afterward, she looked at Trevon with a puzzled expression on her face.

"That's what you call a Haitian bankroll," Trevon explained. "Everything that looks good ain't always good, girl! What was you thinking, Tina? How could you set yourself up for failure again after what happened last night? You can't keep doing the same shit expecting different results. If you take a bottle of poison and label it orange juice, does that mean it ain't poison no more?"

Tina shook her head. "No."

"That's right—it'll still kill your stupid-ass if you drink it! I could've brought your stupid-ass here to get raped again, or even killed, and for what? Two hundred fifty dollars? 'Cause that's all you are holding. That's what the problem is with y'all females. Y'all think a nigga ballin' 'cause he sitting on twenties and got a bankroll. That's the shit that will get you fucked up—look what happened last night! Listen to what the fuck I'm telling you: a nigga ain't about to give you shit unless you're fuckin' him or suckin' his dick. I can't believe you was about to do it again."

"What else was I supposed to do, Tre? I don't have any money!"

"How the fuck you broke and you were born with an ATM machine between your legs?"

"I-I-don't know," Tina answered, wiping away the snot dribbling from her nose.

"Look..." Trevon said, wiping the tears from her face, "If you want my help—I'll help you—but you have to help yourself first. I'ma ask you this one time, and all I want from you is a simple yes or no, understand?"

Tina shook her head yes.

"Do you want my help?"

"*Yes*," Tina answered without hesitation.

"Okay then..." Trevon replied, shaking his head, "these next couple of days, I'm 'bout to give you the game. You ever seen that movie *The Karate Kid*?"

"Yeah."

"Good, 'cause that's exactly what this shit gon' be like... I'm Mr. Miyagi, and you're Danielson; don't ask me no muthafuckin' questions when I tell you to do something. If I tell you to wax on—you wax the fuck on. If I tell you to wax off—you wax the fuck off. If I tell you to sand the floor—you sand the fuckin' floor. If I tell you to paint the fence, what'choo gon' do?"

Tina smiled. "I'ma paint the fence."

"Exactly..." Trevon replied. "If you pay attention, I promise that you'll be right by the end of phase three."

"Phase three? What's phase three?" Tina asked curiously.

"I'ma about to take you through three phases," Trevon answered, holding up three fingers, "phase one starts right now. I call this phase self-awareness..." Trevon turned Tina around, so she could look at herself in the mirror. He stood behind her and pulled her hair back while they both looked at their images as they reflected off the mirror. "Do you see what I see?" Trevon asked, speaking softly into Tina's ear.

"Yeah," she answered, "I see me and you."

Trevon smiled. "This isn't about me, baby. This is all about you, all about Tina. Now, I'ma ask you again: do you see what I see?"

Tina looked into the mirror for a short moment. "I see me."

"That's not what I see," Trevon said, gently stroking his fingers over Tina's cheek. "I see a young woman—a lost young woman—and under all that make-up, a beautiful lost young woman... No matter how much of that crap you put on your face, you can't hide what's underneath. You don't have any idea of who you are, do you?"

"I'm Tina Baptiste."

"*Naw, baby...*" Trevon chuckled, "you're a precious jewel—look at you," he said, pointing into the mirror. "You don't see that? You're so beautiful, how can you not see that? You're special, Tina. Why do you treat yourself like a nobody?"

"I don't know, Tre."

"Close your eyes..." Trevon whispered in Tina's ear. When she did, he caressed her neck with his fingers. No one had never caressed her before, so she couldn't understand the feelings that invaded her body; she started breathing heavily and her vagina began to moisten and ache with a need she couldn't comprehend. "...now I want you to picture yourself," Trevon whispered in her ear, so close his lips touched her earlobe. "Can you see yourself, your beauty?"

"Yes..." Tina answered softly, "I see my beauty."

"Say, I'm beautiful."

"I'm beautiful."

"Say, I'm somebody special."

"I'm somebody special."

Trevon kissed Tina's neck. "And you are, baby," he said afterward. "Open your eyes..." When Tina opened her eyes, she really thought the image she was staring at was suddenly beautiful, like Trevon had induced her into some sort of hypnosis. "You were born a winner, Tina," Trevon said as they looked at each through the mirror. "You beat millions of other muthafuckers from day one."

"What's that supposed to mean?" Tina asked curiously.

"You beat millions of other sperm cells and fertilized your mother's egg, so you were born a winner, you feel me?"

"Yeah," Tina answered with a big smile.

Trevon turned her around and grabbed the sides of her face. "Say I'ma winner."

"I'ma winner."

Trevon grabbed Tina's hand. "Come'ere and sit down," he said, guiding her to the bed. "If you took your pussy to the pawn shop to get a loan, how much do you think you'll be able to get?"

"I don't know...maybe a couple of hundred."

"*That's it?*" Trevon asked in disbelief. "That's all you think your pussy is worth? Don't ever sell yourself short, Tina. One thing I know, and two things fo sho: pussy and drugs gon' always sell. That shit between your legs is a jewel. Pussy is such a beautiful thing when it ain't beat the fuck up..." Trevon looked at Tina in silence for a short moment. "Take off your panties—"

"*What?!*" she replied in shock.

"You heard me," Trevon said, "wax on, wax off—take them shitz off!"

Reluctantly, Tina did as she was told.

"Open your legs," Trevon ordered. Tina did, and he stuck two fingers inside of her; the walls of her vagina was taut, gripping his fingers like a fist. "How long that dude E had you turning tricks?"

"About three or four months."

"How old are you, Tina?"

"Seventeen."

Trevon gazed into Tina's eyes; they testified to the pain she endured. They were older than seventeen, prescient with adulthood. "You've been fuckin' but your pussy ain't gutted-out, and that's a good thing..." Trevon stared at Tina, searching for the right words. "Check this out," he finally said after a short moment, "if you buy a car and don't get it serviced like you're supposed to, it ain't gon' last long. You gosta keep the tires rotated, the oil changed, and the engine tuned up. If not, that bitch gon' be on the side of the road broke down... Pussy ain't no different... think of your pussy as if it were a car. What's your favorite kind of car?"

Tina thought for a moment, "A Jaguar."

"Okay then, from this moment on, this is your brand-new Jaguar," Trevon said, patting Tina's silky pubic hair. "It got a couple hundred miles on it, but we gon' pretend like it's brand new, straight off the lot, a'ight?"

"All right," Tina answered with a big smile.

"Now a Jaguar is a high maintenance car, so if a mufucker wanna ride in it, they gon' have to put some money into it to keep it up. If you had a brand-new Jag for real, would you let a nigga jump in it and dog it out?"

"*Hell naw!*"

"Well, this Jag can't be no different. You have to keep your shit running good, keep it tuned up. This is your transportation," Trevon said, patting Tina's pubic hair again. "If you take good care of it, it's gon' get you from point A, to point B. If not, it's gon' break down on you and leave you stranded; this is Florida, baby, it's too damn hot to be walking. Now you can always catch the bus if you wanna spend the rest of your life depending on a no good-ass nigga..." Trevon spread Tina's legs and stuck his fingers back inside of her and smelled them afterward. "Smell that," he said, holding his fingers under Tina's nose.

"*What'choo tryin' to say*?!" she said angrily. "My pussy stank?!"

"Naw, I'm not saying anything—just smell it."

Tina smelled Trevon's fingers.

"What that smell like to you?" he asked afterward.

"It smell like coochie."

"It smell like fish!"

"That's what coochie is supposed to smell like."

"No it goddamnit ain't!" Trevon said irritably. "Pussy has a real distinctive smell. It ain't supposed to smell like roses, but it ain't supposed to smell like crab cakes either. Your pussy good and tight, but it could be better if you keep it fresh..." Trevon stared at Tina a moment, letting his words marinate. "You like to get your pussy sucked?"

"Nobody never ate my pussy before," Tina answered earnestly.

"*I wonder why*," Trevon replied sarcastically. "How you expect a mufucker to put they mouth down there and your shit smellin' like a tuna steak? How that shit look, you riding around in a brand new dirty-ass Jag? That shit ain't what's happening, and it don't make sense. Its like wearing a brand-new outfit with some dirty-ass shoes. You got a new Jag; you gotta keep that shit clean..."

Tina sat there with her head down, feeling embarrassed.

"Don't look like that, girl," Trevon said sympathetically, "I'm not trying to make you feel bad, I'm just trying to give you the game. Take heed to what I'm telling you and don't take it to heart. I'm not about to sugar coat nothing. If I do, that means I don't give a fuck about you..." Trevon grabbed Tina's chin and tilted her head up. "Are you paying attention to what I'm saying, Tina?"

"Yeah, I hear you."

"I don't want you to hear me, I want you to listen—it's a big difference between the two..." Trevon stood up. "Watch TV or somethin', I'll be back shortly."

Tina stood up, too. "Where you going?"

"To pick up a few things," Trevon answered, "I won't be gone long..."

After Trevon left, Tina laid down and stewed in everything he'd said. It all made sense; she couldn't help but comprehend the way he explained and broke everything down.

Tina closed her eyes and began to think of the way he caressed her neck as she touched herself. *Do my pussy really stink?* she thought to herself as she smelled her fingers. She had never been so humiliated in her life when Trevon told her it did.

Since the day she lost her virginity, Tina had never wanted to be with a man. The men she did sleep with, she slept with them because she felt she was obligated to...

Not Trevon, though.

She wanted him, wanted to feel him inside of her, and the fact he hadn't tried to sleep with her made her want him even more.

Tina put her panties back on and flipped through the channels on the television when she saw Eric's picture, along with the pictures of the two brothers, on the Channel 12 News. She turned up the volume and caught the last part of the breaking news: "...*had been shot execution-style in what police believe to be a robbery.*"

Trevon returned two hours later with several bags. "Here," he said, handing three bags to Tina. One bag was from Miami Subs, with a shrimp dinner and a piece of strawberry cheesecake inside.

Tina looked in the second bag and pulled out a beautiful sundress, a pair of Victoria's Secret panties with a matching bra, and a pair of sandals. In the third bag, there was a bottle of body wash, deodorant, toothpaste, a toothbrush, lotion and a douche.

"Eat..." Trevon said, pulling out a bag weed and a cigar, "then go in there and take a shower and wash that shit off your face... and douche."

Tina thought about asking Trevon about Eric but decided not to. Instead, she put the items back in the bag and did as he was told.

Tina stepped out of the bathroom, looked in the mirror, and loved what she saw. She looked so different; the sundress set off her figure to perfection. She was so amazed at how she could look so sexy but elegant, all at the same time. Whatever it was Trevon was trying to do was working, because she was already starting to feel like a new woman...

"Always remember," Trevon said as he smoked his blunt, "a man ain't gon' treat you no better than you treat yourself—first impressions are everything. If you dress like a hoe and act like a hoe, then guess what?"

"I'll be treated like a hoe."

"*Aaaah, very good, Danielson,*" Trevon said, sounding like Mr. Miyagi. "You've completed phase one. Are you ready for two?"

"Um-hmm," Tina answered, sitting on the bed beside Trevon.

"Phase two..." Trevon said, inhaling a mouthful of smoke, "phase two is all about game."

"*Game?*"

"Yes, game—something your dumb-ass lack and know nothing about. I'm about to teach you all about it. This phase is very complicated, so I need you to pay close attention. Before we begin, I'ma give you rule one of the game: Keep people out of your gameroom... Do you know what I mean by that?"

Tina shrugged her shoulders.

"When I first saw you in McDonald's, I noticed that you and your homegirls were in there shakin' y'all asses. If you're doing what everyone else is doing, then you're doing the wrong thing—you gotta cut them hoes loose."

"Those aren't my friends, they just wo—"

"Will you let me speak? D*amn!*" Trevon said, inhaling another mouthful of smoke. "You gosta keep your grass cut so you can see the snakes, girl. You have to keep your number of associates to a minimum, 'cause once you start doing good, a bitch gon' hate it. That's how niggas are— I don't know why—that's just how it is. A nigga don't ever want to see you do good. They're like a bunch of damn crabs in a bucket. Every time one makes it to the top, it's one at the bottom tryin' to pull it back down. Always remember: it's better to be eaten by a shark than nibbled on by a bunch of goddamn crabs. You gosta learn how to say fuck'em! Let 'em hate; haters gon' hate, doubters gon' doubt—that's what the fuck they do. You have to feed off the shit, let a hater be your motivator, you feel me?" Trevon inhaled another mouthful of smoke. "Rule two..." he said as he exhaled, "rule two is be true to the game and the game gon' be true to you, baby..." Trevon pulled a Bible from one of the night stand drawers and placed it on Tina's lap. "Before I can teach your lame-ass game, you have to first understand what game is."

"What'choo need a Bible for?"

"Because there's nothing better than the Bible when it comes to explaining the game. Nobody had the game on lock like Solomon and Jesus. You remember last night when I told you that there's nothing you can tell me that's gonna make me look down on you?"

"Yeah, I remember."

"Who am I to judge you? Who am I to judge anyone? In the book of John, Jesus was in the temple speaking to a crowd when the Pharisees brought a woman who had been caught in the act of adultery. They put her in front of the crowd and said to Jesus, *'This woman was caught in the act of adultery. The law of Moses says to stone her. What do you say?'* But see Jesus had already peeped game. He knew they were trying to trap him into saying something that they could use against him later. Jesus remained cool, calm and collected. He stooped down and wrote in the dirt with his finger before standing up and saying, *'All right, stone her.'* Then Jesus took the same game they were trying to run on him and flipped it back on them. Jesus said, *'But let those who had never sinned throw the first stone,'* and left 'em lookin' stupid. That's such a powerful scripture, Tina. That means we all have skeletons in our closet, that none of us are perfect."

"I never took that scripture in like that," Tina said earnestly.

"It's a lot of stuff in the Bible you just ain't gon' take in," Trevon replied. "Jesus and Solomon's teachings are filled with so much knowledge. Jesus spoke in parables because his knowledge was so powerful the human mind couldn't comprehend it. Jesus gives you the game, but you have to dissect it and decipher what he's trying to say."

"What do you mean?" Tina asked.

"Just what I said: you have to take it apart and put it back together and ask God to give you an understanding when you do. For instance, take Genesis, the very beginning, where game first originated. See, people read it but don't read between the lines. When you read Genesis, you have to first understand one thing."

"What?"

"That Moses was the author of Genesis, and he wrote the book fourteen hundred-fifty years after the creation of man. How?"

"I don't know, Tre."

"Through a vision, God gave him...answer this: what did Eve do that caused us to be born in sin?"

"She ate an apple from the tree of knowledge," Tina answered.

"*Wrong*! You show me where it say Eve ate a damn apple! That's what I mean by reading in between the lines. Remember Genesis was written from a vision—Moses wasn't there. He wrote what he saw in is vision, so you have to pray and ask God to give you your own understanding. So many people have the impression Eve ate an apple when the Bible says, 'she ate fruit from the tree in the midst of the garden'. That's a parable, a metaphor. So many people have the impression that Adam and Eve was stupid—I can't believe that! I can't believe that neither Adam nor Eve was stupid due to the fact that Adam walked through the Garden of Eden with God and named every tree, every creature—he couldn't have been stupid! And I can't believe that Eve was dumb enough to talk to a snake, and then listen to the muthafucker when it told her to eat the fruit. Eve spoke to a serpent, but I don't think it was in the form of a snake."

"What do you think it was then?"

"When the Bible says 'serpent', understand that a serpent is a creature with a split tongue, a forked tongue, a tongue that speaks lies. Satan is the father of lies; he's the serpent that the Bible is speaking of, we all know that. There's no doubt Eve spoke to Satan, but I don't think he was in the form of a snake... Again, this is my understanding. You may read it and get your own understanding, but I assure you, Eve ain't eat no damn apple, and she sure as hell ain't talk to no damn snake!"

"What do you think happened?" Tina asked curiously.

"Game..." Trevon answered, "Satan gave Eve the game, plain and simple. The fruit Eve ate was sex, that's what I think. The Bible clearly states that God said, 'don't eat the fruit in the midst of the garden,' right?

"Right."

"The word midst means in the middle, or the center... Where is the penis and the vagina located on the human body?"

Tina smiled and shook her head. "In the middle," she answered.

"Um-hmm, now again, this is my understanding, I could be absolutely wrong. Anyways, I think Satan introduced Eve to sex. The Bible clearly states that Eve ate the fruit and it was pleasurable to her—note the word pleasurable—and she gave the fruit to Adam, and when he ate the fruit it was pleasurable to him—again, note the word pleasurable... The definition of the word is: satisfied, amusement, happiness. I don't know about you, but I ain't never ate no fruit that made me feel satisfied, happy, nor amused, but I have ate some pussy that made me feel all of the above."

"So, you think Satan had sex with Eve?"

"Yes, and I think Cain was conceived through that intercourse. That's why God didn't want to have nothing to do with him. Again, this is my understanding. All I'm trying to do is show you how far the game dates back; Satan tricked woman and woman been trickin' man ever since. You ever heard the expression 'this is a man's world'?"

123

"Yeah."

"A bunch of bullshit! This y'all world, baby, we're just living in it. Pussy is a muthafucker, you hear me? It can give life, and it can take life away...dudes will kill for that shit. Everything we do is for that fruit in the midst of the garden. We get money, get fresh, try to ball and floss, for what?"

"Pussy," Tina answered on cue.

"That's right, no matter what we say, we do it all in hope of getting some pussy and to see who can get the baddest bitch. Pussy some dangerous shit! It bleeds one a month for a week straight and don't die—"

"You're so crazy, boy," Tina chuckled.

"It ain't funny, Tina, I'm tellin' you some real shit. Good pussy is a muthafuckin' gold mine, and you know what the golden rule is?"

"What?"

"The golden rule is, the one with the gold makes the muthafuckin' rules...it's called pussy control. That shit between your legs will make the smartest man jackass stupid..." Trevon picked the Bible up and turned to Judges, Chapter 14. "It's right here in black and white. Samson's wife tricked him into telling her the answer to his riddle, then right after that, Delilah put that good pussy on his stupid ass and made him tell her the secret to his strength. And what make it so bad, he knew she tried to trick his dumb-ass three times, but the pussy was so good to him, he broke down and told the bitch what da lick read anyways! Now that's what you call pussy control. Delilah broke down the strongest man in the world by just spreading her legs..." Trevon pulled on the blunt and blew a mouthful of smoke. "Look at King Kong..." he said, "fucked up some shit in New York about that lil' white bitch; he was another bad muthafucker that got broke down by the power of pussy. If he hadn't climbed his dumb-ass up that building trying to protect that bitch, he would've never got shot the fuck down, and it would've been a King Kong part two! Sheiit—it might've even been a part three! The story itself is fiction, but the concept of the story ain't nothing but the truth. What I'm trying to get you to understand is what you possess between your legs, and how to use it with the power of the tongue."

"What'choo mean by the power of the tongue?"

"Just what I said, your tongue is a weapon. Again, the Bible gives you the game on that, too: James, chapter three, verse five. It tells you how the tongue is a small thing that can do big damage. Once you learn how to use it, your tongue can be a dangerous weapon..." Trevon pulled on the blunt again. "I can make my mouth fry chicken..." he said, blowing out a mouthful of smoke, "you know what I mean by that?"

"No."

"That means I can make my mouth say anything, just like any other nigga can make his mouth say anything, so you can't believe everything you hear... Now the difference between making your mouth say anything and running game is what?"

"I don't know."

"When you can make a bitch believe your shit really can fry chicken—that's muthafuckin' game! When you can make a mufucker believe what you want them to believe. My mouth really can fry chicken if you let me tell it. I can talk a cat off a fish truck, baby, and if you listen to what I'm tellin' you, you'll be able to do the same. You don't have to fuck a nigga to get in his pockets. If your game is tight, you can play on his intelligence and fuck his mind and get off in that nigga savings account—fuck the pockets! See how I played on your intelligence today when we were at T.G.I. Friday's? You told me everything I needed to know... I knew what you wanted, I knew what you needed, you gave me power over you. Information is power; never give anyone power over you! You have to learn to be a puzzle, a mystery, how to create illusions. I told you a bunch of bullshit today and your dumb-ass went for it all! None of that shit was true, matter-of-fact, it was the complete opposite. I don't sell drugs—I use'em. I got a real bad cocaine habit and I eat pills like Tic-Tacs. I'm not ballin', 'cause due to my drug habit, I rob Peter just to pay Paul. And that Chevy out there sitting on twenties...that just look good. We were riding with the windows down because the AC don't work. I need four new tires and the back driver's side window don't go down. I have no occupation... I live off the land... I get money by out-thinking and out-talking those I come in contact with. I've been doing this shit since Moby Dick was a goldfish. Now, I'm telling you what God loves, and that's the truth. I got a baby momma and she—"

"Are you and your baby momma together?" Tina asked suspiciously.

"Naw, we're not together, but we're friends, why?"

"I just wanted to know if you had any commitments, that's all."

"Yeah, I do... to my son..." Trevon looked at Tina in silence. "Look, Tina, I hope you've been pickin' up what I've been putting down. I'm trying to get you to realize that you don't have to necessarily fuck someone to get what you want, and if you do have to fuck 'em, make sure you get what you want from 'em..." Trevon looked at Tina as she digested the verbal food he was feedin' her. "You know the difference between a hoe and a slut?"

"They're both the same thing," Tina answered lamely.

"*Wrong!*" Trevon quipped. "Sluts get laid—hoes get paid! A muthafucker gon' always have something to say, so when they say something about you opening your legs, let 'em call you all the hoes they want, just

125

don't let 'em call you broke. Don't ever think of yourself as a hoe; playin' a nigga is a hustle...you're a hustler and you're a customer when you're in the presence of a hustler. Every time they see you have something to sell'em—even if it ain't nothing but a dream. It's too many bitches out there suckin' and fuckin' for hairdos—them peanuts! If a nigga wanna ride in your Jag, you already know what da lick read. Remember what I said earlier about being born with an ATM machine between your legs? Ain't no reason you should be broke, Tina. Your pussy really is an ATM machine. Think of dick as a debit card, and like all debit cards, it's a pin number... I'm giving you the access code to activate any debit card, Tina. Remember, don't ever sell yourself short! If you fuck someone, it's gon' be on your terms or none at all. That way you can say, 'I did it because I *wanted* to', not 'I did that because I *had* to'... that's what being a true player is all about; a player do what they want; a buster do what they can..."

There was a short silence as Trevon stared at Tina. He looked into her eyes and thought: you are so beautiful, Tina. He saw what no one else seen, and he thanked God they didn't see it. He thought about all the men that had Tina in the palm of their hands, not realizing what they were holding. Time after time, they picked Tina up, thinking they were holding an ordinary stone and threw her away. Trevon picked that same stone up and noticed there was something unique about it. He cleaned it, polished it, and realized he wasn't holding a stone after all...

He was holding a diamond.

"Tina..." Trevon said, breaking the silence, "I want you to understand something...I'm doing some shit I'm not supposed to be doing. First, I broke rule one; I let you in my gameroom. I'm not a sucker-ass nigga—don't get it misconstrued. I did it because you touched my heart last night, so I wanted to help you, and by doing so, I went against the grain, against the code—"

"What code?"

"Never give a lame no game. The jewels I gave you, they aren't for everyone... I'm not supposed to give them to you, you're supposed to earn them through trial and error, just like I did. By law, I'm supposed to keep you lame, keep you beneath my heel. I hope you understand the ammunition I gave you. I hope didn't waste my time..."

Tina gazed into Trevon's eyes as tears welled up in hers. "Oh Tre..." she whispered, blinking them away, "you've done more for me in twenty-four hours than anyone has ever done my entire life...and you don't even know me. You've touched my heart...my mind...you don't know how much I appreciate all you have done..." Tina grabbed Trevon's hand and kissed his knuckles as if he were the Pope. "*Thank-you-so-much-Tre!*" she said, getting choked up on her words. "I-I-I don't have anything to offer you, but I swear, one day I will show you how much I appreciate you, that you didn't waste your time."

Trevon wiped the tears from Tina's face as tears welled up in his eyes. "You want to show your appreciation? Take what I told you and never look back...that's all I ask of you, Tina... excel and be successful."

A tear fell from Trevon's eyes. "The Chinese believe," Tina said, wiping Trevon's cheek, "that if you save someone's life, you're responsible for it...I'm yours, Tre...from this day forth, I'm yours. Until the day I die, I'm yours..." Tina spoke her last words with a chilling sincerity.

Trevon smiled, knowing that she meant every word wholeheartedly. "Okay..." he said, "now we're ready for phase three...Now that you know the fundamentals of the game, now it's time to learn how to peep game. This is harder than runnin' game, and unfortunately, it's a skill that can't be taught. It's a gift—a God-given gift—that only you can activate. Some of us possess it, some of us don't. All I can do is give you the fundamentals of it—the rest is up to you..." Trevon pulled on the blunt. It went out. He re-lit it and took a deep pull. "There's different kinds of shit..." he said, blowing out a mouthful of smoke.

"You got dumb shit...you got stupid shit... you got fuck shit...then there's the almighty bullshit...then there's the type of shit I like to deal with— the only type of shit I'll deal with..." Trevon looked up in the air "... the *real* shit! You just learned about spitting game, but in order to spit it, you have to learn how to listen for it so nobody won't be able to spit it on you... You ever wonder why we have two ears and one mouth...? It's because we are supposed to listen twice as much as we speak. It's a hard job, but you have to always be on your toes, you have to constantly analyze people's words and actions to decipher the real from the fake. And I promise, if you listen, everything will come to the light if it's fake. All-you-have-to-do-is-listen! Not only listen to what's being said but learn to listen to your instincts as well...Instincts are warning devices, they warn you when something ain't right..."

Trevon stared at Tina in silence for a short moment. She sat beside him on the bed, crossed-legged, hands folded in her lap, digesting every word. Her pupils were flared, her eyes attentive, her brain in over-drive, trying to process everything Trevon said.

His words gave her life, gave her strength, gave her something to lean on. He saw eagerness in her eyes; she wanted more...

Trevon got up and put on his shoes. "I gotta go, Tina."

"Go where?" she asked pitifully.

"I gotta get home before my baby momma start trippin'—"

"I THOUGHT YOU SAID YOU AND YOUR BABY MOMMA WASN'T TOGETHER!" Tina yelled.

"*Aaaaah—very good, Danielson,*" Trevon said, sounding like Mr. Miyagi again, "you've been paying attention. See what listening does? I'm proud of you; you have successfully completed phase three."

"What'choo mean?" Tina asked, looking confused.

"I did that to see if you would peep what I said about my son's mother, and you did. That's what I mean by analyzing...now it's time for the third rule: Never give anyone any space to play on your intelligence. It never fails, if you give 'em a little *space;* next thing you know they gon' wanna be an *astronaut.* But all the true players know the first space shuttle blew up in '86, just like a situation will blow up in your face if your game ain't tight. You can't lose with the shit I use, you feel me, shawdy?"

"I feel you, baby," Tina replied, wrapping her arms around Trevon. "Lay down with me and hold me, Tre... *please...*"

Tina was in heaven as she laid in Trevon's arms. She has never had anyone to stand up for her the way he did. He made love to her mind; therefore, making her body burn for him. Tina had never wanted something so bad in her life. This is what she was thinking when she fell asleep in Trevon's arms...

The next morning, they woke up and went to get Tina's hair and nails done. Afterward, they stopped by Sassy Cat's (a lingerie shop) and Trevon had Tina try on several things before picking a skimpy schoolgirl's costume and a black lace sheer lingerie set.

"What about my bracelet?" Tina asked when they pulled up in front of the motel. "I'ma lose it if I don't get it by tomorrow."

"Don't worry," Trevon replied, "just take a shower so we can get going."

"Where are we going?"

"Quit asking questions and get'choo ass in the shower so we can get going..."

An hour later, they were parked in front of Cheetahs (the strip club).

"What are we doing here?" Tina asked curiously.

"It's time to put your skills to work, Danielson—"

"*I'm not about to dance in front of nobody!*"

"Why not? You was shakin' your ass up in McDonald's the other night."

"That was different!"

"You're absolutely right," Trevon replied, "that was different; you was doing it for free there—you gon' get paid for it here!"

"*I can't, Tre!*" Tina whined.

Trevon buried his face in his hand and inhaled and exhaled deeply, trying to find the patience *and* the right words to help Tina. After a short moment, he leaned against the door and looked at her. "Look, Tina..." he said, grabbing her hand, "It's rules for every game, and the rules are designed to keep the game within the game... You can't apply the rules of a football game to a basketball game, just like you can't apply the rules of a soccer game to a baseball game... Whatever game you play, you have to play by the rules of that game. And like each game has its own rules, it has its own field or court on which that game is played... You can't play soccer on a basketball court; however, there are some games that can be played on other fields. What I mean by that is, a baseball game can be played on a football field if the football field has been altered to accommodate the requirements of the baseball game..." Trevon looked deeply into Tina's eyes and she stared back at him, digesting. "This is the game you chose to play, Tina. There're two fields you can play it on: here, or on Broadway...now you pick the field you want to play on."

Tina looked at the club, stared at it in silence. "Why can't you just let me borrow the money, Tre?"

"THEN WHAT, TINA?!" Trevon yelled. "WHAT'CHOO GON' DO WHEN YOU NEED MONEY AGAIN?! WHAT?! KEEP DEPENDING ON A NIGGA TO FEED YOU?! I WASTED MY MUTHAFUCKIN' BREATH YESTERDAY!"

"No, you didn't Tre!"

Trevon went in his pockets, pulled out a wad of money, and threw it on Tina's lap. "Here, Tina," he said, "it's about five hundred there, more than enough to get your bracelet! If that's what you want—there it go—but if you take that money, you can't get nothin' else from me, and I put that on ere'thang! But if you go in there and put down what you picked up yesterday, I'll match whatever you make tonight..." Trevon grabbed Tina's hand. "I'm not tryin'a fuck over you, girl! I'm tryin'a help yo ass! You gotta trust me."

"I do trust you, Tre!"

"Then listen to what the fuck I'm tellin' you! I could easily just give you the money for your bracelet—but then what? Just like if you were hungry, we could easily go to *Miami Subs*, and I could buy you another shrimp dinner—that ain't no problem—but I care about you, girl! So, instead of buyin' you that shrimp dinner, I'ma teach you how to fish...so I can feed you for life. I'm tryin' to show you how to live off the land, how to survive anywhere..."

Tina sat there looking at the club for a long moment before looking at Trevon with tears in her eyes. "Okay, Tre... I'll do it. Are you gonna stay with me?"

Trevon smiled. "Of course I am, princess."

Tina returned the smile. "Let's go then, Mr. Miyagi..."

Tina sat at the bar while Trevon talked to Rick (the guy that ran the club). She was underage, so Trevon had to woo Rick to let her dance. Whatever he told him must've worked because five minutes later, he came back to the bar smiling from ear-to-ear. "Take this," Trevon said, placing a Xanax in Tina's mouth.

"What was that?" she asked after washing it down with a Hennessy and Coke.

"A Xanax," Trevon answered, "it'll help you relax."

Tina looked around the club, terrified. "I'm scared, Tre."

"Don't be! Don't pay attention to these folks, you hear me? When you come out, just look at me a'ight? It's just me and you; we gon' be in our own world, baby."

Tina finished the rest of her drink. "Okay, baby."

"What's your name?"

"Tina."

"*Naw, your stripper name?* Like Hypnotic, or Lexus, or Peaches, or—"

"Caramel," Tina interjected.

"Caramel..." Trevon said, shaking his head. "Okay then, Caramel. I'ma go line shit up with the DJ. Put that schoolgirl outfit on and stick to the script."

"*What script, Tre?!*"

"When you hear the music—*dance*! Now go get dressed."

Tina picked up Trevon's drink and downed it in one gulp before getting up...

"She's new on the scene, and is every man's dream," the DJ announced as the lights dimmed, "she sho is sweet, so y'all give it up for— CARAMEEEL!"

Tina strutted out on the stage like a thoroughbred in her schoolgirl outfit and spiked heels. She had her long hair pinned up in a bun with a pencil and had on a pair of reading glasses; sexuality came off of her like humidity from a slab of asphalt on a hot summer afternoon. Just as Trevon instructed, she kept her eyes on him and blocked everyone out...

When Shabba Ranks started playing through the speakers, Tina set Cheetah's on fire: *"Ding-a-ling-ling, school bell ring, knife an fork fight fa di dumpling—BOOYAKA!! BOOYAKA!!"*

The way Tina moved her body put every man in the club in a trance, and the way she made her hips whined and tic made them drool. She let her long hair down before revealing her beautiful, firm breast, and by the time she stripped down to her thong and made her ass clap to the beat, the entire stage was covered with money.

Trevon looked around the club; Tina had the whole place sewed up.

"Oh my gawd, Tre!" Tina said excitedly, sitting on the stool next to him. "Look at all this money!"

"What did I tell you, girl? I knew you could do it, you looked like a superstar out there! And the night just begun, all them dudes out there waiting for you..." Trevon pointed with his chin and Tina looked out into the club at all the men staring at her; there was practically a line waiting.

Every 20 or 30 minutes she had to bring Trevon money to hold for her because there was no more space to keep it on her. Trevon looked on with pride as Tina maneuvered through the crowd: flirting with the customers, whispering in their ears, and teasing them until they left around 4am.

They were in the parking lot, on the way to the car, when one of Trevon's teachings manifested: "Hey Tre! That's yo girl?" a man Tina gave a lap dance to asked.

"Naw," Trevon replied, "but she can be yo girl if that check right."

"Sheiit," the man said, going in his pockets and pulling out a wad of $100 bills, "what da lick read? What that ticket lookin' like?"

Tina looked at Trevon, not knowing what to say.

"Say somethin', girl," Trevon muttered, "dude waiting."

"How much should I tell him?" Tina whispered.

"I don't know," Trevon whispered back, "that's your pussy."

Tina looked at the man and blurted out, "Four hundred dollars."

"Sheiit," the man replied, peeling off four $100 bills, "you ain't said nothin'!"

Tina was incredulous, remembering what Trevon said about selling herself short. Nevertheless, she wanted to be with Trevon. "I'm tired..." she said to the man, "maybe some other night."

"I got five hundred," the man insisted, peeling off another $100 bill.

"I'm sorry, sweetheart," Tina replied apologetically, "not tonight."

131

"A'ight then, lil' momma," the man said in disappointment, "I'll catch you later."

"Was he really gon' give me five hundred?" Tina asked after they got in the car.

"Yeah," Trevon answered, "you gave dude the first impression you about money, so he was gonna spend money to get what he wanted. You put a price on your shit and he called it."

"How much did I make?"

"I don't know, girl," Trevon said, pulling out several wads of cash.

"Is all that my money?" Tina asked in disbelief.

"Yep, so start countin'..."

Tina counted money all the way back to the motel and still wasn't finished by the time they parked. "I made twelve hundred dollars, Tre!" she exclaimed, but it looked more like $12,000 with all the one and five dollar bills she had.

"Naw, you made seventeen hundred," Trevon said, pulling out the $500 he'd promised her for tryin'. "I know I said I'll match whatever you made, but I wasn't expecting you to make so much."

Tina pushed the money back. "I can't take that money, Tre."

"You're not taking it—you earned it. We made a deal and you fulfilled your end of the bargain, so I gotta fulfill mines."

Tina stared at the money. "I don't want it, please don't make me take it."

"*Sheiit*—you ain't gotta tell me twice," Trevon said jokingly, shoving the money back in his pocket.

"Thank you for everything, Tre..." Tina said, counting some of her own money to give Trevon. "Here take this..."

Trevon looked at the money and smiled. "I'm not a pimp, I don't want your money, girl. That's your come-up, not mines."

Tina didn't know how to respond to what Trevon said, better yet, to what he'd done. She had never met a man who didn't expect anything from her. Trevon had not tried to sleep with her yet and she didn't know why. She wanted to give herself to him so bad. When she got out of the shower later on that night, her wish was fulfilled...

"Come'ere, Tina..." he said seductively, lying in the bed naked, covered from the waist down. Tina unwrapped the terry cloth towel she had wrapped around her and let it fall to the floor. She stood there in just her panties, her breast plump and pert, he nipples firm and fully extended.

Trevon reached out and Tina grabbed his hand. He pulled her to him, cradled her in his arms, and kissed her passionately. After doing so, he gazed into her eyes; her pupils were flared, her breast heaving as she rubbed her thighs together, trying to suppress the tingling sensation she felt between her legs.

"You're so beautiful, Tina," Trevon said, gently rubbing the side of Tina's face. He sucked on her neck before leaving a trail of kisses down to her breast, sucking her nipples one-by-one. He continued a trail down Tina's abdomen, and her legs parted as he positioned himself between them, trailing a path up the inside of her thigh with the tip of his tongue. He touched the crotch of her panties; the fabric was wet, soaked with pussy juices. He hooked his fingers in the waistband and slid them down. Tina's pubic hair was dark and silky. A wave of emotions flowed through Trevon as he looked down at her. He felt dizzy. Disoriented. He had never been so intrigued by the physical beauty of a woman.

Trevon pushed Tina's legs back and she instinctively grabbed the back of his head as he shoved his face between her legs. She couldn't find the words to explain the pleasure that jolted through her body as the tip of Trevon's tongue flickered across her clitoris. "*Oh, Tre,*" she whispered, one hand squeezing the back of Trevon's head and the other squeezing her breast. A current surged through her body that made her breath in quick gasps and bite her lower lip. Her whole body trembled and throbbed with tremors of pleasure she had never felt before. The muscles in her pussy spasmed and her body jerked from a big burst of pure ecstasy, making her convulse. It took a moment for the spasms to fade away, and for that moment, Tina was unable to move. She laid there confused and quivering from a sensation that was so intense it made her cry. But her tears weren't from pain and sorrow... they were from pleasure and fulfillment...

"I — I'm sorry, Tre," Tina said as Trevon came up and positioned himself between her legs.

"Sorry for what?"

"I-I- in your mouth...I don't know...it felt like I..." Tina said, holding her head down, trying to find the right words for what she just felt: Her first orgasm.

Trevon grabbed Tina's chin with two fingers and tilted her face up to his, and her lips parted as his mouth came close to hers. He kissed her deeply and she sucked the musky, salty essence of her cum from his lips. "You just came in my mouth," he said with a smile. "You ain't never cum before?"

Tina shook her head no.

Trevon entered her smoothly; he was drawn into the slippery, wet warmth of Tina's pussy. She wrapped her legs around his waist and moved with him instinctively. Their bodies moved in unison, their love making synchronized: Trevon's hips moved in a circular motion and Tina matched

133

his thrust with slow upward lunges. Sweaty skin brushed against sweaty skin, pubic hair tangled with pubic hair, pelvic bone smacked against thighs until finally, Trevon's semen mingled with the slick, milky fluid that secreted out of Tina's glands.

Tina had never known what love was, but at that moment she knew it had to be what she was feeling for this man she'd just met. She laid in Trevon's arms, feeling complete for the first time in her young life. Her skin was bright with a thin sheen of sweat, glowing in the soft light of the television. The cool cotton sheet was damp with perspiration. Tina looked at Trevon, her upper lip beaded with sweat. "I love you, Tre," she said sincerely.

"You're full of passion right now," Trevon replied. "Trust me, you don't know what love is yet, shawdy."

Tina looked back at Trevon with tears in her eyes. "Yes, I do... it's what I'm feeling it right now... I know it is ... I just know it."

By Tina's 18th birthday, she had a Honda Accord and her own apartment. She and Trevon spent so much time together his son's mother ended up kicking his ass out, giving Tina exactly what she wanted.

Cheetahs became Tina's domain, and Trevon became a fixture in the club; Tina was quick to let everyone know that Trevon was her domain, too...this is the reason their relationship took a drastic change.

While Tina was giving a customer a lap dance, she saw another stripper, named Chocolate, all over Trevon with her hands down his pants. Tina cut the lap dance short and stormed over to where they were sitting. She snatched Chocolate off of Trevon and snatched Trevon up by the shirt. "What the fuck is wrong wit'choo, nigga?!" she yelled, causing a big scene. "Why the fuck you got this bitch all over you in my muthafuckin' face?"

"You need to quit trippin', Caramel," Chocolate said, clinging to Trevon's arm.

"*Shut up, bitch!*" Tina hissed. "You best go find you some business and stay up outta mines before I fuck you up in here, hoe..." Tina gave Chocolate a look that could kill.

Chocolate took heed to the warning: "It ain't even that serious, Caramel."

"*Naw, bitch!*" Tina yelled as Chocolate walked off. "It is that serious about mines—*fuck wrong wit'choo*?!"

"What's your damn problem, girl?" Trevon asked, pulling Tina by the arm, "You're not my girlfriend, so you're steppin' out of bounds right about now."

"What am I then, Tre?"

"I don't know, Tina, but you ain't my keeper, just like I'm not yours. I can't say nothin' about all these niggas laps you're sitting on 'cause that's not my place, so how you gon' run up on me with that bullshit? You're supposed to be a player, Tina...but you're actin' like a real buster..." Trevon shook his head and left the club, leaving Tina standing there looking stupid. His words stabbed her in the heart, but like everything else he'd ever told her, they were the truth.

Tina wasn't going out bad; she had to straighten her face. She called Trevon when she got off work that morning: "Hello, Tre?"

"What da lick read?"

"I've been really thinking about what you said earlier. You were right, and I just wanted to say that I'm sorry."

"You don't have to say sorry, baby. You just need to know what position you play in my life and play that position. We need to have an understanding about that or shit gon' be crazy. I come home to you every night, just like you come home to me. So, when I see you with all them dudes it don't faze me, 'cause I know where I stand in your heart, just like you need to know where you stand in mines."

"Does that mean you're coming home tonight?"

"I'm on my way now, why?"

"Because I want to make it up to you."

"Make up what?"

"For actin' like a *buster*," Tina chuckled.

"I'll be there in a hot minute."

"I'll be waiting..."

Trevon opened the front door and followed a trail of clothes to the bedroom. He opened the bedroom door and smiled. "What a sweet surprise," he said as he undressed. "Caramel and Chocolate... I got a big-ass Twix up in this bitch -y'all mind if I have a piece?" Trevon laid between Tina and Chocolate from the club.

"Is that what you wanted, baby?" Tina asked, guiding Chocolate's head as it bobbed up and down on Trevon's dick. She and Chocolate took turns sucking and licking, licking and sucking, looking like two hungry lionesses fighting over a piece of meat. "You wanted to fuck this bitch earlier when she was all over you. What'choo hesitating for now?" Tina said, talking as if Chocolate wasn't there. Chocolate laid on the edge of the bed and Tina straddled her legs over her face, facing Trevon as he positioned himself in front of them. "Open up," Tina said, grabbing the back of Chocolate's knees, putting her in the buck. She began to grind her pussy on Chocolate's mouth, pulling Trevon toward them as she rubbed the fingers

135

of her other hand in Chocolate's pussy. She spread her lips open, guided the head of Trevon's dick into her, and watched as he rocked back and forth inside the stripper, going in deeper and deeper with each stroke.

Between hearing Chocolate moan and watching Trevon's shaft slide in and out of her, Tina was turned on to the highest degree. She popped her hips, grinding her pussy on Chocolate's lips, shooting orgasm after orgasm in her mouth while Trevon fucked her viciously. He and Tina looked at each other and smiled. She grabbed the sides of Trevon's face and pulled him toward her. *"Don't you ever call me a buster again, nigga,"* she whispered before shooting another orgasm down Chocolate's throat.

SMACK! "Take that dick!" Tina hissed, slapping the back of Chocolate's thighs, holding them back so Trevon could plunge in deep. *SMACK!* "This what'choo wanted, ain't it?" Tina said, slapping the back of Chocolate's thigh again—*SMACK!* "Get that pussy, Tre! Give that bitch what she wants!" *SMACK! SMACK! SMACK!*

"Oh shit," Chocolate purred, her face flushed, he body gleaming with perspiration. Her insides churned, and like a volcano, she erupted and white, foamy cream poured out of her like lava.

SMACK! "Yeah—cum on that dick!" Tina said as she continued to smother her with pussy.

Seconds later, Trevon's body shuddered. He pulled out and warm cum gushed on Chocolate's abdomen. "Mmmh," Tina moaned, her head bobbing back and forth in unison with her hand as she slurped on the head of Trevon's dick until she started to feel him go limp in her mouth.

Afterward, she got straight up, went into the bathroom, and grabbed a towel. When she returned she threw the towel at Chocolate, "I'll see you at work tonight, girl," she said, picking up Chocolate's clothes and throwing them on her lap.

"Damn!" Chocolate said in shock. "It's like that Caramel?"

Tina smiled. "I'm not sayin' you have to go home, I'm just saying you have to get the fuck up outta here," she said nastily, and she felt bad for doing so because she knew exactly how it felt to be skeeted on then told to wipe off and kick rocks.

It was a hurtful feeling—but hey—that's how the game goes; she didn't make the rules, she was playing by 'em like a true player was supposed to.

Life was going so well for Tina. She had everything she had ever wanted. The things Trevon taught her were engraved in her mind and heart. She would fall asleep in his arms every night, thanking God for bringing him into her life...

Until the night it all came crashing down.

Tina had just finished giving a customer a lap dance when Carlos came from out of nowhere and grabbed her arm. Tina snatched away and told him to leave her the fuck alone. In return, Carlos threw his drink in Tina's face, and in a blink of an eye, the bouncers threw him out of the club.

When it was all over, Tina searched the club looking for Trevon but couldn't find him. That's when Chocolate came running in the dressing room: "Caramel! Them crackers out there arresting Tre!"

Tina ran out the door just as the police was putting Trevon in the back of the car. Carlos was lying in a pool of blood about 20 feet away with his head bashed open. It felt as if someone had punched Tina in the stomach as she watched them ride off with the love of her life.

It took almost two days for Trevon to get booked and processed. After he was, she called only to find he had no bond. Then she had to wait another two days until he was able to have a visit...

It was the longest four days of Tina's young life.

"Hey, baby," Tina said, putting her hand on the two-inch glass that separated them.

"Hey, princess," Trevon replied as he did the same.

Hearing him call her princess broke Tina down: "I'm going crazy! I miss you so much, Tre!" she said, tears pouring from her eyes.

"I miss you too, boo..." There was a short silence as Trevon stared into Tina's eyes. "Tina, I need you to be strong in this spot, you hear me? I need you to pull yourself together."

"I can't, baby! I miss you so much. I can't think, Tre! I haven't even been to work."

"You can't do that, Tina. You have to keep it pushin', you hear me? You have to keep everything together out there."

"I can't, Tre! I need you—it feels like I can't breathe!" Tina said, burying her face in her hand.

"Look at me..." Trevon ordered.

Tina kept her face buried in her hand crying.

"Look at me!"

Tina looked up, her eyes red and swollen.

"I want you to listen to what I'm about to say, okay?"

"Okay, baby..."

"You remember that day we were in the motel room and I kept pushing you down and telling you to get up only to push you down again?"

"Yes..." Tina answered, "I remember."

137

"I wasn't trying to bully you, Tina... I was teaching you something. You know what it was?"

"No."

"I was teaching you how to pick yourself up, and you did. You picked yourself up then, and you're gonna pick yourself up now, girl, and I don't want to hear no shit about you can't, 'cause I know you can, and I know you can 'cause I done seen you do it! This is life; we gotta take the bad with the good. Now you can roll with it, or get rolled over—it's all on you, Tina. This isn't a time for you to be weak. I need you to be strong...matter-of-fact, I don't need you to come back up here until you are..." Trevon hung up the phone and left Tina sitting there crying...

That was all she needed to hear.

After she left visitation, Tina sat in her car crying for an hour, staring at the county jail, thinking about what Trevon said.

"I'ma be strong, baby," she whispered to herself, looking at the jail one last time before cranking up her car and driving off.

It was time for Tina Baptiste to pick herself up. She swore that she was going to be there for Trevon the same way he was there for her. She was going to make him proud. It was time to play the game.

As you already know by now...Tina Baptiste fucked the game up.

Going In
The Present

Like clockwork, Monique Baker's workdays began at 6:00am. After taking her morning shower, she studied herself in her bedroom mirror. She was looking at the image of a woman with lustfully beautiful features: Beautiful light brown eyes, radiant skin, even white teeth, and a curvy healthy figure. The most unique part of her persona was that she was completely unaware of her attributes...

"*Uuugh*—I hate my shape!" Monique muttered to herself. "I need to start going back to the gym; I'm getting too fat."

After examining herself in the mirror, she walked into her closet and through her everyday routine of contemplation, which took at least 15 to 20 minutes. Because of her figure, finding clothes that fit her right was a tedious task. A skirt had to be just right in the waist. If not, pulled across her protuberant hips. Her solution to the problem was wearing jackets and long blouses; she had no idea how erotic she looked without them.

A half hour later, she was wearing a tan skirt with a matching jacket, and a thin, white silk blouse. After another 10 minutes of contemplating which shoes she should wear, she was fully dressed and out the door, ready to conquer another busy day at Fetterman & Associates and the Palm Beach County Courthouse.

Along the way, she stopped by *Dunkin' Donuts* and got a cup of Mocha Java and purchases a copy of the *Palm Beach Post*. Minutes later, she pulled into her reserved parking space. At 8:00am, Fetterman & Associates was already wide open. As Monique walked to her office, her boss, Mr. Fetterman, approached her with a big smile...

"Good morning, Monique. How's the Baldwin case going?" Mr. Fetterman inquired. He was in his sixties, with salt and pepper hair, and an exuberance that was infectious.

"It's coming along well," Monique answered.

"Is that so?"

"Um-hmm."

"Good."

"I just received the discovery Friday, so I really haven't had a chance to look through it yet."

"What about the depo?"

"I took the victim's deposition last week and there's a lot of conflict in what she said in the police report. There are a lot of discrepancies in the story she told during the depo, from the story she told the police the night it all happened. She's not being truthful about something—there's no doubt about that—but I assure you, Mr. Fetterman, that I will find out and get out client acquitted."

"Well, I'm glad to hear that, Monique. I also want to thank you for taking on the Jenkins case as such a short notice. I really appreciate you."

"Not a problem, Mr. Fetterman. I went out to the jail to see him the day before yesterday. We're set for a bond hearing this morning, 9:00am, Judge Berman."

"Well, that means you have to get going," Mr. Fetterman said, bringing the conversation to an end. "Keep up the good work, Monique."

"Will do, Mr. Fetterman."

Trisha and Faleasha stood less than 20 feet away. They were standing by the water cooler watching Mr. Fetterman and Monique talk...

"Look at Monique—she makes me damn sick! Ole stuck-up bitch!" Trisha said contemptuously as Faleasha nodded in agreement.

"Boujie ass bitch," Faleasha replied, "she think she's better than everybody else."

"She looks like she ain't had no dick in years. Look at the way she walks, with her uptight-ass," Trisha said as Monique walked toward them.

Trisha and Faleasha were paralegals and hated Monique and Naomi, Monique's best friend, who was also an attorney for Fetterman & Associates, because Trisha worked for Monique and Faleasha worked for Naomi, and they didn't like the fact they were Monique's and Naomi's "do girls."

"*Heeey, Monique,*" Trisha whined as Monique approached them.

"*I like your outfit, girl,*" Faleasha complemented, producing a fake smile. It was the most artificial thing Monique had ever seen; the result of Faleasha's brain giving orders to her mouth.

"Good morning, Trisha, Faleasha," Monique replied, giving the same fake smile in return. "Did you get the pictures from the Baldwin case I asked you for a week ago?" Monique asked Trisha in an irritated manner.

"*Yes, ma'am,*" Trisha answered sarcastically, "I'll bring them to you at my earliest convenience."

"Good," Monique continued, "because I have some more errands for you to run. We have a new client: Trevon Jenkins. I really don't have time to chat right now because he's scheduled for a bond hearing at 9:00am. I'll tell you exactly what I need before I go, so please be where you can be found..." Monique looked at Faleasha. "Maybe you can help her fetch some of the things I need."

"I don't think so," Faleasha answered nastily, "I have my own shit to do."

"Very well..." Monique replied, "maybe I'll have a little talk with Naomi to make sure your *'shit'* gets done. Trisha — have those pictures on my desk by the time I get back."

"Did you hear that bitch?!" Trisha screeched as Monique walked to her office. "Talkin' bout some *'maybe you can help her fetch some of the things I need',* "Trisha said, mocking Monique in the most proper tone she could muster.

"*Bitch*!" Faleasha said under her breath, but loud enough for Monique to hear it.

Monique ignored the remark and kept walking. "Good morning, Mary," she said to her secretary. Mary was a plump white woman in her late forties. She was far from beautiful, but yet, there was something about her persona that gave her and angelic glow. She was always smiling, as if she knew something everyone else didn't know.

"Good morning, Monique," Mary replied. "I put the rest of the Jenkin's file on your desk."

"Thank you, Mary. I don't what I would do without you."

"Not a problem, Monique — it's my job... You are aware that you're scheduled for a bond hearing in forty-five minutes, right?"

"I know," Monique answered, "I just stopped by to get the rest of the Jenkins file."

"It's right on top of the Baldwin file," Mary said, standing to open the door for Monique. "You better get going."

Once inside her office, Monique flopped down at her desk, turned on her computer, and punched in her password. She checked her schedule, making a list of things she needed Trisha to do. Afterward, she looked at the two files she had stacked on top of each other on the left side of her desk; these two files were top priority. One file was the Jenkins file, the other file — the most important one — involved a sexual assault: one night, a young girl gets drunk, leaves the club with two older men, wakes up in the morning, and screams rape. She was neither bruised nor injured during the assault. However, one of the accused so happened to be Alex Baldwin, the mayor's son, so that's why the case received top priority.

Monique turned her computer off, picked up the Jenkin's file, and put it in her briefcase. That's when Naomi, her best friend, stepped into her office...

"Hey girl!" Naomi said excitedly. She was an attractive woman, with rich mahogany skin, shoulder length black hair, and enormous hazel eyes. She and Monique had been friends since elementary school and had even went to the same college. Although they grew up together, they were complete opposites. While Monique was soft-spoken and soft-hearted, Naomi was vociferous and vulgar; they were like night and day. "I know you heard that skeezer call you a bitch, 'cause I heard it way in my office," Naomi said, leaning against the door and crossing her arms.

"Girl, I don't have time to be playing them childish-ass games with Trisha and Faleasha!" Monique said, as she walked toward the door. "I'ma grown-ass woman, and they're little girls, so I expect them to do little girl things."

"I don't care if they're younger, Monique! You need to quit letting them hoodrats call you everything but a child of God—and I got something for Faleasha's ass!" Naomi said as they were about to walk out the door.

When they opened it, they were greeted by Trisha and Faleasha.

"May I help you?" Naomi asked nastily.

"Here them pictures you asked for," Trisha replied, shoving a large manila envelope in Monique's face.

"Thank you," Monique said, snatching the envelope out of Trisha's hand.

Trisha looked at Faleasha with an expression that said: *no this bitch didn't just snatch them pictures out of my hand!*

"I'm glad you're here," Naomi said to Faleasha. "I'm going to be in court all day, so I don't have *shit* for you to do, so you can help Trisha do some *shit* for Monique." Naomi looked at Monique. "Now what was it you said you needed done, girl?"

Monique smiled and held up the list she'd just made.

Naomi grabbed it, folded it up and slipped it into Faleasha's shirt pocket. "Y'all have fun now," she said as they walked off towards the elevator.

"*Hmph! No-that-bitch-didn't!*" Faleasha said through clenched teeth.

"Oh, yes that bitch did," Trisha said under her breath as Monique and Naomi entered the elevator...

"Now that's how you do it, girl!" Naomi exclaimed, nudging Monique in the side with her elbow after the elevator door slid closed.

"I'm not about to sit up there and bicker with them ghetto-ass girls!"

"You don't have to bicker—just get ghetto right back with they ass, and if they wanna get stupid, we can turn this mug into *SMACK DOWN*, girl!" Naomi said, imitating like she had someone in the headlock.

"*You're so damn crazy,*" Monique chuckled.

"What'cha got scheduled after the bond hearing?" Naomi asked in a more serious tone.

"I have a meeting with the mayor at ten thirty."

"You wanna do lunch?"

"What time?"

"Twleve o'clock."

"Where?"

"T.G.I. Friday's—you know I gosta have my J.D. steak and shrimp, bitch! *Stop playin!*"

"I'll see you at twelve, fool," Monique giggled as the door slid open.

●　　●　　●

Trevon was escorted into the courtroom at 8:50am, shackled down, wearing the bright orange jumpsuit inmates wear when they are in confinement. One of the first people he saw when he walked in was Mr. Bryant, his parole officer, who was sitting in the front row, with Tina and Fresh sitting right behind him.

Tina looked at Trevon with a devious smile and winked before whispering something in Mr. Bryant's ear. Fresh was trying to tell Trevon something, but was cut short by the deputy that was escorting him: "No communicating with the prisoners," the deputy said. "If I tell you again, you'll be escorted from the courtroom."

Reluctantly, Fresh ceased communication and Trevon sat down in the booth that's used for the inmates that are in custody.

At 8:55am, Monique walked in, put her briefcase down, and walked over to the booth where Trevon was sitting. "Morning, Mr. Jenkins."

"Good morning, Moni–," Trevon caught himself "–I mean, good morning... Ms. Baker."

This brought a smile to Monique's face. "Your parole officer is here to speak on your behalf," she said, "so I don't see any reason, why you shouldn't get a bond. However, I don't know what the amount will be."

"Just get me a bond and I'll take it from there," Trevon replied.

"Have you had a chance to talk to the prosecutor yet?"

143

"No, not yet," Monique answered, "and that's what I need to talk to you about. In order to help you, I need to know what I'm up against, Mr. Jenkins. I need to know exactly what happened, and only you know what happened, so you need to tell me the truth."

"You want the truth?" Trevon asked casually.

"Yes, I do."

"Do you believe in love at first sight, Ms. Baker?"

"No, I don't."

"Neither did I... until the day before yesterday."

"And what happened the day before yesterday?" Monique asked curiously.

"That was the day I saw you for the first time... the first sight ...love at first sight."

Monique's cheeks blushed. "And what does that have to do with anything?" she asked bashfully.

"I just gave you what you asked for," Trevon answered.

"I asked you for the truth, Mr. Jenkins."

"*And I just gave you the truth, Ms. Baker.* Two days ago, you set my heart on fire. They say the truth will set you free... I just told you the truth... now set me free, Ms. Baker."

"You think she gon' be able to get Tre a bond?" Fresh asked for the umpteenth time.

"*Damn!* How many times you gon' ask me that shit, Fresh?" Tina said irritably. "I told your stupid-ass yeah the first time you asked! Yeah, she gon' get him a bond, now will you please quit fuckin' with me—*damn!*"

"Don't get me started up in here!" Fresh shot back. "I don't care if we are in the courthouse—I'll go ham in this bitch!"

"I swear; a bitch can't take you nowhere! Why you always act so damn ignorant, Fresh?"

"Because I'ma fuckin' Grimlin," Fresh replied, pinching Tina's arm.

"*Stop, boy!*" Tina exclaimed in a loud whisper, snatching her arm away, and everyone in the courtroom stopped what they were doing to look at the two of them. At the same time, Monique was walking back from the booth where Trevon was sitting smiling from ear-to-ear.

When Tina looked at Trevon, he was smiling even harder as he brushed off his shoulder and silently mouthed the words, "*I got her.*"

Tina sucked her teeth, swatted her hand at him, and silently mouthed the word, "*Whatever.*"

"*Issa wrap,*" Trevon replied silently, twirling his index finger in the air.

"All rise!" the bailiff announced. "Court is now in session. The Honorable Judge Joseph Berman presiding."

"You may now be seated," Judge Berman said. "First case on the docket please..." Judge Berman was a pudgy white man in his late fifties, with a no-nonsense authoritative manner. In the 20 minutes Trevon waited for his case to be called, he got the impression Judge Berman was a fair man as he listened to him make decisions in the cases that were called before his.

When Trevon's case was called, he and Monique approached the podium and Monique explained to Judge Berman how he had strong ties within the community, had a job waiting upon his release, a child to support, and a parole officer who spoke highly of him.

Mr. Bryant approached the podium and explained how all this must have been some kind of mistake because Trevon Jenkins was a model parolee, and how he wished he had more clients like him. He also told the Judge how Trevon abided by all the terms of his prerelease commitment, found a job within days of his release, and passed all his drug screenings (imagine that ☺)... By the time Mr. Bryant was finished, he made Trevon look like an angel.

Damn, Tina! Trevon thought to himself. *I love you, girl!*

After Monique finished, the prosecutor brought up Trevon's criminal history and went about the regular routine of trying to make him look like a terrorist. Afterward, Judge Berman read over some papers in silence for a short moment before saying, "Bail is set at twenty thoudsand dollars, under the conditions the defendant doesn't possess or come within 100 feet of a firearm, and reports to the S.O.R. (supervised own recognizance) office weekly...court is now in recess," Judge Berman said before tapping his gavel and disappearing from the bench.

"Call me as soon as you get out so I can schedule you an appointment," Monique whispered in Trevon's ear.

By the time, Trevon looked back, Tina and Fresh were already gone. He walked back to the booth and watched as Monique tossed papers into her briefcase. When she looked in his direction, he shot her a wink. Monique shot him a smile in return as she placed her hand to her ear, imitating a phone, and mouthed the words, "*call me*" before walking out of the courtroom.

●　　　　●　　　　●

145

Tina and Fresh went straight to Vicky Owens (the bail bondsman) from the courthouse to pay Trevon's bail before he got back to the jail, but it wasn't nothing Vicky could do until the paperwork from court was processed. So, Vicky took the money, did all the necessary paperwork, and told Tina she would have Trevon bonded as soon as the bond was entered into the system...

●　　　●　　　●

"Count time! Everybody get on their bunk!" the deputy yelled as he stepped into the confinement cell block. He went from cell to cell conducting his count before stopping in front of Trevon's cell: "Get on your bunk, state baby," he said in a nasty tone, "It's count time, you know the procedure."

"*Fuck that!*" Trevon replied before pulling down his pants and swinging his hips from side to side, making his balls jiggle. "Count deez nutz, *pussy-ass cracker!*"

"I'm writing you a D.R. (disciplinary report) for that one, you stupid motherfucker!"

"I don't give a fuck," Trevon countered. "You gon' be writing that shit for practice 'cause I'm up outta here any minute—FUCK BOY!"

"Oh Yeah?" the deputy chuckled. "Done finally talked one of your baby mommas into using her welfare check to come get'cha, huh?"

"Naw," Trevon chuckled, "I done finally talked your wife into sellin' some of that good pussy, so don't come home too early tonight... I'll be there; you might see some shit you don't want to see."

"I swear to God, if you ever—"

"*Oooh—I'm scared,*" Trevon said, cutting the deputy off. "I hit a nerve talkin' about that snow bunny, huh, white boy?"

"I don't have time for your bullshit, Jenkins. I have better things to do."

"Well, then leave me the fuck alone. Kick rocks, go count something', honky," Trevon said just as his name was being called over the intercom:

"Jenkins, Jenkins, Trevon Jenkins—pack it up all the way!"

Trevon looked at the deputy and smiled. "Well, I guess that's my cue, peckerwood. It's time to go repay your wife for her kindness."

"Keep running your mouth and you're gonna be talking out the other end of your ass, you stupid motherfucker."

"*Out of the other end of my ass...?*" Trevon said, looking up in the air as if he were pondering something. "That doesn't make any sense, what-so-ever, you fool. Out of the end of my ass — now that would make sense — *but out the other end?* What the fuck is that supposed to mean? Isn't the other end of my ass my mouth? I'm already talking out my mouth, you big dumb-ass redneck."

The deputy laughed, looking Trevon up and down. "That's your problem, state baby...you think you're so smart, but in all essence, you're dumber than a box of rocks. You're too smart for your own good, state baby, that's exactly why you'll be back."

"You can get your nuts off my shoulders," Trevon said as he stripped the sheets off his mat. "You can bet your ass you won't see me again."

"You'll be back, state baby," the deputy teased.

"If I do, it's gonna be for killin' a cracker just like you."

"Why are you so ignorant, Jenkins?"

"Why are you so fuckin' ugly, honky? Why y'all smell like German Shepherds when y'all get wet?"

"German Shepherds? Is that all you can come up with? I'm not about to sit up here and play these childish-ass games with you, state baby."

"Fuck you then, bitch!"

"That's all fine and dandy, state baby..." the deputy chuckled, "mark my words: *you-will-be-back...*"

●   ●   ●

Tina and Fresh were sitting in the release lobby of the Palm Beach County jail. They had been there ever since they left the bondsman's office, waiting for Trevon to be released. Tina was sitting, rocking her leg back and forth, looking irritated, as Fresh walked back from the vending machine opening a bag of Skittles....

"Aye, Tina," Fresh said, smacking on a mouthful of Skittles.

"What, Fresh?"

"You're lookin' like a black Jesus at The Last Supper right about now."

"What the fuck is that supposed to mean?"

"That means break bread wit'cha boy—*beeouch!*"

"Damn, Fresh! I just gave you a dollar for some Skittles—"

147

"Exactly! That was for some Skittles—Fresh need a soda now! So, break bread, chicken-head."

"You're getting on my last nerve," Tina said, going in her bag and shoving a dollar in Fresh's face. "Here! And don't ask me for nothing else! You got money to pay that footdragon rent, but you don't have a dollar to buy a soda."

"I done told you about callin' my boo a footdragon!" Fresh yelled defensively, and once again, Tina and Fresh were the center of attention as everyone in the lobby looked in their direction.

"Y'all have to excuse my little brother," Tina said to the audience. "He has Down's Syndrome, he don't know any better."

The lobby erupted with giggles.

"Fuck y'all laughing at?" Fresh asked angrily. "That shit ain't funny."

At that moment, the door buzzed and Trevon walked through it. When Fresh saw him he smiled and sang: *"Let-my-peoplee-gooooo!"* at the top of his voice.

"What da lick read?" Trevon said, throwing his arm around Fresh's neck.

"Damn, I'm glad you're out, homie," Fresh replied, wrapping his arm around Trevon's waist. "The way Tina was talking, I thought you were through dealing."

"You and me both," Trevon said, looking at Tina.

"*Hey, baby,*" she said, spreading her arms.

Trevon hugged her tight. "Hey, boo."

"I kept my word."

"You did."

"I told you I would be here to pick you up today."

"I knew you would."

"I missed you so much, Tre," Tina said, gazing deeply into Trevon's eyes. "I've been fiendin' baby."

Trevon pecked her on the lips. "Fiendin' for what?"

"For some of that dope head..." Tina replied, pecking him back on the lips, "and for some of that dope dick...I need a fix; think you can help me out?"

"I'm the dopeman," Trevon said, pecking her again, "of course, I can help you out."

"*Mmmmh,*" Tina said, rubbing her thighs together as if she had to pee, "you got my pussy tingling already—"

"Tre ain't got your shit tingling," Fresh intervened, "that shit got your shit tingling—you need to go to the clinic and get checked."

"Fuck you, Fresh!" Tina exclaimed. "All up in a bitch conversation—you done fucked up the whole script!"

"Well, Tre ain't Denzel Washington," Fresh fired back, "and you sure as hell ain't Jada Pinkett Smith, and this ain't Hollywood—this the release lobby of the county jail. Don't none of these people wanna hear nothin' about no dope dick, or your infected—ass pussy tingling, and neither do I, so could y'all please save the role playing for the bedroom and drop me off? Fresh do have better things to do."

"I swear, you're so aggravating," Tina said, rolling her eyes at Fresh to look at Trevon. "Joey wanted you to call him as soon as you got out. He was real worried about you," Tina said, grabbing Trevon's hand and leading him out the door...

Trevon leaned against Tina's Acura, waiting for her to give him the phone. "Damn, I hope Joey ain't mad," he said as Fresh jumped on the trunk and sat beside him.

"And if he is—fuck 'em!" Fresh quipped.

Trevon looked at him and shook his head. "It ain't even like that. Joey is real good peoples, I fuck with him the long ways — and he's Frank Rosario's son."

"I don't give a fuck!" Fresh countered. "Joey can still get it, just like Frank can get it—I don't see that shit! Frank's scalp can get peeled just like everybody else's scalp."

Trevon looked at his friend and smiled, "Frank in a whole 'nother league, Fresh. People like him invented the graveyard. We don't need them kind of problems."

"Here, Tre," Tina said, handing Trevon the phone, "it's already ringing."

Trevon held his breath, waiting for Joey to answer.

"Hello? Tina?"

"Naw, it's Tre. What's good, Joey?"

"*Tre!*" Joey said excitedly. "How does it feel to be a free man?"

"Feels good," Trevon answered, "and I really appreciate you getting me a lawyer. That was real good lookin'."

"Forgeddaboudit—it was the least I could do, Tre. I got something else for you too, for taking them lumps and keeping your mouth closed, My father would've fuckin' flipped if that shit had gotten back to him."

"I don't want to talk over the phone, so I'll come in tomorrow and give you the four-one-one."

"That's real good news, 'cause Tony really misses you. We've been real busy, so it'll be nice to have you back."

149

"Does that mean I still have my job?"

"*Sheesh, Tre!* Quit bustin' my fuckin' balls, will ya? Of course you still have your job. What kind of question is that?"

"I don't know, I just thought you were mad about taking that loss or hired somebody else or something."

"Getdafuckouttahere! *Me mad at you?* I thought yous mad at me! I'm just glad you're out, that's all that matters. Tina said she got you a real good lawyer, so everything is going to be alright, capisci? I'll see you when yous get here tomorrow."

"Thanks again, Joey."

"Forgeddaboudit...see ya tomorrow." *Click.*

Trevon exhaled and gave Tina back her phone. "Damn, that's a big relief."

"I told you he wasn't mad," Tina said, cranking up the car.

Fresh got in the backseat, pulled out $5,000 wrapped up in a rubber band, and threw it up front on Trevon's lap. "Those bills are the shit, Tre! Ain't nobody peep the lick yet, everything went real smooth. I thought I was gonna have to fuck somebody up, but nobody came back to the trap complaining yet. We need some more of them shitz, son."

"Joey's the man," Trevon said, counting out $2,500 to give back to Fresh. "That's why I was worried about him being mad; I can't fuck this plug up..." Trevon looked at the jail one last time before they pulled out the parking lot and thought about the last words the peckerwood said to him: *You'll be back, state baby...you-will-be-back!*

God, I hope not, Trevon thought to himself.

●   ●   ●

One the other side of the visitation parking lot where Trevon had just left, stood the Gun Club Criminal Justice Complex: Home of the medical examiner, county coroner, and the Palm Beach County Sheriff's Department.

This is where Detective Kurt Price was at the particular moment, snooping through a file he had no business snooping through.

The file he was snooping through...?

Several weeks earlier, a suspect was pulled over and during the search of the vehicle, deputies recovered $50,000 in counterfeit bills and a .380 semi-automatic hand gun. What caught Detective Price's attention was the fact the counterfeiters were printing fake bills that were so real, the detectives that were assigned to the case couldn't tell them apart from the real. If it weren't for the note that was in the bag with the money, they would have never known that the money was fake.

The reason Detective Price had no business snooping through this particular file...?

Detective Price was a homicide detective, and this case was assigned to a task force that handles organized fraud and forgery.

The reason Detective Price was snooping through this particular file...?"

Because Detective Price was as crooked as Nas' chipped front tooth before he got it fixed, as well as Detective Price's crooked first cousin, Detective Larry "Curly Top" Burke, who was a detective for the Riviera Beach Police Department (Narcotics Task Force). Between the two, they had sent more people to prison than Bush did troops to Iraq.

That's why Price was so determined to find the counterfeiters before the task force did and get them to cooperate and cut him a piece of the pie. And if they didn't he was going to send them where he'd sent the rest that didn't want to play ball. Besides, he was getting old and to the point of retirement, and after twenty years with the Sheriff's Department, he refused to retire broke and with nothing to look forward to.

I need to diet. Detective Price thought to himself as he rubbed his beer belly. *I could probably get one of them expensive surgeries if I find these counterfeiters.*

Price was far from attractive. He was in his late forties, had black beady eyes, a hawkish nose, and a receding hairline with salt and pepper hair, all thrown together on a barrel-shaped body.

After his wife left him for a younger Puerto Rican man, he swore to himself that he was going to get her back and make life hell for all minorities. Price didn't feel bad about it either; he paid for their welfare with his hard-earned tax dollars, so he felt that it was only fair to return the retribution. They took his money, wife, and part of his life, so he didn't mind taking from them. Tit for tat, right?

Price still couldn't accept the fact his wife left him for a wetback. It had been almost three years since she left, but he was still dealing with the rejection. "*Bitch!*" he mumbled to himself, as he leaned back in his chair and laced his fingers behind his head. He would spend several hours a day contemplating ways of getting her back, but at this particular moment, he needed to figure out a way of getting Lieutenant Goldberg to give him the okay to get in on the counterfeiting case.

Lieutenant Goldberg was Jewish. Price didn't like Jews, but he put up with LT because he was his supervisor. To be truthful, Price didn't like niggers either, whom he called 'spades' because he knew they didn't like it.

151

And he didn't too much care for chinks or anything else of the Asian persuasion. Come to think of it, he didn't like waps or Russians, Iraqis or Iranians, or any of the Muslim sand nigger types...

But Price didn't consider himself a racist in any way, shape, form or fashion.

Price was just about to call it a day when the phone rang. "Price speaking."

"Hello, detective," a female voice replied. "This is Beth over at the lab. I got something for you."

"Shoot."

"Ballistics came back for that .380 semi-automatic you sent in."

"And?"

"We have a match."

So, there is a God after all, Price thought to himself. Just what he needed, a reason to get in on the counterfeiting case.

"Beth?"

"Yes?"

"Did you tell anyone yet?"

"Not a soul."

"Good, let's keep it that way. I'll be over to pick up the .380 and the ballistics in a little bit."

"Okay, detective."

"Bye." *Click.*

Now, all he had to do was get an arrest warrant, find the suspect, and prep him up for the extortion game. Price opened the file and scanned for the suspects name...

"Jenkins... Trevon Jenkins," he mumbled to himself as he picked up the phone to call his supervisor. "Hello? Lieutenant Goldberg? We got one; I'm gonna need a warrant for a suspect... Trevon Jenkins, I'm going to the lab now to pick up the ballistics, then I'll fill out the application to submit to the judge...Yes, sir." *Click.*

Price leaned back in his chair and smiled. "Trevon Jenkins," he mumbled to himself again. *"Damn, I love my job..."*

●　　　●　　　●

Later on that night, Trevon and Tina held each other's sweaty, drained bodies as they laid in bed...

"I want some more," Trevon said, turning Tina over on her back and positioning himself between her legs.

6

Ready or Not

October 3, 2007 (The Next Day)

"Fetterman & Associates," Mary stated as she answered the phone.

"Yes, ma'am," the caller replied, "with whom am I speaking to?"

"This is Mary, how may I help you?"

"This is Trevon Jenkins... Ms. Baker told me to call to schedule an appointment."

"Oh, hello, Mr. Jenkins!" Mary replied enthusiastically. "I'm glad that everything worked out in court yesterday and that you're out!"

"Thank you," Trevon replied. "Is Ms. Baker in?"

"I'm afraid not, dear. She'll be in court all morning."

"When do you expect her back?"

"It's hard to say...she usually spends her break in her office catching up on paperwork. I can schedule you for an appointment tomorrow."

Trevon inhaled and exhaled deeply. "I was hoping to see her today."

"Hold on a minute..." Mary said, before checking Monique's schedule for the day. "Sorry, Mr. Jenkins, but she has a case deposition scheduled for one thirty, and a deposition for two thrity. There's no way I could schedule you for today."

"You said that she spends her lunch break in her office, right?"

"Um-hmm, usually."

"*Well...*"

"Well what?"

"What time will that be?"

"Anytime between eleven and one."

"Do you think you can get me in then?"

"I don't know if—"

"*PLEEEASE!*"

"You needs to be saving that energy," Tina replied.

"For what?"

"'Cause after you lose this bet, you gon' need it."

"I'm not gon' lose."

"Yes, you are Tre."

"Girl, stop playing! You ain't see how I had Monique smiling in that courtroom today?"

"Cause her firm just made twenty grand off your black ass. Shit, I would be smiling, too."

"That ain't got shit to do with it, she was smiling at me. Monique was choosin' ya boy."

"She ain't one of them hoodrats you're used to scoopin', Tre. You gon' have to come better than that shit you use, and if that's what you're planning on using, you might as well save your time, 'cause Monique gon' ball that shit up and throw it in the trash."

"You're sounding like a real hater, Tina."

"I'm not hatin'. I'm just tellin' you what it is. You done lost, negro. You'll see."

"Naw," Trevon chuckled, "You'll see—Monique already mines and you don't even know it. You gon' quit doubting my capabilities."

"I'm not doubting you; I'm flat out tellin' you it ain't gon' happen."

"Yeah, it is."

"Well, you got fifty-nine days, Mr. Jenkins, and the clock is ticking..."

Little did Trevon know, the clock was really ticking...

"Well," Mary answered reluctantly, "I guess I could squeeze you in some kind of way."

"What time?"

"Like I said, anywhere between 11:00am and 1:00pm."

"I'll be there at 12. If she comes in before then, hold her hostage."

"I'll try my best," Mary chuckled.

"Please! Don't let her leave, I'll make it worth your while."

"Alright."

"Thank you so much, Mary."

"You're welcome, Mr. Jenkins."

"See you soon." *Click.*

●　　　●　　　●

Inside the Gun Club Criminal Justice Complex, Detective Price was sitting in his office scanning through Trevon's criminal history when his telephone rang...

"Detective Price speaking."

"Hello, detective, this is Kathy over at N.C.I.C. (National Crime Information Center). I have that information on Trevon Jenkins you called for earlier."

Price picked up a pen. "I'm ready when you are."

"The most recent information I came across was from the Department of Corrections. His community control was just terminated, so everything should still be active. Are you ready?"

"Go ahead."

"Okay, the address is four-eight-six-two Palm Bay Drive, Royal Palm Beach, Florida three-three-four-one-four. Got that?"

"Um-hmm."

"Phone number is five-six-one, three-one-three, six-two-seven-eight. Place of employment is Amici, it's an Italian restaurant on the island of Palm Beach."

"Yeah, I know where it is. Thanks Kathy."

"No problem." *Click.*

Price leaned back in his chair and rubbed his chin with his index finger and thumb. "Amici..." he mumbled to himself, "something isn't adding up."

Trevon's criminal history gave him the impression that he was a blue-collar criminal with a possible drug addiction. He didn't fit the profile

155

of a white-collar counterfeiter. His entire criminal history was violent: armed robberies, a carjacking, aggravated assault, aggravated battery, and a few drug possessions.

"How in the hell are you connected to these counterfeiters, you sonofabitch," Price mumbled to himself before looking at his watch.

In any minute, Lieutenant Goldberg should be calling to inform him that the judge signed off on the arrest warrant. When that's done, via Trevon Jenkins, Price would be just that much closer to nailing the counterfeiters to the cross.

Something still isn't adding up, Price thought to himself as he picked up the phone to call 411...

"*What city?*" the operator asked.

"Palm Beach," Price answered.

"*What listing?*"

"Amici Italian Restaurant."

"*One moment please...*"

●   ●   ●

"Your total is five eighty-six, my friend," the Arab cashier said as he placed Trevon's merchandise in a plastic bag.

"Let me get a scratch-off," Trevon said, pointing to the lottery tickets.

"What kind?"

"The Money Bags," Trevon answered.

After ringing up the ticket, the cashier placed it into the bag with the Peach Snapple and Newports Trevon just purchased. After walking out the Quick Stop, Trevon stood by the door with his head down, scratching off his ticket when he heard a familiar voice...

"Long time no see, stranger," Chris boasted as he stepped out his car.

Trevon looked up and saw Chris standing there smiling as if nothing had ever happened. "*What'choo said, nigga?*" he asked in disbelief.

"I said long time no see."

"Naw, dirty...." Trevon said, giving Chris the coldest stare he could, "it ain't been long enough."

"You've been out for almost a year and you ain't try to find ya boy. What's up with that, Tre?" Chris asked nonchalantly.

"If I wanted to find you, I would've found you."

"What's that supposed to mean?"

"Just what the fuck it sounded like! If I wanted to find you, I would've found you. I didn't find you, 'cause I wasn't looking for you. After that shit you and Desiree pulled, I should've found you and put yo ass where nobody else could find you—straight up!"

"*Is that a threat*?!"

"It is what it is, bruh. Take it as you will."

"It's like that?!" Chris asked angrily. "You done caught feelings over that shit that happened between me and Desiree?"

"Who the fuck you raisin' your voice at?!" Trevon snapped. "How the fuck you gon' beat me getting mad, Chris?!"

"Cause you're trippin' for nothin, Tre. How you gon' let a bitch come between us, huh?"

"That's the whole point, Chris... Desiree ain't some bitch... she's the mother of my child, and you were supposed to be my partner—my ace boon coon. I would've never crossed you like that, Chris—*never!*"

"Look, Tre...I'm sor—"

"Save that sit, pussy-ass nigga! Yous'a real fuck nigga, you know that? Of course you do... I know a bitch gon' do what a bitch gon' do, and that it takes two to tango, but I blame you more than Desiree. Ain't nobody put a gun to her head to make her do what she did, but you did take advantage of her."

"Ain't nobody take advantage of De—"

"Didn't I tell you to save that shit, pussy nigga? You done stabbed me in the back once... I never was to give you the chance to do it again..." Trevon looked at the lottery ticket he'd just scratched off. "*Hmph!*" he chuckled with a smirk. "I just won two dollars...why don't you take it, 'cause that's all you're worth, two-dollar-ass nigga! Trevon threw the ticket in Chris' face, got in the Acura, and left his used to be best friend standing there looking stupid. It took everything he had to restrain himself from going ham. One thing he'd learned was that everything had its time and place; now wasn't the time and the Quick Stop wasn't the place...

"*In due time...*" Trevon mumbled to himself, looking at Chris one last time before cranking up the car, "*just be patient, Tre. You gon' get his ass in due time...*"

●   ●   ●

After stopping by the flower shop and purchasing a few things, Trevon went to Amici to straighten things out with Joey. The last thing he

157

wanted was for Joey to think he wasn't trustworthy; therefore, he had to set the record straight by all means.

Trevon arrived at Amici an hour before they opened for lunch, so everyone was running around busily as usual. When he couldn't find Joey, he was just about to call his cell phone when he came up behind Trevon and tapped him on the shoulder...

"Lookin' for me?"

"Wussup, Jay?"

"Glad you're back, Tre. Shit has been real crazy around here. Think you can come in tonight?"

"*Hell, yeah*! I need the money. I gotta lot of catching up to do."

"Don't worry, I got you covered."

"Come outside so I can let you know what's going on," Trevon said, heading out the door. Once outside, they walked to the Acura and got in. "First off," Trevon said, "I just wanted to let you know that what happened wasn't my fault. They pulled me over for no reason and—"

"Shit happens, Tre," Joey said, cutting Trevon off. "Yous kept your mouth shut and that's all that matters. The money can be replaced, so don't worry about it, bro."

"I don't know, Jay... I feel like I let you down."

"It's all good, Tre. You didn't let me down, so quit thinking like that. You got pinched and didn't scream. That shows me your character, so if there's anything you need, let me know and I got you, Capisci?"

"I'm glad you said that, 'cause I need some more of them bills," Trevon said, opening the glove compartment and pulling out the $2,500 Fresh had given him the night before. "You said you would charge me thirty dollars every hundred, right?"

"Right."

"Well then I need twenty-five hundred worth."

"I already got you covered, bro." Joey replied, pulling out an envelope and throwing it on Trevon's lap. "Bada bing! That's five thousand, keep your money, that's on me, Capisci?"

"Damn, that's good lookin', Jay!"

"Forgeddaboudit."

"I'ma still need twenty-five hundred worth. My people said they were getting rid of them shitz like government cheese."

Joey took the money from Trevon. "I'll have it for you by the time you come in tonight."

"This top-notch shit, Jay. If you wouldn't have put that note in the bag, they wouldn't have ever known. They questioned me for hours, they really wanted to know where the bills came from."

"You don't know how much I appreciate yous keeping your mouth closed."

"I live by a code, Joey, and cooperating with law enforcement isn't a part of it, you feel me?"

"Oh yeah," Joey said matter-of-factly, "some dude called here earlier looking for you."

"Did he leave a name?"

"Naw, he just said that he'll call back."

Trevon thought for a short moment. "It was probably my homeboy."

"Naw," Joey replied, "it was an older white dude."

"Probably my parole officer then. He sounds white..." Trevon said, brushing it off.

Afterward, he went inside, put on his chef jacket, and went to work. Twenty minutes later, he placed some spaghetti with tomato garlic sauce in a to-go container, topped with chicken and eggplant parmigiana, and wrapped several pieces of garlic bread in aluminum foil.

"I'll be in at three," he said to Joey before leaving.

"I'll have that for you by then," Joey replied.

With that said, Trevon was out the door. He had a deadline to meet that was 59 days away, and patience was an element he had no time for. In order to get Monique, Trevon knew he had to go in head first, and that's exactly what he was about to do...

●　　●　　●

Mary was on the phone when Trevon stepped off the elevator, so she didn't see him when he approached her desk holding two bags; what caught her attention was the smell of fresh garlic bread. She hadn't eaten lunch yet because she had to wait for Trevon to get there before she could leave. Come to find out, she didn't have to go anywhere after all...

"I'm so flabbergasted," Trevon said casually as Mary hung up the phone.

"Excuse me?" Mary replied, not knowing who Trevon was or what he was talking about.

"I said I'm so flabbergasted," Trevon repeated. "You look astonishing in person than you sound over the phone."

"*Oh, thank you, Mr. Jenkins!*" Mary replied with a big smile, realizing who Trevon was now.

"For you..." he said, holding out one of the bags he was carrying, "I hope you like Italian food."

"I love it!" Mary said, taking the bag from Trevon's hand. "You're right on time. Monique just stepped into her office, I'll let her know that you're here..." Mary picked up the phone. "Monique, Mr. Jenkins in here... Alright, I'll send him in..." Mary stood and opened the door for Trevon.

"Thanks again, Mary," he said.

When Trevon walked into Monique's office, she was on the phone speaking to someone as she looked at him and signaled to give her a minute with a finger. His eyes took everything in as he sat down, using the things in her office to build a personality profile: There was a picture of an older couple on her desk, and from the resemblance, Trevon came to the conclusion that they were her parents; he also noticed that there were no other pictures of boyfriends or kids. There was also a bookshelf in the corner filled with law and philosophy books, along with some poetry, spirituality, and inspirational material.

From his observation, Trevon gathered that Monique was single, had no kids or siblings, and liked literature and debating. He also got the impression that she was in love at some point, but had been heart broken and had a complex about whatever caused her relationship to turn sour, therefore she was doing some soul searching, which explained the inspirational material...

This is going to be harder than I thought, Trevon thought to himself as Monique hung up the phone.

"Good afternoon, Mr. Jenkins."

"That it is."

"What is that supposed to mean?"

"That means that this is a good afternoon, Ms. Baker. Any time frame spent in your presence is good, being morning, afternoon, or night."

Monique smiled, looking Trevon up and down. He had on a baggy, powder blue Polo sweat suit, snow white Reeboks, a white Polo hat, and his jacket was unzipped, revealing his white tank-top and Cuban link.

"You look..." Monique paused, trying to find an appropriate adjective, "different. You look different."

"Is that good or bad?" Trevon asked suspiciously.

Monique smiled. "Good, definitely good," she answered reassuringly. "I think anything beats looking like an inmate."

Trevon reached into the bag he was holding, "I got something for you," he said, pulling out a small package and placing it on Monique's desk.

She picked it up and examined it a moment before saying, *"Seeds?"*

"Flower seeds," Trevon replied, "Dahlia flower seeds."

"And what am I supposed to do with flower seeds, Mr. Jenkins?"

"Plant them."

"In what?"

"In this..." Trevon said, pulling out a flower pot and a small bag of soil. "I think that giving someone flowers is kind of..." Now it was Trevon pausing, trying to find the right words. "...I think it's kind of elderly...it's also very boring; you give someone flowers, they enjoy them for a few days, and then they die. I don't think you would've found gratification in that. You seem like the type of woman that would appreciate the process."

"What process, Mr. Jenkins?"

"The process of growing, Ms. Baker. Something we do each day but fail to communicate with it because we're so intertwined in irrelevant activities. That which is relevant, we cease to acknowledge."

"And what's that?"

"Life...the beauty of it, the complexities of it. To me it's so amazing how something so small and so simple—such as those seeds—can grow into something so complex and beautiful..." Trevon leaned forward and looked into Monique's eyes. "You and those seeds have a lot in common, Ms. Baker."

"How is that?" Monique asked curiously.

"You're both fragile and delicate, therefore you can be easily hurt or damaged. You both need certain elements to grow, and when given those elements, you'll blossom into something beautiful... without those elements, you'll wither up. You've blossomed, Ms. Baker, but you still have more growing to do."

Monique was at a loss for words as she gazed into Trevon's eyes. The things he said were so interesting and sincere. She had completely underestimated him. He was a complete stranger, but somehow, he made her feel like she'd known him for years. As bad as she wanted to finish the conversation, she knew she couldn't—business was business, and Trevon was a client; that was a line Monique refused to cross.

"Thank you, Mr. Jenkins. This was very thoughtful of you."

"It was the least I could do. I'm glad you liked it."

Monique looked at her watch. "I umm... I have another client that should be here momentarily. We really need to sit down and discuss some things about your case; however, we don't have time right now. I could schedule you an appointment for next week, if that's okay with you?"

Trevon smiled, "No-can-do."

"When will be a good time?"

"Tomorrow."

"I can't."

"Why?"

"Catch up day, I'll be tied up all day."

"You're taking a lunch break, right?"

"Yes, I'm taking a lunch break."

"Well, then let me treat you to lunch."

"I don't think that's such a good idea. You're a client, Mr. Jenkins. I don't mix business with pleasure."

"Don't then, we'll keep it strictly business. I promise there will be no pleasure involved."

"I don't... I don't know if..."

"*Pleeeease*," Trevon pleaded, folding his hands and batting his eyes.

Monique smiled. "Don't do that."

"Do what?"

"Make that face."

"I'll make reservations...Amici, in Palm Beach. You ever heard of it?"

"Yes."

"Ever ate there?"

"No."

"The most authentic Italian food in South Florida... Is eleven thirty good for you?"

Monique smiled.

"Does that mean yes?" Trevon asked suspiciously.

There was a short silence before she answered. "Yes, eleven thirty is good for me..."

When Trevon and Monique stepped out of the office, Mary stood and began to smile uncontrollably. There was nothing unusual about seeing Mary smile, but Monique had never seen her smile the way she was at this particular moment.

"Have a nice day, dear," Mary said to Trevon.

"You have a nice day, too, Mary. It was nice meeting you."

"Same here..."

Trevon started dancing as soon as the elevator door slid closed. He was extremely happy because he had Monique right where he wanted her. He knew that if he could get her to have lunch, he knew he could get her to listen to what he had to say during lunch, and if she did listen, he knew that she was his for the taking.

When the door slid open, Dexter was standing there flanked by three of his goons. All four had blood shot eyes and smelled like they just came from a Bob Marley festival. It was the first time they seen each other since the night he got out of prison, but Trevon still got the same bad vibe he'd gotten that night when he looked into Dexter's eyes.

"Wha ha um, my yute?" Dexter asked, swinging his long dreadlocks to the side and extending his hand.

Trevon extended his and they shook. "Same ole, same ole."

"Yuh cum check Monique?"

"Yeah, she's up there waiting for you."

"Da gal dem ah reel good, yuh know?"

"Yeah, I heard."

"Babylon dem fuckin' wit' mi, my yute. Mi have tree lawyers," Dexter said, holding three fingers, "Monique, and two odda crackers mi hire tuh fight mi deportation cases. Everything bout blood-clot money in dis country. All da yankee dem waan: *money, money, money!*"

"That shit makes the world go 'round, dread. Speaking of which, I need some work, I need you to plug me in."

"Link up with' mi when yuh ready fi g'wan, sén?"

"Bet..."

After Trevon got finished talking to Dexter, he sat in the car trying to remember where he knew Dexter from. His instincts told him something wasn't right and that's why it was eating him up, because his instincts were 99.9% accurate.

"Where do I know you from...?" Trevon mumbled to himself. "Maybe I'm just trippin'."

He laid his head against the headrest and thought for a short moment before cranking up the car.

Nah, I'm not trippin', Trevon thought to himself, *something ain't right. Me and Dexter bumped heads before... but where?*

While Trevon was in the car brain storming, Dexter was in the elevator doing the same thing...

"Mi doe know where mi know da bwoy Trevon from, but mi know mi know him from somewhere." Dexter said, walking back and forth between is goons. "It's somethin' about da bwoy ah yammin' mi up. Da bwoy ah snake! Yuh ear me? A bumba-clot snake in da grass! Find out everyting 'bout da bwoy, you ear? Every blood-clot ting..."

7

Opposites Attract

What am I doing? Monique asked herself for the umpteenth time on her way to Amici, the restaurant Trevon asked her to meet him at so they could discuss his case over lunch. She had not been alone with a man, or anything close to a date since she moved to West Palm Beach from Richmond, Virginia.

She moved to West Palm Beach to get away from the painful memories of Keith, her ex-fiancé. She had met Keith two months after she graduated law school and was engaged six months after that. He was the perfect gentleman—or at least that's what she thought—up until the late nights at the office, and the women calling his cell phone at all hours of the night, which led to the arguments and the arguments led to the beatings.

Monique would leave and Keith would promise that he would change, so she would come back only to be beat again. Naomi, her best friend, begged her to move to West Palm Beach with her the first time Keith put his hands on her. "If he did it once, he'll do it again..." Naomi used to say after Keith put his hands on her. Monique would take up for him and make excuses for his actions. She had to find out the hard way just how right her friend was...

Finally, after almost two years of abuse, Monique was fed up. One week before their wedding day, Monique packed up whatever she could in her Mercedes SL 500 while Keith was at work and headed south...

Destination: West Palm Beach, Florida

That was three years ago... the first year she tried to adjust. South Florida and Richmond were like night and day. There were so many different nationalities in South Florida, people from all over the world. There were so many different cultures, and so many different languages.

Monique thought that she would never be able to get used to it, but as time moved on, she became immune to Floridians. Now she was used to all the ratchet-ass women, the gold teeth, and the cars with huge rims and loud music.

She was used to the drugs, the violence, and the money. Between the hurricanes, alligator attacks and killings, Florida was a crazy place to live, but Monique learned to love it.

Three years ago, when Monique used to hear of West Palm Beach, the first thing that came to mind was Donald Trump and the Kennedy's. Once she moved here, she found out that it wasn't all about mansions and palm trees. Shortly after Monique started working for Fetterman & Associates she learned that Palm Beach County was ranked #2 in the nation for bank robberies—behind Los Angeles—and that West Palm Beach was labeled on of the most dangerous cities in the country—ahead of New York, Los Angeles and Miami.

Monique had to learn that Palm Beach and West Palm Beach were two different places. Palm Beach was an island where Donald Trump and a host of other filthy rich people lived. The only thing that separated Palm Beach and West Palm Beach was the intercostal and a bridge...

Once you crossed that bridge you were in another world.

All the cities that made up Palm Beach County were flooded with cocaine and assault rifles. People were being robbed and murdered on a daily basis, which meant business was booming in the criminal justice field.

Monique had just gotten one of her clients acquitted on drug trafficking charges. Now he's requesting her services again. This time the DEA raided his house and found several uncut kilos of cocaine, a scale, and three AK-47 assault rifles. She didn't know how she was going to explain this one to the jury, but she was sure she would find a loop hole like she always did.

Monique loved her job, the money was good and there was plenty of work to do, which she didn't mind because it kept her busy, therefore she had no time to think about Keith, which is one of the reasons she agreed to have lunch with Trevon. She'd been so busy that she had practically lived off Taco Bell and McDonald's. Monique couldn't remember the last time she had a decent meal. Besides, she'd heard a lot about Amici: how good the food was, and the excellent service. Very expensive, but well worth the dining experience.

As Monique crossed the Flagler Bridge leaving West Palm Beach, she thought about how opulent Palm Beach was. Everything on this side of the bridge was so perfect.

There wasn't a piece of paper on the ground, a lawn that wasn't perfectly manicured, or a tree that wasn't perfectly trimmed. All the cars were exclusive, and all the mansions were huge. It was a whole new world over here. Monique still couldn't believe that on the other side of the bridge was one of the most dangerous cities in the country...

This made her think of Trevon.

He didn't seem like the type that would step foot on the island of Palm Beach, better yet, make reservations at one of its most exclusive restaurants. He was tall and handsome, with the most succulent lips, but he was a client and Monique made sure she let that be known before accepting his invitation.

When Monique pulled up in front of the restaurant her Mercedes fit right in with the rest of the luxury cars and SUVs that were being parked by the valet. After she was given a ticket, she watched her car disappear into the bowels of the parking garage.

When Monique reached the front door, there was a tall Hispanic man with curly, black hair, standing at a podium, which held a reservation book.

"Hello, how may I help you today?" he said, producing a warm smile.

"Yes, reservations for two, I believe it's under the name Jenkins."

"Oh, yes!" the host said, excitedly. "I've been expecting you—right this way, Ms. Baker."

As Monique was being led to her table, she noticed that she was the only African American in the whole restaurant. She instinctively smiled and nodded her head at couples as she passed them, and they did the same. When she reached the table, she saw that Trevon wasn't there yet.

"Here you go," the host said, "Mr. Jenkins will be with you shortly. Can I get you anything while you wait?"

Monique smiled. "No, thank you, I'll wait for Mr. Jenkins."

After about five minutes, Monique cursed Trevon for being late. She was just about to get up and leave when he walked through the door talking on his cell phone. The man that walked through the door looked nothing like the inmate she visited at the county jail, nor did he look like the man that visited her office the day before wearing a sweat suit.

No, this man was different: he wore a cream-colored suit with a tan shirt with cuffs and gold links, and a cream and tan tie that begged for attention; his goatee and sideburns were trimmed so perfect it looked as if he drew them on.

As he walked, no, glide is more like the word Monique would use to describe the way he moved—as if he were on roller skates.

As he glided toward her, Monique couldn't take her eyes off of him. Treon looked nothing like the criminal she thought he was; he looked professional, like a doctor or a stockbroker.

As he glided toward her, Monique noticed that everyone stared at him the same way they starred at her, but they were different kinds of stares: for the men, it was stares of envy; for the women, it was stares of lust...

"Please forgive me," Trevon said apologetically, "I got caught up in traffic. How long have you been waiting?"

"Not long," Monique answered.

"Thank you so much for accepting my invitation, Ms. Baker. You don't know how much I appreciate you coming," Trevon stated warmly as he turned off his phone and placed it inside his jacket pocket.

"It's my pleasure, Mr. Jenkins. Thank you for inviting me."

Trevon smiled. "As usual, you look ravishing."

Monique looked around the restaurant at all the other women with elegant jewelry, expensive dresses, and nice hairdos.

"I think I look rather plain compared to all these other women," she replied.

"That's exactly what I mean," Trevon countered. "You don't need fake nails, make-up, or any of the other accessories these women need to be beautiful. Their beauty is cosmetic—it's applied—therefore, it can be taken off the same way it's put on. You, on the other hand, have no other choice but to be beautiful all the time. Every woman in here will kill to have what you possess, Ms. Baker."

Monique felt her heart skip a beat.

"Well, thank you," she said bashfully.

"Just speaking the truth."

Monique smiled.

"Did I do that?" Trevon asked.

"Do what, Mr. Jenkins?"

"Make you smile?"

Monique smiled even harder. "Yes..." she answered, "you made me smile, Mr. Jenkins."

The host from the front door appeared holding two menus. "Your server will be with you shortly," he said before leaving.

When Monique opened her menu she noticed that there were no prices displayed, which meant one thing: if you were worried about the prices, you were in the wrong place.

"What do you recommend?" she asked as she scanned her menu.

"The chef is from Bari," Trevon replied, "so he specializes in Tuscan dishes and whatnot."

"Bari? Where's Bari?" Monique asked curiously.

"On the southeast coast of Italy," Trevon answered. "The risotto is good, but the steak Florentine is off the meat rack."

"*Off the meat rack...?*" Monique said, looking confused.

Trevon smiled. "I'm sorry, Ms. Baker. I forgot you don't speak the lingo. 'Off the meat rack' means, off the chain, off the hook..."

Monique gave Trevon a puzzled look.

"Very well," he said, "let me translate it for you: The steak Florentine is delicious. Sensuous. Scrumptious. Exquisitely delightful if I do say so myself, my dear lady," Trevon said, sounding as proper and distinguished as he could.

Monique burst out laughing as she closed her menu. "I'll have the steak Florentine, Mr. Jenkins."

Trevon closed his menu as well as waved for the waitress. A short, friendly lady sped to the table and wrote down a long list as Trevon spat out what they wanted. Shortly afterward, she came back with a bottle of Vidal and poured some in each glass, filling them halfway. Monique practically gulped down the first glass and the alcohol went straight to her brain.

"*Whoa!*" Trevon said. "You better take it easy, killer. I don't think it's a good idea for you to go in front of the judge intoxicated."

Monique smiled. "I appreciate your concern, but I don't have any more appearances at the courthouse this afternoon..." The warmth of the alcohol embraced Monique as she spoke; the wooziness caused her to loosen up a little. She picked up an advertisement display that had the day's special listed on it and tried to pronounce the words on it: "Pep-ero-"

"It's peperonata with ricotta crostini," Trevon corrected. "It's a pepper stew."

Monique looked at Trevon through squinted eyes. "Okay, how about the ricotta and cream filled bur-burraa—"

"That's burrata," Trevon corrected again. "It's a fresh cheese known as *latticini.*"

"Okay," Monique replied, "What's the difference between a crostini and a crostini bagnati, Mr. Smarty pants?"

Trevon leaned back in his chair and smiled. "Crostini are large crostini. Here they are called '*bagnati*'—which is Italian for wet—because they're bathed in olive oil."

"*Are you making this up?*" Monique asked suspiciously.

The waitress appeared before Trevon had a chance to answer and placed a tray of bread, olives, and mixed meats with a small bowl of olive oil on the table.

Trevon began eating. "This is the anti-pasta," he said, between bites.

"Huh?" Monique replied.

"Italians..." Trevon said, "dinner is like a ritual to them, and there's a procedure as to how it's served. First is the anti-pasta, which is usually a plate of mixed meats such as this..." Trevon said, pointing to the tray, in front of them. "Then there's the first course—primi—which is usually pasta or soup. Then there's the main course—the secondi—which is usually a dish of chicken, fish, beef, or lamb..." Trevon spent the next fifteen minutes answering all of Monique's questions; lunch turned out to be a learning experience for her.

"How do you know so much about Italian food?" she asked curiously. At that moment, their server returned with their first and main course; Monique couldn't help but admire the presentation of it as the waitress placed the plates on the table. They were decorated so well she was almost afraid to touch them.

Monique cut into her steak and placed a piece in her mouth. "*Mmmh! This-is-so-delicious!*"

They are in silence for a short moment.

"I work here," Trevon said, breaking the silence.

"Huh?" Monique replied, dumbfounded.

"I'm answering your question," Trevon explained. "Remember? You asked me how I knew so much about Italian food—I work here, that's how."

"Oh...yeah...umm," Monique stammered, "the wine. I hadn't had a drink-"

"I understand," Trevon said reassuringly. He saw Monique's cheeks blush and smiled to himself.

"I-I'm sorry," she said apologetically.

"It's okay, there's no need to be."

Monique took another sip of wine. *So, that explains why he knows so much about the chef,* she thought to herself.

"So, what's your occupation? Are you a waiter?"

"No, a chef...Well, I'm not technically a chef, but I'm training under one."

"*A chef?!*"

Trevon smiled. "Yes, a chef."

"*Wow!* I didn't know you knew how to cook, Mr. Jenkins."

"You never asked, Ms. Baker."

"I'm speechless," Monique said, but deep down she was completely fascinated. The man sitting before her was so mystical, so mysterious, so unpredictable. He was like a puzzle with none of the pieces fitting. It seemed like every time he was in her presence he never ceased to amaze her.

"It was hard at first," Trevon explained, "but I caught on eventually. Tony, the executive chef, doesn't' speak English very well, but he was very patient with me. I studied the menu at home and absorbed the lingo. Over time, I picked up on their culture."

"I think you've done a good job."

"Really?"

"Yes, really."

"May I take that as a compliment?"

"You may."

"Well, thank you." Trevon said. "I guess I'm good at blending in with my surroundings... If you ask me, I think Italians and Blacks have a lot in common."

"How is that?"

"We both love money, jewelry, and have no respect for authority...we also like a lot of meat and a lot of seasoning in our food."

Monique smiled. "You know, I've never looked at it like that, but now that you've mentioned it, we do have a lot in common. I see that you're full of surprises, Mr. Jenkins. You caught me completely off guard with all of this."

Trevon took a sip of wine, replaced his glass, and looked Monique directly in the eyes. "Never underestimate your opponent, Ms. Baker. The element of surprise can be a dangerous weapon."

Monique looked Trevon directly in the eyes. "I never knew we were opponents, Mr. Jenkins. The last time I checked I was your lawyer, so in my book that makes us allied, not opposed."

"That, Ms. Baker, is true to an extent. Yes, you are my lawyer, so yes we are allied from that point of view. But from my point of view, opposed is exactly what we are."

"And how it that?" Monique asked suspiciously.

"Opposed means to act against something, or try to prevent something. Resisting."

Monique picked up her glass and took another sip of wine. "I never knew I was acting against you."

"No, you aren't, but you are trying to prevent something."

"*Am I?*"

"Yes, you are."

Monique placed her elbow on the table and placed her hand under her chin, looking Trevon dead in his eyes. "Tell me, Mr. Jenkins, what am I trying to prevent, what am I acting against?"

Trevon got stuck, trying to find the appropriate words, not knowing how honest he should be. He had never had a problem with getting his point across or speaking his mind. He didn't want to be too honest and make Monique feel like he was being disrespectful in the process. There was no way to sugarcoat what he had to say, so he let intuition lead the way...

"Well," Monique said impatiently, "I'm waiting."

Trevon picked up his glass and leaned back in his chair. "I'm not one to beat around the bush, Ms. Baker. I believe in being honest, and at times, I'm too honest."

"I love honesty," Monique replied, her speech starting to slur; the wine was taking its toll. "I don't know a woman who doesn't appreciate honesty. So tell me... as honest as you can, what am I resisting, what am I trying to prevent?"

That's your cue, Tre, Trevon thought to himself. *It's show time!*

"Ms. Baker..." he said, pausing to take a sip of wine as if he needed the fortitude to continue, "I've learned that people will forget what you say... they'll forget what you did... they'll forget what you gave them... but they'll never forget how you made them feel. I'll never forget the first time I saw you, the feeling I felt when I saw you. It was a need, an ache, an ache so deep it touched every part of me. Since the day I met you there's not a minute that goes by that I don't think about you and it's driving me crazy. The way you intrude my thoughts, it's as involuntary as blinking..." Trevon put his glass down and gently grabbed Monique's hand. "I want to get to know you, to be a part of you," and in almost a whisper he said, "*to please you*—I want to make you happy..."

Monique didn't realize it, but she held Trevon's hand tight. Her breast heaved as her breathing got heavier.

Trevon smiled inwardly; he had her right where he wanted her.

"What I feel for you, Ms. Baker, is beyond lust, beyond infatuation. What I'm trying to tell you is that I need you, I must have you, and some day, some way, you will be mines. It may not be today or tomorrow, but you will be mines. I will make love to you, and when I do, I'm going to make your body feel things your mind can't comprehend. And that's what you're trying to prevent, that's what you're resisting. For whatever reason, you have a wall built up around your heart. You're trying to find a flaw or any kind of discrepancy in anything I say or do—"

"That's not true!" Monique snapped.

"Yes, it is," Trevon countered. "when I told you I worked here, I could read your thoughts as if they were printed on ticker tape and running across your forehead. You said it yourself, remember? '*Oh, you're so full of surprises, Mr. Jenkins, you caught me completely off guard'.*" Trevon said, doing his best impersonation of Monique. "What's so surprising about me being a chef? Why is it so hard to believe that I'm head over heels for you? It's too good to be true, and somewhere in the back of your mind it's this little voice saying '*girl, he's up to no good, he just want some coochie'.*"

Monique laughed at Trevon mimicking the voice in her conscience.

"You're trying to figure me out," Trevon continued, "but there's nothing to figure out. There's no catch to it—it is what it is, raw and uncut. You can't keep listening to that voice in here..." Trevon said, pointing to his temple. "You have to follow what you feel here..." he said, placing his hand over his heart, "and quit trying to prevent me from getting in there..." he said, leaning to the side and looking between Monique's legs. "So, see, you're resisting. Resisting what you feel. And you're trying to prevent me from getting into your mind, your heart, and your panties. Now do you see how we are opposed? I'm trying to do the complete opposite of what you're trying to prevent. So, now that you see things from my point of view, you make the call, Ms. Baker, you tell me what we are: allied or opposed?"

Monique felt exposed. She looked around the restaurant to see if anyone had been listening; it was now filled to capacity. No one was paying attention to them with the exception of an elderly lady sitting with a companion at the table next to them. When she saw Monique look at her, she smiled and waved, and Monique did the same. From the look on the elderly lady's face, Monique knew she heard the whole conversation.

When Monique looked back at Trevon her face was impassive. She was still trying to absorb everything she had just heard.

This is what she went to school for, to debate and defend. She could stand in a courtroom full of people, in front of a judge and jury, and exculpate her client, arguing the complexities of their case, rather innocent or guilty. Now here she was, sitting before a man she barely knew, unable to defend herself. Guilty of everything he had just said.

Monique felt vulnerable; Trevon had read her like the front page of the *PALM BEACH POST*. His brown, knowing eyes pierced down to her soul, exposing all her thoughts:

How did he know about the voice in my head? How did he know I have built a wall around my heart? How did he know I was trying to find fault in everything he said and did? How did he know I had been fighting to keep him out of my mind? Then Monique thought: *Oh my God! Does he know how bad I want him? Does he know how bad I want him to make love to me? Is he aware of the fire that's burning inside of me?*

Monique had to regain her composure. She couldn't let Trevon know her true feelings, not yet anyways. So, he was right; they were opponents. The game had begun and he was up one point. Monique knew she had to score. Somehow, she had to take control of the situation, but first she had to regain control of herself...

That's when she realized she was still holding Trevon's hand.

Monique let go, hoping he didn't notice how sweaty her palms were, or how tight she was holding on. It took everything she had to gather her thoughts. She sat as poised as she could, and even though her head was spinning from the wine, she picked up her glass and took a long sip before gazing into Trevon's eyes...

"You have a way of getting your point across, Mr. Jenkins, or should I say, you have a way with words. Tell me, do you talk to all the women you meet like that?"

"No, I don't," Trevon answered coolly. "I explained to you what I feel, now it's up to you to do with it what you will."

Monique giggled.

"What's so funny?" Trevon asked curiously.

"You are, Mr. Jenkins... your arrogance, your confidence," Monique now did her best impression of Trevon, *"'I'm gonna make you mines, I'm gonna make love to you, and when I do I'm gonna make your body feel things your mind can't comprehend...'* It's going to take a hell of a lot more than a steak, a couple glasses of wine, and that crap you just told me to get in between my legs."

Trevon laughed.

Now it was Monique asking, *"What's so funny?"*

"Is that what you think this is all about?" Trevon asked.

Monique crossed her arms and leaned back in her chair.

"It's a shame," Trevon continued, "a shame that you're so intelligent, but yet, you're slow. Do you really think that all this was about getting between your legs? I'm not sexually deprived, Ms. Baker. Do you think I thought all I needed was a steak and a couple glasses of wine to get off? If that's the case, I could've gone to McDonald's, grabbed a six-pack and jacked my dick—it sure as hell would've been a lot cheaper. So, no, this is not about getting in between your legs. Don't get me wrong, it would've been nice if I could, but if not it's okay, because I've already gotten into what I intended to get into."

"And what is that?"

"Think about it."

"I thought you said you're not one to beat around the bush!"

"I thought you said you loved honesty," Trevon countered, "and I'm not beating around the bush, I'm just giving you something to think about."

"I think you've given me more than enough to think about!"

"You said you appreciated the truth. How do appreciate something you can't handle? I should've told you a bunch of bullshit!"

"How do I know all that crap you just told me wasn't a bunch of bullshit, huh...?" Monique looked around the restaurant before she continued. "Oh, the smooth operator can't answer that one, huh?" Then through squinted eyes, she said, "My mother warned me about you!"

"Well, your mother's a goddamn lie!" Trevon said defensively.

Monique shot forward quickly. " *You don't know my mother to be speaking of her like that!*"

Trevon shot forward in the same manner. "*My point exactly!* Your mother don't know me, so how is she gonna warn you about me?"

"You know what I mean?"

"Actually, I don't."

"I didn't mean you specifically—I meant she warned you about your kind."

Trevon poured more wine in both glasses. "Tell me," he said before taking a sip, "what's my kind?"

"You know what you are, who you are, I shouldn't have to tell you about yourself, Mr. Jenkins."

"Please do, Ms. Baker. I would love to hear how you see me."

Monique picked up her glass and stared at Trevon a short moment. "You have a one-track mind, and you want thing and only one thing only. At first, it's the sweet talk and the wine and dine thing. Then after you get what you want, it's a whole different ball game. You don't care about nobody's feelings but your own. All you care about is your own desires."

"*That's not true!*"

"Yes, it is, and I'll prove it!"

"How do you plan to do that?" Trevon asked curiously.

"By your answer to this question."

"Shoot."

"Okay..." Monique said, taking a sip of wine and studying Trevon suspiciously. "If I allowed you to sleep with me right now, would you?"

"What the hell is that, some kind of trick question?"

"Just answer the question!" Monique snapped.

Trevon held up both hands, signaling a truce. " *Whoa!*" he said. "First of all, am I under oath? I don't know why, but I feel like a witness being cross examined."

"If that's the case, yes, you are under oath, Mr. Jenkins. Now will the witness please answer the question."

Trevon leaned back in his chair and smiled. "Yes... what was the question again, Ms. Baker?"

"If I allowed you to sleep with me, would you?"

"Is Wesley Snipes black?"

Monique tried her best not to laugh at Trevon's answer but failed. "Will the witness give a yes or no answer, please," she said, trying to wipe the smile off her face.

"Well, then yes," Trevon answered, "I'll tear that ass up!"

"*See what I mean?* How could you sleep with me and you don't even know me, know nothing about me?"

"I know enough."

"Oh yeah?"

"Yeah."

"And what do you know about me, Mr. Jenkins?"

Trevon raised a hand quickly. "*Objection, Your Honor!* Ms. Baker is badgering the witness!"

"Maybe because the witness is being hostile!"

"Far from it. You asked the witness a question and the witness answered the question as truthfully as he could. Now, if I would've sat here and said no, I wouldn't sleep with you, then I would be telling a bald face lie... You did advise me that I was under oath, and lying under oath is perjury, and that's exactly how Lil Kim got fucked up. At least I was honest. You could ask a thousand different men the same question and get a thousand different answers, but when it all boils down, it's only one truth. The one that says no, they wouldn't, that's the dude you need to watch — not me!"

"Answer my question, Mr. Jenkins: what you know about me?"

"Why do you keep badgering the witness with the same question, Ms. Baker? I've already answered your question."

"No, you haven't!" Monique interjected. "You're giving an exculpatory testimony."

"*Exculpatory,*" Trevon chuckled, "I like that. *Exculpatory.*"

"Oh, I'm sorry, Mr. Jenkins... I forgot you don't speak the lingo," Monique said, using Trevon's line back on him. "Let me translate it for you: giving an exculpatory testimony means — "

"*I know what it means, Ms. Baker,*" Trevon said irritably. "It's a fancy way of saying that I'm trying to remove blame from myself, that I'm trying to confuse the judge and jury..."

Monique leaned back in her chair and crossed her arms. *Impressive*, she thought, *very impressive.*

"Don't let the Ebonics fool you; I have an extended vocabulary," Trevon said. "I like to say things where you can get more meaning with less effort. I try not to waste words, Ms. Baker. Why use a fifty-dollar word when a five-dollar word can be just as effective?"

Monique smiled.

175

"I'm not the bad guy, Ms. Baker. I'm not that dude who broke your heart."

"Who ever said someone broke my heart?" Monique said defensively.

"Somebody did something to you!" Trevon quipped. "I know I didn't! I don't know why you're trying to sit up here and scrutinize everything I say and pass judgement on me. Truth be told, I don't think it's a fair question to begin with. I'm in a no-win situation: if I tell the truth, you get what you want and get to say I have one track mind. If I tell a lie, you'll know that I'm lying then you'll criticize me for that... I think it's fair to say that you should modify your question."

"And how should I modify my question, Mr. Jenkins?"

"Don't ask me *if* I would make love to you—we both know the answer to that—instead, ask me what I would do *after* I've made love to you."

Monique felt herself losing control of the situation again. She knew if she asked the question, Trevon would see straight through her and fall into his trap. Then she thought: *what would he do after he made love to me?*

Her curiosity got the best of her.

"Okay," she said, "what would you do after making love to me...?" There was desperation in her voice.

She bit the bait; Trevon had her right where he wanted her.

"After making love to you, I would embrace you and wrap my arms around you like a blanket. I would think about the yearning I felt for you the first time I saw you and cherish the moment and thank God for answering my prayers. I would caress your neck and lips with kisses and search your face for any signs of displeasure, and after your eyes have acknowledged that I have pleased you to the fullest—like I know they will—I would explore your mind the same way I would've explored your body: slowly, patiently, making sure I don't miss a particle of your being..."

Monique had no recollection of what was said afterward. Trevon's voice was so warm and filled with promise; it was almost hypnotic. She couldn't look him in the eyes. They were so intelligent and seemed as if they were looking right through her, exposing her most secretive thoughts.

Monique found herself only being able to make eye contact for a few seconds at a time, therefore she focused her attention on Trevon's mouth when she couldn't bear to look in his eyes after those few seconds were up. She studied his lips as he spoke. They were moving but no sound was coming out of his mouth, as if someone had hit a mute button and silenced everything around her.

Then she thought to herself: *His lips... he has the softest, most sensual lips a man could have.* They had the look of pleasure and made her imagine what they would feel like sucking on her lips. Then she imagined herself lying in Trevon's arms after he made love to her...

Monique banished those thoughts and anchored back to reality. That's when she realized that she'd been daydreaming—*damn!*

"Ms. Baker?" Trevon called out.

"*Huh?*"

"Are you okay?"

"*What?*"

"I said are you okay?" Trevon asked cautiously, over-pronouncing his words as if he were speaking to a hearing-impaired person.

"*Yes—I was just—I'm okay,*" Monique replied, getting choked up on her words. "*I—I was just...*" she didn't have to say anything else, the glimmer in her eyes testified to everything she felt. "Excuse me," Monique said, backing away from the table, "I need to use the restroom."

Trevon backed away from the table and stood as well.

"I think I can manage to find it myself, thank you," Monique said rudely.

"Knock yourself out," Trevon replied. "It's located in the hall beside the bar, second door on the left."

Monique turned and walked away, leaving the faint smell of her Victoria's Secret body spray behind. As she walked away, Trevon's eyes locked in on Monique's back, from the length of her slender torso and wide hips, to her knee-length skirt, then to her ass...

"*Um-um-um—goodness gracious!*" he said, under his breath. He could see the print of her panties and couldn't help but wonder what they smelled like.

Trevon looked over to the table where the elderly lady and her husband were sitting.

They smiled at him.

Trevon smiled back and raised his glass, gesturing a toast. "*Salud.*"

They did the same. "*Salud.*"

●　　　●　　　●

Tina had just got off the phone with Trevon when she heard a knock on the front door. Curious, she went to go answer it, wondering who it was because they never called from the security booth to inform her that she had a guest,

177

When she opened the door, standing before her was a short, barrel-shaped man flanked by two Palm Beach County Sheriff deputies.

"May I help you?" Tina asked rudely.

"Yes, I'm Detective Price with the Sheriff's department. Sorry to disturb you, but is this the residence of Trevon Jenkins?"

"No, it isn't," Tina answered nastily.

Price produced a phony smile. "Well, our records show that it is. Please ma'am, I don't have time for games. My patience is wearing thin. Now, is Trevon Jenkins here?"

"What is this all about?" Tina asked suspiciously.

"We just need to ask him a few questions," Price answered.

"About what?"

"That's on a need to know basis, and right now, you don't need to know."

"Is he in trouble?"

"No, we just need to ask him a few questions."

"Well, he's not here."

"Do you mind if we come in and take a look?"

"Do you have a search warrant?"

"No ma'am, but if you —" SLAM!

Tina slammed the door in the detective's face and ran straight to the phone to call Trevon. She dialed his number and got sent to his voice mail. So, that meant his phone was off.

Tina had been around long enough to know that it doesn't take three law enforcement officers to ask someone a few questions. Something was definitely wrong. Some kind of way, she had to get in touch with Trevon to let him know...

●   ●   ●

When Monique walked away she could feel Trevon's eyes burning a hole in her back. She tried to walk away as sexy as she could without making a fool of herself. When she stood up the wine went straight to her head and the room spun so hard she thought she was on a merry-go-round.

Was it the wine, or did Trevon stimulate her mind just that much? Or was is a mixture of both? Whatever it was, it had Monique gasping for air because her heart was racing.

When she made it to the restroom, she entered the nearest stall and locked the door behind her before sitting on the toilet to catch her breath. Being in Trevon's presence repulsed Monique, but at the same time it awakened feelings that had been lying dormant inside of her. Emotions that had been buried long ago were suddenly being aroused.

Trevon was everything Monique didn't want in a man: He was rude, arrogant, and obscene, but at the same time he exuded a sense of power that was unexplainable. A power that was like a magnet, and Monique felt like a helpless piece of metal being drawn to him.

Monique thought about when Trevon came to her office the day before, how Mary couldn't stop smiling at him, staring at him adoringly. Then she thought about how all eyes were on him when he walked into the restaurant.

There was no doubt in Monique's mind that Trevon could have almost any woman he wanted, so why was he after her? Her instincts told her that he was the type of man to have three or four women at a time simply because he could, so why should she play with her emotions only to be rejected when the next beautiful woman comes along and catches his eye?

Never again, she told herself. Especially after all the hell she went through in her last relationship. All this time, she had hid her feelings, guarding them against the pain that comes with rejection. Somehow, Trevon made all of this evaporate. She wanted him just as bad as he wanted her, if not more. The way he spoke to her with authority aroused her. Though, she didn't realize how aroused she was until she touched herself and saw how wet her panties were...

They were soaked through with her juices.

Monique couldn't recall ever being so wet. He pulled the crotch of her panties to the side and stuck two fingers inside of her. She pulled them out and rubbed her fingers and thumb together, feeling the slippery slickness of her pussy juices.

She closed her eyes and thought of Trevon's lips as nasty images began to cloud her mind: Her hand on the back of Trevon's head while it was shoved between her legs; the sound of his lips slurping on her pussy, glistening with her juices.

Monique was so caught up in her pipe dream she was unaware her hand was back inside her panties, biting her bottom lip as she stroked her clitoris...

The sound of the restroom door opening and closing brought her back to reality. Someone entered the stall next to hers, and seconds later, Monique heard the sound of urine splashing in the toilet, followed by the toilet flushing.

179

When Monique came out of the stall she saw the same elderly lady that was sitting at the table next to theirs. She was standing at the sink washing her hands. Monique noticed that they were veiny and frail, and the same color as parchment paper. They caught Monique's attention because the lady had on one of the most beautiful wedding rings she'd ever seen; the diamond was huge, almost the size of a nickel.

Monique stood beside her at the sink and washed her hands as the lady looked into the mirror at Monique's reflection. When she finished she grabbed a napkin and dried her hands as Monique did the same.

"I'm Julie," she said, offering her hand to be shaken, producing the same warm smile she displayed earlier.

"Monique," Monique said, grabbing Julie's hand and pumping it gently before letting go.

"Stop resisting..." Julie said, staring deeply into Monique's eyes. "He seems like a sweet guy, your friend out there—*and he's gorgeous!* Whatsdamatter with you, huh?" she said with a heavy Italian accent. "Hell, I'll take him if you don't want him. We could switch, you and me. You can have my Paulie out there. Just make sure you give him his insulin shots and pressure medication. Oh, and he has real bad gas, too, but you'll get used to it after a while..." She whispered the last part, looking around as if it were a classified secret. "So, do we have a deal?"

Monique giggled. "I don't think Paulie would like that so much. Why would he want me when he has such a beautiful companion?"

"You're full of shit," Julie chuckled, "but thank you anyways for the compliment..." There was a short silence as she gazed into Monique's eyes. "You only live once. Take it from me, time flies, kid. Enjoy life, because before you know it, you're gonna be sevety-five and wishing you would've followed your heart. You only get one shot at this life, so don't let it pass you by. Take my advice and go for it."

"I...I don't know," Monique said, hesitantly, "I would love to give it a chance, but I'm so afraid of being—"

"Don't be afraid," Julie said, cutting Monique off, "be willing. How would you ever know what could have been if you don't give love a chance, sweetheart? Trust me, Monique. You're talking to a woman that has been there and done that."

Monique smiled, "I hope you're right."

"I am. Now, go get'cha man."

"Thank you for the advice."

"*Ah, forgeddaboudit,*" Julie replied, "Now, let's get out of here before they think somebody kidnapped us..."

When Monique and Julie stepped out the restroom they heard the sound of someone laughing hysterically. That someone was Julie's husband, Paulie, better known as Paul Palmieri throughout Palm Beach. Paul was a multi-millionaire and the owner of P&J Jewelers, therefore he was well-known.

Monique and Julie returned to their tables and found Trevon sitting with Paul with a fresh bottle of wine. Mr. Palmieri was laughing so hard he was gasping for air.

"*Paulie!*" Julie exclaimed. "This is no good for you!" She looked at Trevon. "If I would've left you here a moment longer, I would've been a widow."

"*He's fuckin' hilarious!*" Paul said in between breaths. "I love 'em! I haven't laughed like this in years!"

Trevon stood and gestured for Julie to take a seat where he was just sitting. "Sorry, if I caused any trouble, Mrs. Palmieri," he said apologetically. "Paul was just telling me how wonderful it was to be married to such a lovely woman." Trevon continued, giving Paul a devilish wink.

When Monique saw what happened, she thought: *Damn! Is there anyone this man can't charm?*

Paul reached into his pocket and pulled out a business card. "Here," he said, handing Trevon the card. "Give me a call when the two of you are ready to make that move. We have some beautiful rings at the store this young lady would love."

Trevon's head bounced back and forth from the card to Paul before saying, "You own P&J Jewelers?"

"Yep, that's me," Paul answered. "I'm Paul and that's Julie."

"I see your commercials all the time!" Trevon said excitedly.

"Make sure you call me, Tre," Paul said before looking at Monique. "We'll get her into something nice."

Trevon looked at Monique and smiled. "How would you like that sweetheart?"

"That would be lovely," she answered sarcastically.

"Thanks, Mr. Palmieri," Trevon said, "I really appreciate it, and sorry for disturbing your lunch, Mrs. Palmieri."

"Not a problem, sweetie," Julie replied. "Don't be a stranger, make sure you call us."

Trevon and Monique returned to their table. After they sat down Monique stared at Trevon in silence...

"What were you and Paul really talking about, Mr. Jenkins?"

"I told him a joke."

"A joke?"

"Yeah, a joke."

"It must've been a helluva joke."

"Just some man stuff, nothing you would find funny."

"Enlighten me, you never know."

Trevon smiled and picked up the bottle of wine. "Would you like another glass?" he asked as he poured some for himself. "And no, I'm not trying to get you drunk so I can take advantage of you."

"I never said you were."

"No, you didn't, but isn't that what you were thinking?"

Monique smiled. "Actually, I was thinking that I would love another glass," she lied, "and why do you always do that?"

"Do what?" Trevon asked as he poured more wine in Monique's glass.

"Always assume, always think you know what someone is thinking?"

Trevon picked up his glass and leaned back in his chair. "Do you play chess?"

"No."

"Too bad, it's an interesting game. To be good at it, you have to learn how to get into the mind of your opponent."

Monique picked up her glass. "So, you feel it's necessary to get into my mind?" she asked before taking a sip of wine. "Is that what this is for you? Some kind of game?"

"Yes," Trevon answered truthfully. "That's exactly what this is. Not just this situation, though—life in general is one big-ass chess game. Some may not view it like that, but to me, that's exactly what life is. Life and chess, they are two different games, but you have to use the same strategy if you want to be successful in either one of them: stay two or three steps ahead of your opponent. There's an old saying: No man is your enemy. No man is your friend. Every man is your teacher... That's my perception of life, Ms. Baker. We should all rationalize and learn what each man or woman has to teach us. My whole life, I've strived for intuition. After doing so for so long, I don't have to try to figure anything out... things just come to me instinctively."

"Oh yeah?"

"Yes," Trevon answered with a smirk.

Monique studied Trevon suspiciously. "Okay...tell me what I'm thinking, and why do you keep smirking?"

"Because I knew you were gonna ask me that."

"See what I mean?!" Monique snapped. *"There you go again!"*

"I'm sorry, it's just a bad habit."

"A very bad habit, one that you need to break." Monique put her glass down. "So...are you going to answer my question?"

Trevon starred at Monique in silence for moment. "Do you really want to know, Ms. Baker?"

"Yes, I do. I wouldn't have asked if I didn't."

Trevon sighed uncomfortably before he began: "You find me attractive—very attractive—which is why you agreed to have lunch with me. You many not mix business with pleasure, but so far, it's been a real pleasure doing business with me. So, you said to yourself, '*what the hell, it won't hurt anything to discuss his case over lunch.*' Besides, this is a business arrangement, right? Well, that's what you thought it was gonna be, up until you conversed with me and got to know me a little better. And the more you speak to me, and the more you listen to me, the more you realize I'm not the person you thought I was. I'm no longer some criminal you're defending, am I? You can't quite figure me out and your curiosity is getting the best of you... You can say what you want, Ms. Baker, but deep down inside I know you want me."

"*Hmph!* I do?"

"Yes."

"And what makes you think that?"

Trevon took a sip of wine as he looked deeply into Monique's eyes. "*Your eyes...*" he said, "your eyes are begging me to fuck you... You want nothing more than for me to take you home right now so I could make love to you, but you can't give in that easy because what would I think of you? What would be going through my mind if you gave in that easy? How would I ever be able to respect you?" Trevon leaned back in his chair, flaunting the same devious smirk he displayed moments earlier. "So, am I right? Did I hit the nail on the head, Ms. Baker?"

Monique took a big gulp of wine to keep her composure; Trevon saw straight through her.

"You know what I think?" she asked before taking another gulp. "I think you're a rude, arrogant, egotistical, self-centered, sonofabitch! Yes, you're a handsome man, but that doesn't give you the right to talk to me or any other real woman that way! Who the hell do you think you are? You're not God's gift to earth, Mr. Jenkins. I'm sorry you got the wrong impression when I agreed to have lunch with you, but my intentions were strictly business and nothing more..."

Trevon smiled.

"Wipe that stupid-ass smile off your face!" Monique snapped. "I don't see what's so goddamn funny!"

"You are, Ms. Baker...you contradicted yourself. You said your intentions were strictly business and nothing more, right?"

"Correct."

"Then why haven't you asked me one thing about my case?"

"Because I wanted to... you never gave me... we were..." Monique was at a loss for words. She looked away, unable to look Trevon in his face.

Trevon's smile melted as he reached for Monique's hand. "Look at me, Monique..." he said, gently squeezing her hand, trying to make eye contact with her. "Look at me—please! I want to look you in the eyes when I tell you this."

Reluctantly, Monique held her head up and looked Trevon in the eyes.

"Disrespecting you is the last thing I would ever want to do. When you agreed to have lunch with me, I was ecstatic. I didn't know how to present myself, or how to act, or what to say—you're a friggin' lawyer for chrissakes! I'm pretty sure you came from a good family, went to a good school, pledged some sorority and more than likely, you were on some kind of debate team or whatever it is that Jr. lawyers do... That's your world, and I was like, *wow*, how can I be a part of your world when the world I live in is so far away? I was so overwhelmed because I never pledged any fraternity, shit, I ain't even been to college. So, I asked myself, how can I impress this woman? What should I do? What should I say? How should I act? I came to one conclusion: Be myself. Yes, I'm rude. Yes, I'm arrogant. Yes, my mouth gets a little fly at times, but at least I'm honest. I could've come here and pretended to be everything I'm not, and said everything you wanted to hear, but I could never be something I'm not... I'll tell you what I am, though... and that's crazy about you. I haven't lied about anything yet, so why should I start now? I'm sorry if I came on too strong, but if I see something I want, I'm gonna go after it. Monique, I never wanted anything in my life the way I want you, and I'm willing to do whatever it takes to get you..." Trevon rubbed the side of Monique's face. "You're so beautiful."

Monique felt herself blush.

"I know my past is shady," Trevon continued. "There are a lot of things I would change if I could turn back the hands of time. We all make mistakes; that's why pencils have erasers on 'em. Please don't make a mistake by judging me. Give me a chance to get to know you..." Trevon folded his hands together as if he were about the pray, "*pleeease.*"

Monique smiled, "Don't do that."

"Do what?"

"You know what?"

"What?" Trevon asked innocently.

"Make that face."

Trevon grabbed Monique's hand again. "Look, you don't have to answer me now. All I ask is that you give it some thought, okay?"

Monique looked down for a short moment.

Trevon looked over at Mrs. Palmieri and she gave him the thumbs-up.

"Okay..." Monique said, looking at Trevon, "I'll give it some thought."

"Promise?"

"Yes."

"Pinky swear promise?" Trevon said, sticking his pinky out.

"Yes," Monique chuckled.

"Come on, lock it in," Trevon said, wiggling his pinky. "You can do it, you can do it."

Slowly, Monique raised her hand and locked pinkies with Trevon.

"Thank you," he said, bringing her hand up to his mouth and kissing her knuckles. "I promise you won't regret it."

Trevon's lips brushing against Monique's skin sent chills throughout her body. Reluctantly, she pulled her hand away and took a deep breath, trying her best to keep her composure...

"I have to get back to the office, Trevon."

Trevon took note that she called him by his first name for the first time since they met.

I'm getting somewhere after all, he thought to himself.

Trevon waved for the waitress. "Check, please."

●　　　●　　　●

Detective Price was parked across the street from Amici in an unmarked car, with two marked units parked behind him. He went in an hour earlier to see if Trevon was working when he saw him sitting at the table having lunch with a female companion. There were too many people in the restaurant, so they decided to apprehend him when he comes out.

"Come out, you sonofabitch," Price mumbled to himself, and seconds later, Trevon came out with his female friend. *"That's our man!"* Price barked into his radio. With his hand on his Glock, he and two deputies rushed across the street. "Trevon Jenkins?!" Price called out.

Trevon turned around with a puzzled expression on his face. "Who wanna know?" he asked suspiciously.

185

Price flashed his badge. "Palm Beach County Sheriff's Department. We need to ask you a few questions."

Monique jumped in front of Trevon. "About what?"

"I'm not at liberty to say right now," Price answered.

"Well, then Mr. Jenkins isn't at liberty to speak to you," Monique fired back.

"And you are?"

"His lawyer."

"I'm afraid he has to come with us," Price replied as the two deputies flanked Trevon, one of them pulling out a taser.

"Put your hands on top of your head," the other deputy ordered, pulling out a pair of handcuffs.

"AIN'T THIS 'BOUT A BITCH!" Trevon yelled in disbelief.

"Is my client under arrest?" Monique asked, blocking the deputy.

"Put your hands on top of your head," the deputy ordered, "I'm not gonna tell you again."

Reluctantly, Trevon put his hands on top of his head and the deputy secured his hands behind his back as Price stood in front of them.

"Don't say a word until I get there, Mr. Jenkins," Monique ordered. "What's my client being charged with?"

"Murder," Price answered now that they had Trevon in custody. "You have the right to remain silent. If you give up the right to remain silent, anything you say may be used against you in the court of law. You have the right to an attorney. If you cannot afford an attorney, one will be appointed to you. Do you understand these rights?"

"Get the *fuck* out of my face, cracker," Trevon hissed.

Price smiled. "Very well... haul his ass."

"Don't say a word until I get there!" Monique yelled as they drug Trevon to the car. "Not a word!"

Less than 50 feet away, Frank Rosario watched Trevon get arrested from upstairs in his office window...

"Isn't that the kid that works for us?" he asked his bodyguard, Eddie.

"Yeah, boss," Eddie answered nervously.

"What the hell is going on around here? This ain't good for business," Frank said, looking at John, his other bodyguard. I want you to call one of our people down at the Sheriff's Department and find out what's going on, capisci?"

"Okay, Frank," John answered.

"And Eddie, go downstairs and get Joey. Tell 'em I said, get up here—*now!*"

"Okay, boss," Eddie replied before going to do as he was told.

As soon as Eddie stepped out of Frank's office, he loosened his tie because it felt as if someone was choking him. Beads of sweat started to form on his forehead because he knew the shit was about to hit the fan. It was just a matter of time until Frank found out Trevon got arrested because of Joey, and that meant it as just a matter of time until Frank found out that Eddie had been helping Joey do business with Victor Pagan...

As soon as Frank found out, Eddie knew he was as good as dead.

8

Deja Vu

Trevon was escorted to an interrogation room that bared a clock, a metal table and four metal chairs that were bolted to the floor. After entering the room, he sat in one of the chairs that was directly in front of a gigantic 2-way mirror and smiled. He'd watched enough movies to know what the mirror was for, and that the fat-ass detective that had arrested him was on the other side smiling himself.

"Let's get this show on the road, fat boy. I ain't got all day," Trevon said before leaning back in the chair.

"Fat boy?" Detective Price chuckled as he looked at Trevon belligerently. "You ain't gon' have nothing but time if you don't play ball, nigger." Detective Price mumbled under his breath. He decided to let Trevon sweat a little bit before going into the interrogation room, and though he didn't show it, that's exactly what Trevon was doing. He was scared to death. He knew he was being charged with murder, but who's murder? He was brainstorming, trying to remember some of the dirt he'd done as questions began to emerge: Who? When? Where? Did they have any evidence? If so, how much did they have?

Trevon wanted answers, and he wanted them desperately. Anticipation became more and more vivid as the clock on the wall ticked like a time bomb, waiting to explode. *How in the hell did I slip?* Trevon thought to himself. The past was finally coming to haunt him.

The door unlocked and opened. Detective Price walked in holding a tape recorder and a folder. "Hello, Mr. Jenkins," Price said as he sat down. "We got off on the wrong foot earlier, we never got a chance to get acquainted...I'm Detective Price," Price said as he extended his had to be shaken.

"Man, what da lick read?" Trevon asked, ignoring Price's hand.

Price looked confused. "*What da lick read...?* I'm afraid I don't understand the lingo. What exactly does that mean, Mr. Jenkins?"

"That means wussup? Wushappening? That means why the fuck do you have me here? You ain't talking 'bout a goddamn thang! I ain't got shit to say to you—I want my lawyer!"

"Your lawyer can't help you right now, Mr. Jenkins. The only people that can help you right now are you and I... if you allow me to."

"I ain't friendly, dude. You're wasting your time."

Price turned on the tape recorder and then turned if off before saying, "Mr. Jenkins, may I ask you a logical question—off the record?"

"Yeah... you're just gonna get a null answer—off the record."

"I like that," Price chuckled, producing a phony smile. He opened the folder and took out a picture and slid it across the table to Trevon. "You know what that is?" he asked.

Trevon picked it up. It was a picture of a .380 semi-automatic, the same .380 Eddie had given him the day Joey asked him to meet Victor Pagan's people with the counterfeit money. "It's a gun," Trevon answered casually, "a .380 if I'm not mistaken."

"Does it look familiar?" Price asked suspiciously.

"Why should it?"

"Because that's the gun that was found in your possession... the same gun you used to kill Louie Gurino—"

"Louie who?" Trevon asked feeling relieved. He'd done dirt, but he knew he didn't kill anyone named Louie Gurino—he didn't even know anyone name Louie.

"You know what I think, Mr. Jenkins?"

"No, I don't know what you think. Who the fuck I look like—Ms. Cleo?"

"I think you got the gun from the same people that gave you the counterfeit money—the same people that killed Louie Gurino. You think they give a fuck about you? If they did, they wouldn't have given you a piece they used to whack somebody with."

"I don't know what you're talkin' about," Trevon replied, "cause nobody ain't give me shit! I never seen that gun or money until they pulled it from out the car... If you let me tell it, y'all put that shit in there." Trevon was trying his best to conceal his anger. He couldn't believe Joey gave him a gun that had a body on it.

"Bullshit, Jenkins! I've been doing this shit for over twenty years! You were still suckin' yo mama's titty when I started sending shit like you to the chain gang! The same chain gang you're going to if you don't start yappin'. I could help you... you could walk right out of here if you play your cards right. If not, I'll put you under the jail."

Trevon sat in deep thought before he spoke. "All right, what's in it for me?"

"Your life. Your freedom... I could make all this disappear—no court dates, no prosecutors, no judges."

"What do you want in return?"

189

"The whole enchilada," Price answered with a devious smirk. He knew Trevon was going to play ball—they all did—but he didn't know it was going to be this easy. "I wanna know where the money came from, how it's being printed, and who's printing it."

"What assurance do I have?"

"My word," Price answered reassuringly.

Trevon thought in silence for a short moment before saying, "All right, I'll talk. Turn the recorder on 'cause I'm only gon' say this shit once."

Price grabbed the recorder, turned it on, and placed it in the center of the table. "Today is Thursday, October fourth, two thousand seven. I'm Detective Price, badge number three-eight-six, and I'm present with suspect Trevon Jenkins... Mr. Jenkins will you please stated your name and date of birth for the record, please."

Trevon folded his hands and leaned toward the tape recorder. "Trevon Jenkins. Date of birth: eight twenty-nine seventy-eight."

"Mr. Jenkins, where did you get the counterfeit money that was found in your possession?"

"From an associate that's been hanging with me for years."

"What's his name?"

"Malong."

"Malong...? Malong who?"

Trevon picked up the tape recorder and spoke directly into it: "Malong dick, bitch! And you can suck it if you think I'ma fuckin snitch! Now go take that to the grand jury."

"Fuck you, Jenkins!"

"Naw, don't fuck me—fuck with me—that's what you do, ole pussy-ass cracker!"

Price turned the recorder off. "I'ma railroad you somethin' terrible, boy. You're gonna wish you did snitch."

"Run that shit then, bitch! Let's crank that jury up—you ain't got yourself nothin'! You stink, muthafucker! You're supposed to be investigating a murder and you're in this bitch asking me about sum muthafuckin' money—fuck you take me for, pig?"

"What I take you for...?" Price chuckled. "What I take you for isn't the question... the question is, what I'm about to take you for, boy? I'm about to take you for a ride... for a real long time."

●   ●   ●

"At the tone, please state your name—beep," the automated voice instructed.

"Aye, Fresh, this Tre, accept the call," Trevon stated.

Seconds later, Tracy, Fresh's girlfriend, answered the phone, "Hello, Tre?"

"What da lick read?"

"What happened? Are you okay?"

"I don't know yet, shawdy. Where my nigga at?"

"Hold on—FRESH PICK UP THE PHONE!" Trevon heard Tracy yell.

"Who dis?" Fresh asked, inhaling a mouthful of smoke.

"It's me, bug... these crackers got me in the weaver."

"What...?"

"I'm locked up, nigga—"

"You're what?!"

"I'm back in jail, dirty."

"For what?"

"A body."

"Say it ain't so, son!"

"Yeah... I'm good, though. Some dude named Louie somethin'... never heard of him, so I know they ain't got shit."

"Why poe-poe keep fuckin' wit'choo, son?"

"That hammer I got popped with last month—it had a body on it. Do you believe that shit...? After all the shit—after all the bullshit—and I get bagged for somebody else's bullshit."

"What'choo need for me to do?"

"Call correctional billing and put some money on your phone pre-paid so I can call your cell phone."

"It's done, nigga. Tina know yet?"

"Naw, call her on three-way for me."

"A'ight, you ready?"

"Yeah, go ahead," Trevon answered before he started blowing into the mouthpiece while tapping on it with his finger so the phone wouldn't hang up. The phone company implemented a new program to prevent callers inside correctional institutions from doing three-way calls. So, if the system heard the line click over, it would automatically terminate the call. But you already know how black people are...

They'll find a way to buck the system: "Hello? Tre?" Tina called out after Fresh clicked back over. "What happened, baby?"

"Shit crazy, you hear me? Shit fucked all up. Where are you?"

"With Casey?"

191

"I need you to get in contact with Joey. I can't talk over these phones, but you already know what da lick read."

"I know, Tre, I know."

"Just stick to the script, a'ight?"

"Jenkins!" a deputy yelled. "Time to go—wrap it up!"

"I gotta go, y'all—Fresh?"

"Yeah."

"Don't forget to do that."

"No doubt."

"I love you, Tre," Tina said sincerely.

"I love you too."

Minutes later, Trevon was standing in a stall where he was told to strip naked. He was searched and told to lift up his testicles, and to squat and cough before trading in his $1,500 Armani suit. In return, he got a set of county blues, a toothbrush, toothpaste, and a bed roll...

"Jenkins, grab a mat. You're going to West-Six, A block," the deputy said, when they reached the elevator.

When Trevon stepped into the open bay dorm he was scrutinized by a gang of inmates that were in the dayroom watching TV. Like a lion claiming his domain, he dropped his mat and made eye contact with all of them one-by-one, with a screwed-up face, until they all turned to watch TV again.

It's an unspoken rule of the jailhouse: never tuck your tail and cower. Jail is a jungle... a concrete jungle. And just like any other jungle, a predator can smell fear like a heavy cologne. The first 30 seconds determine how one will do their time in the jungle...

Trevon was letting it be known that he was at the top of the food chain.

"Aye, you can't leave your mat right there, homeboy," an older dark-skinned dude said in a nasty tone.

"I'm not a new cock, nigga!" Trevon replied, matching his tone.

"I'm not saying that you are, dawg," the man said in a more civilized manner. "I'm just telling you 'cause I'm the houseman, that's all."

Reluctantly, Trevon picked up his mat and threw it in the bunk area before getting on the phone. He tried calling Tina's and Fresh's cell phones, but they were still collect call restricted. He tried calling Fresh at home but got no answer, so he called Desiree...

"Why the fuck you back in jail, Tre?!" she demanded after accepting the call.

"Don't start that shit, Dee. I'm not trying to hear that shit right now."

"I'm just sayin', Tre! You just got the fuck out, and you ain't even come see you son. Yeah, that's right, nigga. I know exactly when you bonded out the day before yesterday because I called up there, mutherfucker!"

"Will you please shut the fuck up—*damn*! You're always talkin' muthafuckin' shit! I didn't have a chance to go see Lil Tre."

"Why?"

"Fuck you mean 'why'? 'Cause I got locked up—that's why."

"For what?"

"Murder."

"Murder?!"

"Did I stutter?"

"Well goddamn, Tre! Who the fuck you done killed?"

"I ain't killed nobody... Look, it's a long story—"

"Well then start talkin'!"

"Desiree, please—"

"Please?! What the fuck you going through? Yous about to tell me somethin'!"

"All right, but not now—now ain't the time, Dee. Please understand what the fuck I'm tellin' you... please."

The was a short silence.

"Are you okay?" Desiree asked sympathetically.

"I'm good. Where's my son?"

"Running the streets, where else? What am I supposed to tell him, Tre?"

"I didn't do it—I swear I didn't. It's a mistake—a big mistake."

"I hope so, Tre; your son needs you."

"You don't think I know that?"

"I know you do, it's just... he needs you in his life, Tre."

"I'm gonna be in it... I'm getting out of here, Dee."

"I really hope so, Tre."

"I am... Look, I need you to do a three-way call for me."

"All right, who you want me to call?"

"Tina—"

"Tina?! Nigga! You might've tried me! I ain't callin' that bitch!"

"Goddamn, Dee! Will you please let that shit go for a minute?" Trevon heard Desiree suck her teeth and could visualize her rolling her eyes.

"All right... I'll call her this one time, but don't ask me to call that bitch again, Tre—you ready?"

"Yeah," Trevon replied before tapping on the mouthpiece.

193

"Hello?"

"Tina?"

"I put money on my cell phone, but they said it could take up to twenty-four hours for the line to open up. Did you try to call?"

"Yeah, it's still blocked. Did you get up with Joey yet?"

"No, not yet."

"I really need you to get in contact with—"

"I got you, baby, I got you."

"Please, Tina ... it's important that you get in contact with him."

"I got you, Tre. I've been callin' but can't get in touch with him. What else you want me to do?"

Trevon sighed. "I know you're doing everything in your power. Just keep trying, ok?"

"I will..." Tina replied. "I love you, Tre. I'm gonna get you out, okay?"

"Aw, bitch!" Desiree exclaimed. "I'm not about to sit here and listen to this shit, Tre! *Fuck wrong wit'choo?* You gots me fucked up!"

"Why don't you grow the fuck up?" Tina said.

"Fuck you, bitch!" Desiree retorted. "I paid for the muthafuckin' call!"

"WILL Y'ALL PLEASE STOP?!" Trevon yelled.

"Y'all?!" Tina quipped. "It ain't no y'all—that's yo baby momma!"

"That's right, bitch," Desiree said, "the baby momma—and you better goddamn respect it—" *Click.*

The line went dead.

"SHIT!" Trevon yelled.

"Hey, people back there trying to sleep. Hold it down a little, bruh," the houseman said.

Trevon hung up the phone and took a deep breath. "Look here, homeboy..." he said as calmly as he could. "I'ma tell you this one time and one time only: It's a fuckin' gorilla in that tree you're barking up—a fuckin' gorilla—you hear me?"

"Whatever," the houseman mumbled under his breath.

"That's strike two... strike three you're out," Trevon said before picking up the phone to call Desiree again. "What's your problem, girl?" he asked after she accepted the call.

"I don't want to hear that shit, Tre! And I'ma crack yo muthafuckin' head when I see you again, nigga! You know I don't play that shit—and I'ma fuck that bitch up, too! Talkin' 'bout some *'I love you, Tre. I'm gonna get you out, okay?'"* Desiree said, doing her best impression of Tina. "I don't wanna hear that shit! You know I hate that bitch, Tre!"

"DESIREE, PLEASE!" Trevon yelled.

"Hold that muthafuckin' noise down—I'm trying to sleep!" someone yelled from the bunk area.

"Fuck nigga—bond out!" Trevon yelled back. "This jail; sleep when you can, not when you want—fuck wrong wit'choo?"

"Who the fuck you talkin' to?" the man asked, sitting up to put on his sneakers.

"Who the fuck you strappin' up for?!" Trevon asked, hanging up the phone and running toward the man, trying to catch him before he had a chance to tie his shoes. When he got close enough, he saw that the man was bigger than he looked from a distance...

A lot bigger.

DAMN! Trevon thought to himself when he saw how big his neck and arms were- it was too late though.

Trevon swung and hit him on the chin with all he had before putting him in the headlock. The man still got up and lifted Trevon like a rag doll, swinging him from side-to-side. Trevon stayed locked on his neck like a pit bull locked on a tire. That's when the houseman came from the blind side and popped Trevon in the eye; at that very moment, he understood what it meant to see stars.

Trevon squeezed the man's neck as tight as he could and used his body as a shield to keep the houseman from landing another blow. Seconds later, the block was stormed by a bunch of deputies and the altercation was broken up.

Trevon had never been so happy to see the police.

"Y'ALL NIGGAS DONE FUCKED UP!" Trevon yelled, being handcuffed and hauled off to lock down. "If I ever catch one of you niggas—issa wrap!"

●   ●   ●

Déjà vu was an understatement for what Trevon felt as he stared into the mirror. Here he was, back in lock down... in the same jail... on the same block... and in the same cell he'd left from two days earlier.

"Ain't this 'bout a bitch?" he mumbled to himself as he rubbed his eye.

That's when he heard the same irritating voice...

"Ahh, haa, haa—didn't I tell you that you'd be back, state baby?" the deputy chuckled.

"You ain't got nothin' better to do, peckerwood?" Trevon asked as he stared in the mirror.

"You know what, state baby? A couple of days ago, you had the audacity to call me a fool, to call me dumb. Who's the fool now, state baby? You just couldn't stay away, huh?"

"I'm back in here for the same shit I didn't..." Trevon cut short what he was about to say and looked at the deputy. "Man, fuck you! You don't know me, muthafucker! I'ma human being just like you—"

"Well the quit acting like a fuckin' animal, Jenkins. Look at you— you're in a freakin' cage. My dog doesn't have to sleep in a cage, and you do..." There was a short silence as the deputy stared at Trevon, shaking his head. "You say that you're a man, Jenkins; a man doesn't get himself caged up. Do you really think I enjoy coming here to see a grown man caged up? You're right, you're not an animal. You're a human being, just like me, and under this uniform, I'ma human being, just like you. This is my job, this is what I do—I don't enjoy doing it—but it's what I do, what I have to do to take care of my family. A family I get to go home to every night... Get your shit together, Jenkins. This isn't living, my friend."

The deputy opened Trevon's cell.

"What, you're about to kick my ass now?"

"For what?" the deputy asked. "That's not my job; my job is care, custody, and control."

"What'choo open my cell for then?"

"Because you have an attorney visit, state baby... you wanna go or not?" the deputy asked with a smile.

Trevon stepped out the cell with his hands held out in front of him. "You gon' cuff me up or what?"

"For what, state baby? The deputy asked. "Do I need to put handcuffs on you?"

"Naw..." Trevon answered as he lowered his hands, "I'm straight."

"Well, let's get going, state baby," the deputy replied, "and we'll stop by medical on the way back to get you an ice pack for that eye."

Trevon looked at the deputy, not knowing what to say...

"Thank you," he said moments later.

●　　　●　　　●

When Trevon arrived at the attorney visiting room, Monique was already there waiting. He could see the unmistakable look of concern in her eyes when she saw how black and blue his eye was...

"Oh-my-god! What happened to your eye?" she asked sympathetically.

"I'm okay. I just got into a little altercation."

"Are you, all right?"

"I'm good," Trevon chuckled, "you should see the other guys, though."

"Guys...?"

"Yeah, guys—plural. They got on my ass. I'm good, though."

Monique studied Trevon suspiciously. "I've been trying to see you for the past eight hours and they've been giving me the run around. I'm glad to see you, although I must say not under these conditions or circumstances..." Monique tried to make herself smile. Truth was, it hurt her to see Trevon locked up gain. "Well, I tried to find out what I could about this new case. It wasn't much, but I do know that you're being charged with the murder of—"

"Louie Gurino," Trevon said, cutting Monique off.

"How did you find out?" she asked suspiciously.

"From the detective."

"Please tell me you didn't speak to him."

"Hell naw."

"Good..." Monique gazed into Trevon's eyes. "Well, did you do it?"

"No—hell no!" Trevon replied, holding his head down. "Look, Monique... I know you think I'm full of shit, but I really didn't do this. Please believe me—I didn't do it. I'm so sick of this..." Trevon looked up with tears in his eyes."

"Sick of what?" Monique asked, grabbing Trevon's hand.

"Sick of being locked up. Sick of this jail," Trevon indicated with a wave of his hand. "Sick of the bullshit... I'm sick of living like this." Tears began to pour as he squeezed Monique's hand.

"Don't cry, Trevon. I'm gonna do everything in my power to get you out of here. I promise, all right?"

"How much more money will you need?"

"We'll cross that bridge when we get to it; right now, we need to focus on getting you out of here. You have an arraignment tomorrow morning."

"Will you be able to get me another bond?"

"You let me worry about that. I already told you; I' good at what I do... You want me to believe in you...? I need you to start believing in me."

"I do."

"Good...then let me get you out of here tomorrow."

197

Monique had to fight back tears as she rode the elevator down to the release lobby. She was getting emotionally involved with a client, something she swore she would never do. She wanted Trevon out and was going to pull whatever trick she had to pull to see that he got a bond.

It was something about him that enchanted her. He was funny, smart, and sensitive, on top of being sincere. He was nothing like the person she thought he was. Something was telling her that he really was innocent and was just a victim of circumstances...

That made her all the more determined to see to it that he was free.

9

A Raw Deal

Tracy was 19, with a chocolate complexion, hazel eyes, plump lips, chunky hips, an even chunkier booty, and long, thick firm legs... This is why Fresh made her his main and spoiled her to death.

There wasn't anything that Tracey wanted that Tracy didn't get. Although Tracy looked like she could be eye candy in XXL magazine, there was one flaw that Tracy possessed: Tracy wasn't too bright...

That was okay with Fresh, though, because not only was Tracy super fine, she could also do things with her mouth that made Fresh's toes curl. So, in his book that made up for her dumbness...

"Get me a pack of Newports and a fruit punch," Fresh said to Tracy as they parked in front of the QuickStop.

"Get me one, too," Tina added, giving Tracy a $5 bill.

Tracy took the money and said, "Okay...what kind of juice y'all want me to get?"

"I told you fruit punch, boo." Fresh answered.

"You know...*the red stuff,*" Tina added sarcastically.

"Oh...yeah..." Tracy replied lamely before getting out of the car and going into the QuickStop.

"Where the fuck you got that dumb, dingy-ass bitch from Fresh?" Tina asked after Tracy got out.

"I done told you about disrespecting my boo!" Fresh replied defensively.

"Fuck *yo' boo.*"

"Naw, muthafuck you!"

"She need to hurry up! If I miss Tre's arraignment, I'ma beat that footdragon to death!"

"She ain't no goddamn footdragon! Stop callin' her that shit!" Fresh demanded as a black Escalade pulled up beside them, banging a Trick Daddy song.

It's occupants, Chauncey and three members of his "O.F.L." clique: Big Cush, Roam, and Killer emerged from the SUV just as Tracy walked out the QuickStop.

"Damn, lil mama!" Big Cush exclaimed.

"When you gon' come fuck wit' a real nigga?" Killer added while giving Chauncey dap.

"Where's your buster-ass boyfriend at anyways?" Roam asked, not seeing Fresh behind the dark tint of Tina's Acura.

"You're callin' my name, you must be lookin' for me—*here I go!*" Fresh said, stepping out the car and cocking a round into the chamber of his Glock .40.

"Fresh, no!" Tracy pleaded, stepping between Fresh and Roam.

"Wussup then, nigga," Roam asked, reaching for his pistol.

Tina grabbed Fresh just as he was about to take aim: "Use your damn head, Fresh!" she said spinning him around.

"Chill out, nigga," Chauncey said to Roam.

"I was just playing with his punk-ass," Roam replied.

"I ain't gon' be nan 'nother punk or buster, pussy-ass nigga!" Fresh said.

Chauncey took a step forward, hands raised in truce. "Everything cool, Fresh. Don't pay that nigga Roam no mind. You know how he is."

"Get the fuck out my face, Chauncey!" Fresh snapped. "I don't know a goddam thing... But I know you know something, though. You know who shot me, muthafucker."

"You're still on that shit, Fresh? Ain't none of my peoples shot you, cuz. You're trippin', my nigga."

"Let's go, Fresh," Tina said, getting back in her car. "We don't have time for this shit."

"Heeeey, Tiiinaaa," Big Cush sang.

"Where's Tre?" Killer asked.

"Yeah—the other buster," Roam added, and all four of them burst out laughing.

"We gon' see who the busters are, bitch-ass niggas," Tina replied defensively.

"Y'all gon' get it," Fresh said, as he and Tracy got back in the car, "that's my muthafuckin' word."

"Whatever, nigga," Chauncey replied as Roam pointed his finger at Fresh, imitating a gun and mouthing the word *"Pow!"*

●   ●   ●

Tina, Fresh, and Tray entered the courtroom just as the bailiff said, "All rise! Court is now in session. The Honorable Judge Kenneth Erwin presiding."

"You may now be seated," Judge Erwin said. "First case on the docket please."

"Yes, Your Honor," said the prosecutor, "That would be the state of Florida versus Terrence Taylor…"

Monique said a silent prayer as she sat, waiting for Trevon's case to be called. She had been up all night thinking about him, and even dreamed of him when she finally fell asleep. No matter how hard she tried, she couldn't get her mind off him. She found herself smiling inwardly when she thought about the conversation they had the day before. He had made her laugh more in the hour they'd spent together during lunch than she had in the past three years…

"Trevon Jenkins, case number 26134FB6FLA," Monique heard, bringing her out of her daze.

Trevon and Monique made their way to the podium.

"Yes, Your Honor," the prosecutor began, "Mr. Jenkins is being charged with murder in the first degree."

"How do you plea?" Judge Erwin asked.

"Not guilty," Monique answered.

"Very well," Judge Erwin replied with a nod.

"Your Honor, we're requesting bail at this time," Monique said before the prosecutor intervened.

"You Honor, the state strongly objects! The defendant is being accused of murder and faces life or the death penalty. If given the opportunity he may flee from—"

"If my client possessed such intentions he would have absconded by now!" Monique interjected. "I would also like to bring to your attention, Your Honor, that my client was already out on bond for the initial case in which this case was conceived. If you would read the probable cause affidavit, you will find that all evidence against my client is circumstantial. And the law states that, and I quote, 'offenses except murder and treason shall be bailable by sufficient sureties. Murder and treason shall not be bailable when the proof is evident, or the presumption is strong,' end quote. In the state versus Brock, our supreme court held that if the state seeks to deny bail to a person charged with murder, it has the burden of proving that there is proof of, or a presumption of the defendant's guilt which is evident or strong. In the light of the Brock case, it appears that the state has the burden—not Mr. Jenkins. And the law also states that the prosecution must prove beyond reasonable doubt that the defendant is guilty… After reading the probable cause affidavit, I'm sure that you will agree that my client has no reason to 'flee' from the state or anywhere else."

Trevon looked at Monique admiringly as the judge read over the probable cause affidavit. He didn't understand half of what she was saying, but it sounded good, and from the way the prosecutor was looking, it had to be on point...

Monique looked at Trevon and smiled.

"I've read the file," Judge Erwin said, "and reviewed the prosecution's affidavit in support of no bond. However, I also read the probable cause affidavit and take into consideration that all evidence against the accused is circumstantial. Therefore, I will set bail at a hundred and fifty thousand dollars... This case is assigned to Judge Berman, Division R, for all purposes. Court is now in recess."

"*A hundred and fifty thousand dollars?!*" Trevon exclaimed after the judge left the bench.

"It was the best we could do, Trevon. It's a murder charge, so of course, the bond is going to be high. At least he gave us bail—"

"*Bail?!* That's not bail—that's a fuckin' ransom!" Trevon replied sarcastically.

"Can you make it?"

"I don't know... ten percent of that is what, fifteen thousand dollars? I think my peoples can get that up, but it may take some time. Like you said: at least we got bail... Thank you, Ms. Baker."

"I told you, Mr. Jenkins—I'm good at what I do. I need you to start believing in me, okay?"

"I have no other choice after that."

"Well..." Monique said with a smile, "let's try this again: Call me when you get out, so we can schedule an appointment."

"Why does it feel like all this has happened before?" Trevon asked jokingly.

"Because it has," Monique chuckled, "and let's hope it's the last time, Mr. Jenkins..."

●　　　　●　　　　●

Tina was so excited that she didn't pay attention to the two men dressed in dark suits that departed with them after the judge stated Trevon's bond. Her mission had one objective: get Trevon out ASAP.

After calling the bondsman she found out she would need 10% of $150,000 ($15,000), and then another $5,000 for collateral... $20,000 total.

Fresh gave her $5,000 to put with the $5,000 she had saved, and after finessing Dexter for the other $10,000, her mission was complete.

After all their scrambling, they went to the bondsman with the intentions of getting Trevon out only to find out that his bond had been paid, and that he was going to be released as soon as the paperwork cleared.

Not knowing what else to do, they made their way the county jail so they could be there when Trevon walked out the door...

•   •   •

Detective Larry Burke got his nick name from his curly, strawberry blond hair. "Curly Top" is what they called him in the streets.

Detective Burke joined the Riviera Beach Police Department around the same time his cousin, Detective Kurt Price, joined the Palm Beach County Sheriff's Department. Since then he'd been a part of every unit and task force the Riviera Beach Police Department had to offer. And of all the units and task forces he'd been a part of, it was one that accommodated him well: The Narcotics Task Force.

Detective Burke was the lieutenant of that task force, and he ruled it with an iron fist. He and his selected few terrorized the drug dealers and prostitutes of Riviera Beach. They would raid one trap house, abusing its occupants before robbing them of money, jewelry, and drugs, then would drop off the drugs to another trap house to be sold by their workers.

Kidnapping. Murder. Extortion. Drugs. Prostitution—you name it, and you could rest assure that Curly Top and his goons had their hands in it...

"This is first class work," Curly Top said, holding up one of the counterfeit bills Price had stolen from the evident room.

"This is our ticket out of the game," Price replied with a smile.

"Is he cooperating?"

"No, not yet."

"Who is it?"

"Jenkins—Trevon Jenkins."

"*Tre?!*" Curly Top asked in shock.

"Yeah, that's him. You know him?"

Curly Top frowned. "Yeah...we got our hands full with him. He's a bucker, not very cooperative."

"He'll cooperate," Price replied, "if not, I'll—"

203

Price's cell phone rang. He answered it as Curly Top continued to examine the bill, trying to find a flaw, but couldn't.

"What the fuck do you mean he bonded out?!" Price yelled into the phone. "How?!" Moments later, he hung up the phone: "The cocksucker bonded out!" Price said in disbelief. "A hundred and fifty thousand dollars, and the fucker bonds out like it's nothin'!"

"That might be a good thing, cousin," Curly Top said. "Use your head, moron... Now we can squeeze him. How could we have done that if he's locked up?"

"Yeah..." Price replied with a twinkle in his eyes, "I guess you're right."

"I know I am. Now all we have to do is sit back and watch him and he'll lead us straight to the jackpot..."

●   ●   ●

Even though Tina was still sitting in the release lobby of the county jail, she still felt nervous sitting there with $15,000 in cash zipped up in her Coach bag.

After she gave Fresh back the $5,000 he'd given her, she was going to stop by the condo to put the money in her safe but decided not to. She wanted to be there when Trevon walked out the door, and she also wanted to know who paid $20,000 to bond him out...

"Do any of these people look familiar to you, Fresh?" Tina asked as they scanned faces in the release lobby.

"Naw," Fresh answered before looking at the faces of the two men that were sitting right across from them. There was something peculiar about the two. What caught Fresh's attention wasn't their faces, but rather the suits they wore. Then it came to him: they were the same men that were in the courtroom earlier.

They seemed out of place, sitting there looking straight ahead like two programed robots, and both looked as solid as rock under their expensive attire. Fresh had never been afraid of anyone, but it was something about them that gave him the chills. As they say: game recognize game, and real recognize real.

Fresh knew, from being a real "head busser", that he was looking at two stone cold killers...

"*I'm hungry Fresh,*" Tracy whined. "*I wanna go get something to eat.*"

Tina rolled her eyes and gave Tracy a look that said: *Bitch! If you don't shut the fuck up, I know somethin'!*

"We're gonna leave in a lil bit, boo," Fresh replied, grateful that Tina didn't roast Tracy like he knew she wanted to.

As if Trevon heard Fresh's silent prayer, the door buzzed open and he walked through it, smiling from ear-to-ear. "What da lick read?" he asked, giving Tina a hug.

"Yo, son..." Fresh said, "why does it feel like I'm in an episode of the Twilight Zone? I could've sworn this shit done happened before... Now this the part where Tina gon' tell you she's been fiendin' for some dope head and dope dick, and that she need a fix. Then you gon' say you're the dope man —"

"Wrong," Fresh heard someone say from behind him. "This is the part where I tell you Mr. Rosario wants to see you," one of the suited men said.

"About what?" Trevon asked nervously.

"You'll find out when you get there," the shorter one of the two answered in a nasty tone.

Trevon recognized him from Amici; his name was John, one of Frank Rosario's goons. "Well, what if I tell you I don't want to see Mr. Rosario?" Trevon said nonchalantly.

"Well, what if I tell you we'll snatch your ass up if you don't comply?"

"Well, what if I tell you to go fuck yourself, John?"

"I'm through speaking in hypotheticals," John said firmly. "I don't think you understand what's going on here, Trevon... I'm not asking if you want to see Mr. Rosario..."

Trevon stared into John's eyes; they were black and soulless. They say that the eyes are the windows to the soul. Looking into John's was like looking into the windows of an empty building.

"What'choo sayin' then, B?!" Fresh snapped.

"It's cool, bug," Trevon said reluctantly. "I'll go."

When they got outside a limousine pulled up to the curb and Trevon walked past it. "Hey!" John called out. "You're riding with us."

Trevon looked at Tina. "Just meet me at Amici. I'll be okay."

"Are you sure?"

"Naw, son—*hell naw!*" Fresh said, opening the door of the limo and climbing in. "It ain't going down like that."

"Get out!" John demanded.

Fresh stuck his head out the door. "If my mans go, then I'm going."

"You're not going anywhere!" John barked.

"I don't think you understand what's going on here, John..." Fresh replied using his line back on him. "I'm not asking you if I can go—Tre, let's get it, son!"

"Well, what if I tell you he's not getting out of the limo?" Trevon chuckled before climbing in behind Fresh.

"Fuckin' smart-ass," John mumbled, getting in behind Trevon.

•   •   •

The lights on the twin towers of the Breakers Hotel illuminated the island skyline as they crossed the Flagler Bridge into Palm Beach, and Trevon wondered if he would ever cross the bridge back into West Palm ever again. Whatever the scenario may have been, he knew the situation wasn't good if Frank Rosario sent his goons to escort him back to Amici.

They parked in the back when they reached the restaurant and took a private elevator up to Franks' office. "Search 'em," John ordered as soon as the door slid open.

Reluctantly, Trevon and Fresh raised their hands and two of Franks' goons searched them. After doing so, they were escorted through gigantic French doors and walked into Frank Rosario's office that was designed to strike visitors with dominance...

Dominance in the huge, expensive Persian rug they were standing on. Dominance in the huge, over-stuffed Italian leather sofa and chairs. Dominance in the huge oak wood desk Frank was sitting behind, and dominance in the 10-foot shark that was hanging on the wall behind him.

There were two chairs in front of Frank's desk. They were positioned low so whoever sat in them had to look up to Frank (another act of dominance). One chair was occupied by Joey, and the other by Eddie, Frank's other goon, the one that gave Trevon the counterfeit money and the gun the day he got arrested.

Eddie just sat there looking constipated as Frank yelled at whoever was on the phone. And Joey... Joey looked up at Trevon and shook his head, and from the look in Joey's eyes, Trevon knew the shit was about to hit the fan.

John walked in and stood behind Eddie, and the two that frisked Trevon and Fresh stood by the door like two sentries. Not knowing what else to do, Trevon walked over and stood behind Joey and listened as Frank barked into the phone...

"Whatsdamatter with you, huh?! Frank my fuckin' balls! What?! I need to make reservations to get in contact with you? Y'know, let me tell you somethin': I need an example—don't let you be that example! I tell you right now, I need the fuckin' exercise! Do you understand me, you fuckin' schmuck mutherfucker you?!"

After hearing that Trevon knew they were as good as dead. He looked back at Fresh, and Fresh shook his head, knowing exactly what was on Trevon's mind: they were going down swinging.

Frank slammed the phone down. "After we're finished here, I want you to go pick that cocksucker up and bring him to me! I'm gonna give him a kick in the fuckin' balls!"

"Okay, boss," John replied.

"And what the fuck is this?!" Frank asked, pointing at Fresh.

"Umm... I'm sorry, Frank, but umm...he wouldn't leave," John answered.

"He wouldn't leave?" Frank asked incredulously. "What the fuck do you mean *'he wouldn't leave'?* I asked for Trevon Jenkins—not Trevon Jenkins and his fuckin' entourage! What the fuck is going on around here?!"

"Excuse me, Mr. Rosario," Trevon said hesitantly. "With all due respect, sir. He's here because I trust him with my life, so if anything needs to be said, it can be said in front of him."

At that time Fresh looked over and saw the handle of the pistol that was on the waistline of the goon closest to him.

"So, you trust your friend with your life, huh?" Frank asked as he stood.

"Yes sir, I do."

Frank walked around the desk, staring at Trevon. "You can leave now, Joey."

"Pop, listen," Joey started to protest, "it's not Tre's fault, he just did—"

"I SAID GET THE FUCK OUTTA HERE, JOEY! NOW!" Frank yelled, making Eddie jump.

Reluctantly, Joey got up and gave Trevon a look that said: *Sorry, Tre.*

When Joey was gone, Frank walked behind his desk and pulled a dossier on Trevon from the drawer. "Trevon Jenkins..." he said, flipping through Trevon's criminal history. "You have a very colorful past. Interesting—very interesting. You wanna tell me how you ended up with some of my money, and a gun that was used in a situation that should have been disposed of..." Frank looked at Eddie and beads of sweat appeared on his forehead. "HOW?!" Frank yelled.

"I-I-don't know, boss," Eddie answered nervously.

"I-I-don't know, boss," Frank said, mocking Eddie. "Y'know Tre... there's nothing I can't find out. I know exactly how you ended up in jail with my money, and I know who gave you the gun...I also know what went on while you were in there."

"Never at any time did I indicate where I got the money or gun from, Frank," Trevon said reassuringly.

"I know you didn't," Frank replied. "If you would've said anything other than what you said, you would've committed suicide. They would've found you with a sheet around your neck, hanging from the bars inside that cell you were in, while in confinement..." Frank stared at Trevon, letting his words marinate. "My arms are long, Tre. There's nothin' I can't reach; I have more eyes than a pineapple. I know all about Kevin Ferrell and Charles Jones."

"Who're they?" Trevon asked curiously.

"The two that beat your ass in west-6A earlier; that's how you got that black eye. I even know you went to medical to get an ice pack after you saw your attorney..." Frank looked at the dossier then back at Trevon. "Ms. Monique Baker. Is all this information accurate?"

Trevon shook his head.

"Sit down, Tre," Frank said.

Trevon sat in the chair Joey got up from moments earlier as Frank walked over stood behind him and Eddie.

"There's one thing I respect more than life itself. Do you know what it is Tre?"

"Loyalty." Trevon answered on cue.

"*Ahhh*—that's right!" Frank beamed. "Loyalty—I respect loyalty! Even after this cocksucker gave you a piece he used to whack somebody with," Frank slapped Eddie across the head, "you still kept ya mouth shut out of loyalty to my son..." Frank turned and pointed to the 10-foot shark hanging on the wall behind his desk. "You see that shark...? Caught it last year, down in the Keys... I fought with that cocksucker for forty-five minutes... Do you get where I'm coming from, Tre, huh? I wouldn't have caught the sonofabitch if he hadn't opened hit fat-ass mouth. LOOK AT IT!" Frank exclaimed. "The most feared predator in the ocean, and I caught it because he couldn't keep his fat fuckin' trap shut! You on the other hand, kept your trap shut, and showed loyalty in the process. Loyalty... that's something my people lack around here, huh, Eddie?" Frank said, slapping Eddie across the head again.

John pulled out a .22 automatic and screwed a silencer on the barrel.

"Boss, please! Let me expl—"

"SHUT THE FUCK UP, YOU FUCKIN' CAZZU!" Frank yelled, cutting Eddie off. "You dishonored me, Eddie! You shouldn't have done that..."

Trevon watched John raise the gun, pointing the barrel of the silenced .22 directly behind Eddie's ear.

"...you know why you shouldn't have done that, Eddie...?"

Eddie didn't answer; he sat there with tears in his eyes, looking horrified.

"...you shouldn't have done that because I'm Frank Rosario, and Frank Rosario lives by a code—you know what the code is, Eddie...?

Eddie still didn't answer.

"Death before dishonor..." Frank hissed, "that's the code, Eddie. That's the fuckin' code, you fuckin' piece of shit—"

John squeezed the trigger three times, and Trevon watched as the .22 spat out three empty cartridges, only making a muffled *"pfft, pfft, pfft,"* sound.

Eddie's limp body flopped on Trevon's lap, and whatever fear he felt turned into rage. That's when Fresh grabbed the gun from the waistline of the man near him and pointed it at John.

"Put that gun down, you sonofabitch!" Frank warned.

"Tre, what da lick read, son?!" Fresh asked nervously.

"Was this shit supposed to scare me, Frank?" Trevon asked nonchalantly, pushing Eddie's body off his lap. "What, you gon' kill us now, Frank?"

"If I wanted you dead, you would've been dead in the county jail."

"Then why am I here?" Trevon asked. "What's the purpose of all this? You said there's nothin' you can't find out; apparently, you didn't do your homework on me. You think I'm just some nigga that cooks spaghetti in your restaurant? Naw, Frank... this shit ain't nothing new to me. This is what we do—we live for this type of shit."

"Wussup, Tre?" Fresh said, shifting nervously. "Give me the word and I'ma pop this nigga top!"

Frank stared into Trevon's eyes. "Tell your friend to drop that fuckin' gun or *so-help-me-god!*"

"Naw," Trevon chuckled, "it ain't going down like that Frank. We're not going out like Eddie..." Trevon stood up. "I ain't taking it sitting down—we gon' set it off in this muthafucker. If we go, then some of y'all are coming with us—"

"If I wanted to kill you, do you think I would've spent twenty thousand dollars to bond you out?"

"Then why did you bond me out?" Trevon asked suspiciously.

"To give you a chance."

"A chance for what?"

"To redeem yourself..." Frank picked up Trevon's criminal history. "I could help you, Tre. You have rare qualities that I admire. I could change your life, no more petty bullshit. But you have to trust me, Tre... tell your friend to put that gun down." Frank spoke his final words with a chilling calm in his eyes.

All Trevon could do was think about his son. Here he was staring down the barrel of John's gun, and after looking into his eyes, he knew there was no doubt John would take him straight to hell with him if Fresh pulled the trigger...

That scenario was out of the question.

"Put the gun down, Fresh."

"What?!"

"I said put the gun down."

"You're crazy as fuck, Tre!"

Trevon turned around and looked Fresh in the eyes. "Put it down, Fresh. Trust me on this...put the gun down, homie."

Reluctantly, Fresh lowered the gun, and Trevon held his breath, waiting for Jon to peel his scalp back. Instead, Frank reached into his jacket pocket, pulled a cigar, and let out a long-wicked laugh...

"Y'know..." he said after he lit his cigar, "yous got cojones, the two of you..."

John lowered the .22 and Trevon exhaled.

"...I like that," Frank continued, "a man with cojones, you know how to keep your mouth shut, you have loyalty and cojones."

"What's all this about, Frank?" Trevon asked impatiently.

"Like I said before: a chance."

"A chance to do what?"

"A chance to make the wrong things right?"

"And what might that be?"

"Pagan!" Frank hissed. "Victor Pagan! That fuckin' cocksucker! He's been going behind my back doing business with my son—*minchia!*"

"So what are you saying, Mr. Rosario?"

"I'm saying that it's a chain of command. As bad as I want to go down to Miami and blow that wetback motherfucker of the map, my boss doesn't think it's in the family's best interest to involve ourselves in a conflict with the Pagans...But you, you're not family. Know what I mean, Tre, huh?"

"Yeah..." Trevon answered, looking at Fresh, "I know exactly what you mean... We'll take care of your problem, but we are gonna need a few things."

"John?"

"Yeah, boss?"

"Make sure they get whatever they need, capisci?"

"Okay, boss."

"And wrap this piece of shit up and get him out of my office," Frank said, referring to Eddie's body. Then he looked at Fresh: "And give my man back his fuckin' piece, will ya? Cojones... he really has cojones. I fuckin' love it!"

Available May 1, 2018

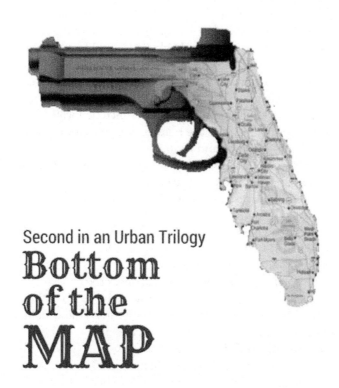

Second in an Urban Trilogy

Bottom
of the
MAP

Steven L. Brown

10

It's going Down

Trevon and Tina sat in the car and watched as Fresh worked the slim-jim, popping the lock of a black, 2001 Fleetwood Cadillac. After doing so, he got in and hit the tilt bar on the left side of the steering column and adjusted the steering wheel so he could have easy access to what he needed to get to.

After chipping away the steering column and unlocking the ignition rod, he pulled the blinker forward a little so he could get a visual of the spring that locked the steering wheel. Once he located it, he stuck the flat head screwdriver inside the blinker box and dislodged it, making the steering wheel sway back and forth.

"Issa wrap," Fresh mumbled to himself before pulling the ignition rod toward him to crank the Cadillac up...

The whole process took less than 60 seconds (grand theft auto 101).

Fresh pulled beside Tina's Acura, rolled down the window, and yelled, "Grab that B.G. CD and let's get it, nigga!"

"Which one?" Trevon inquired.

"*The Heart of The Streets,*" Fresh answered.

"Just stick to the script," Trevon said as he grabbed the CD and the black duffel bag that was lying on the backseat. "Follow behind us all the way and don't let anyone get behind us, a'ight?"

"Be careful, Tre," Tina replied.

"I will," Trevon said, "just stay behind us..."

Fifteen minutes later, they were on I-95 headed south. Destination: Miami Beach.

Trevon and Fresh had the CD player turned up to the max, straining the 6x9s, making them rattle every time a bass line dropped. Their heads bopped back and forth as they recited the words to B.G.'s *What'cha heart beating for?* taking turns hitting a blunt that was the size of a magic marker.

After they finished the blunt, Trevon pulled out a small glassine bag of cocaine and dumped a small mound on his hand in the groove between his thumb and index finger, held it up to his nose and inhaled, sniffing the white crystallized powder.

"Feed me!" Fresh snapped, leaning over with one hand on the steering wheel, and the other covering one of his nostrils.

Trevon dumped another pile on his hand, held is under Fresh's nose, and watched it disappear.

"More!" Fresh demanded. *"Feed me! Feed me, Seymore!"* he sang sounding like the Venus Flytrap from *Little Shop of Horrors.*

Trevon laughed and fed Fresh more of the cocaine before putting the bag away.

As they drove south, Trevon looked out to the western horizon at the sunset; the sight was breathtaking. There's something about South Florida that reaches deep down in your soul and brings out the naughtiness when the sun goes down. You can feel it in the air, like some kind of unseen vibrant force, and Trevon felt like a vampire awaiting nightfall as unexplainable invigoration flowed through his veins...

Thirty minutes later, they got off I-95 at the 135th Street exit and headed east toward South Beach. They made a right on Biscayne Boulevard and followed the directions to the address John had given the day before.

"There it go," Trevon said, pointing to a Cuban café that was anchored by a supermarket, with other mom and pop stores strung out along both sides.

They made a U-turn and Tina followed them to an alley behind an apartment complex two blocks away.

"Pop the trunk," Trevon said to Tina. After grabbing a gas can, he walked around to the driver's side window. "If we're not back in twenty minutes—call the police."

"Ha, ha, ha—that shit ain't funny, Tre," Tina replied, trying to make herself smile. "Please be careful, baby."

"We will," Trevon said reassuringly. "We'll be back before you know it."

"Let's get this shit over with. Me and my boo got a date tonight!" Fresh yelled from the Cadillac, his head bopping back and forth to B.G.

When they returned to the plaza, they parked in a parking spot not too far away from the café. The parking lot was halfway full, so Trevon looked around nervously before unzipping the black duffel bag and pulling out two AR-15 assault rifles, four clips, five boxes of 5.56 mm ammunition, two ski-masks, two pair of gloves, two black hooded sweatshirts, and two bullet-proof vests (all compliments of Frank).

"This how it's going down..." Trevon said as he put on his gloves and began loading shells into the clips. "The North Miami—a hot spot—so

215

we're in and out this bitch, you feel me? The response time should be about a hundred and twenty seconds, so that gives us about sixty seconds to go in here and blow these muthafuckers to smithereens, and sixty seconds to get back to the Acura and get the fuck out of dodge, you with me?"

"Yeah," Fresh answered, smiling like a kid in the candy store.

"This is Victor Pagan," Trevon said, holding up a picture of a pudgy, Spanish man. "All them bitches look the same to me, so to be safe, we're gonna go up in there and wet the whole spot up; ere'body gon' get it. When we walk up out of there we ain't leaving nothing breathin', you still with me?"

"Yeah," Fresh answered, smiling even harder than before.

"What the fuck you smilin' for?" Trevon asked curiously.

"Because my muthafuckin' dawg back," Fresh answered. "This just like the good ole days, B. You were on that cornball shit when you first got out, trying to lecture me about getting my priorities straight... See, I told you homie. I told you that you'll be back to your old self in no time."

"Fresh, we're about to go wet up some shit up. Ain't nothin' funny about this shit; I still feel the same way. It's just..."

"Just what?"

"Just business," Trevon answered, "and these muthafuckers got the short end of the stick. It is what it is, but that don't mean it's right."

"Yeah, yeah, yeah," Fresh replied. "This is a beautiful moment, Tre... please don't fuck it up with that self-righteous bullshit."

Trevon slapped one of the thirty-round clips in the rifle and cocked a round into the chamber before strapping on his vest as Fresh did the same. After they were done, Fresh looked at Trevon with an angry expression on his face...

"Don't look at me like that, nigga," Trevon said. "I don't care nothin' about you getting mad."

"What'cha heart beatin' for?" Fresh asked teasingly.

"My heart ain't beatin'," Trevon answered defensively. "What *your* heart beatin' for?"

"My heart ain't beatin' neither," Fresh replied before they looked at each other in silence for a short moment...

Then they pointed at each other at the same time and yelled, *"YOOOUU SCAAARREEDD!"* and burst out laughing.

"Let's go get it like Drac," Fresh said, pulling the ski ask over his face.

"In blood," Trevon replied as he did the same.

"Look! Look! Look!" Fresh said excitedly, pointing toward the café.

Trevon looked in the direction Fresh was pointing and saw two Hispanic men walking through the front door carrying briefcases.

"Are you thinking what I'm thinking, bug?"

"Umm-hmm," Fresh answered in a daze.

"Change of plans; let's go get them briefcases."

"I second that motion," Fresh said.

At that moment, Tina chirped Trevon on his Nextel, speaking in their cryptic code:

BEEP–BEEP: "Blue Bird to Eagle Team." *BEEP–BEEP.*

BEEP–BEEP: "Go ahead, Blue Bird." *BEEP–BEEP.*

BEEP–BEEP: "What's your twenty (location)?" *BEEP-BEEP*

BEEP–BEEP: "We're at the ten-twelve (Café). We had to eighty-six (cancel) the original plan. Something came up." *BEEP–BEEP.*

BEEP–BEEP: "You said if you wasn't back in twenty minutes, call one-two (the police). You still want me to make that call?" *BEEP–BEEP.*

BEEP-BEEP: "Oh, you got jokes now?" *BEEP–BEEP.*

BEEP–BEEP: "Naw, I was just making sure y'all was fifty-four (okay)." *BEEP–BEEP.*

BEEP–BEEP: "Yeah, we're Gucci... Eagle Team out." *BEEP–BEEP.*

BEEP–BEEP: "Ten-four, Eagle Team." *BEEP–BEEP.*

"It's about to go down in there, bug," Trevon said, setting rifle's rate of fire selector switch to three-round-burst. "Remember, we got sixty seconds. We're in and out this bitch—*let's go get it!*"

Fresh pulled out the parking spot and pulled up in front of the café.

"Sixty seconds," Trevon said, hitting the button on his stopwatch, "starting now!"

●　　　●　　　●

Coming Soon...

PU$$Y
REAL GOOD

STEVEN L. BROWN

Made in the USA
Middletown, DE
12 March 2022

62521833R10126